THE UNINVITED CORPSE

Hope continued down the hallway and stopped at the closed study door. She twisted the doorknob then entered with Drew behind her. A wall of floor-to-ceiling bookcases greeted them, along with the faint smell of cigars. Leather furniture, dark wood, and a massive desk left no question the room belonged to Harrison.

Hope's gaze narrowed on three half-empty glasses left coasterless on the end table. She swiped them up with precision, setting them on the tray, and was pleased to see no rings on the hardwood. A visual search of the room found no other unattended glasses, however it did turn up a messy situation over by the desk.

"Look at this mess. I can't imagine Harrison leaving his study like this."

Papers were scattered on top of the impressive desk that gleamed from regular polishing. Her gaze traveled downward, where she saw more papers and folders scattered on the floor. It was as if someone had been searching for something.

"My career is going nowhere." Drew's head dipped down and he tapped on his cell phone. He was always checking his messages for the next big story.

"That's not true and you know it." Hope knew a thing or two about a career going nowhere and was even more intimately familiar with a career that had crashed and burned. She inched cautiously toward the desk. Something felt off, but she couldn't put her finger on what it was. She froze in place. A shudder zipped th⎯⎯⎯⎯⎯⎯ and her muscles tensed as she look⎯⎯⎯⎯

Peaches McCoy⎯⎯⎯⎯⎯⎯⎯⎯⎯n, on the carpet . . .

The Uninvited Corpse

Debra Sennefelder

KENSINGTON PUBLISHING CORP.
www.kensingtonbooks.com

KENSINGTON BOOKS are published by

Kensington Publishing Corp.
119 West 40th Street
New York, NY 10018

All Kensington titles, imprints, and distributed lines are available at special quantity discounts for bulk purchases for sales promotions, premiums, fund-raising, educational, or institutional use. Special book excerpts or customized printings can also be created to fit specific needs. For details, write or phone the office of the Kensington sales manager: Kensington Publishing Corp., 119 West 40th Street, New York, NY 10018, attn: Sales Department; phone 1-800-221-2647.

KENSINGTON BOOKS and the K logo are Reg. U.S. Pat. & TM Off.

ISBN-13: 978-1-4967-1592-0
ISBN-10: 1-4967-1592-6

First printing: April 2018

10 9 8 7 6 5 4 3 2 1

Printed in the United States of America

First electronic edition: April 2018

ISBN-13: 978-1-4967-1595-1
ISBN-10: 1-4967-1595-0

This book is dedicated to my parents,

Martin and Elsie McCormack.

Thank you for everything.
Love you, always!

ACKNOWLEDGMENTS

Writing a novel is a long, long, long process, and rarely does an author take on the process by herself. Every step of writing *The Uninvited Corpse* I had trusted friends and supportive family alongside me. Then when I was ready to show my baby to the world I found industry professionals who helped turn my manuscript into this novel. I would be remiss if I did not thank those people who stood with me and who now celebrate with me. A big thank-you goes out to my husband, George. Your support and encouragement all these years has meant the world to me. I want to thank my friend and critique partner, Ellie Ashe. You've been one of my biggest cheerleaders, and you've pushed me to step outside my comfort zone time after time. You've helped me become a better writer. You've believed in this book since day one and I am grateful for that. Thank you to my friend Heidi Ulrich. You turned this writer into a plotter and a sticky-note collector. Your encouragement and advice have been priceless. Thank you to my nephews Michael Confield and Erick Kuhlmann for answering my police-procedural questions. Thank you to my agent Dawn Dowdle for believing in this book. Thank you to my editor John Scognamiglio and the team at Kensington for bringing *The Uninvited Corpse* to publication. You all just don't make books, you make dreams come true.

Chapter One

"Thank you, Hope Early, for joining us and sharing all of your tips for spring cleaning. I'm sure you've inspired our listeners to get busy and start cleaning out their homes," Morning Pete of WPTX radio said.

With the cordless phone tucked between her ear and shoulder, Hope refilled her coffee cup for the second time. She'd been on air answering caller questions and promoting her blog, "Hope at Home." Most of the questions were easy—where to begin cleaning out, how to organize the process, and how to stay motivated midway through the important ritual of spring. It was a ritual she participated in every year and one she had down to a science. Then came the question she didn't expect.

She hated being blindsided and she hated being naïve just as much. She should have seen it coming.

"What was it like going from being a successful

magazine editor to becoming a finalist on *The Sweet Taste of Success* to writing a blog about taking out the trash?" Morning Pete asked with a laugh, followed by a chorus of laughter from his morning crew.

Oh, so very funny. Her descent from high-powered editor to baking competition reality show loser to newly divorced blogger was fodder for *Morning Pete.* With no other choice but to laugh along with the morning crew, she bit her tongue and somehow managed to get the interview back on track. "Life throws us curveballs all the time, and sometimes I wish I had a little guidance when I went through all that stuff. Speaking of guidance, I have a free giveaway, and it's called 'How to Survive Spring Cleaning.' I invite everyone to visit my blog and download your copy today."

Finally her time was up. "It was my pleasure," she said through gritted teeth and then clicked the phone off. As she set the phone back into its base, footsteps sounded in the mudroom. There was only one other person who would be up so early.

Chief of Police Ethan Cahill greeted her with a smile. He'd always looked damn good in his uniform. The classic cliché—tall, dark, and handsome—always fit him. But on this chilly late-March morning, he looked even better to her because he held a white pastry bag from her favorite coffee shop, The Coffee Clique on Main Street.

"You're a good man." She snatched the bag and moved back into the kitchen island. She should eat something healthier like yogurt and granola or whole-grain toast with an egg white. But after dealing with the morning crew circus, she deserved something sweet and delicious.

The cinnamon bun, not Ethan. Then she sucked in a deep breath at the thought.

Whoa. Where did that come from?

Ethan was her rock. The friend she leaned on. The person who helped her through the darkest period of her life. So when did he go from all that to sweet and delicious?

He settled at the table and gestured to the bag. "There's one in there for me, too."

She glanced down. Better to focus on the food. She quickly plated both gooey treats and set the plates on the table, along with two filled coffee cups.

"You handled yourself well, even when that jerk asked about the reality show." Ethan bit into his cinnamon bun, then licked a drop of icing off his bottom lip.

Slightly distracted by Ethan's mouth, it took a second for Hope to register his comment. "Yeah, I didn't expect that question. Guess it's always going to come up." She'd made peace with the fact that when her name was searched on the Internet, it would always be associated with *The Sweet Taste of Success*. A baker's dozen of wannabe culinary stars competed for a prime-time slot on the Culinary Channel. She walked away from the twelve-week experience—just losing the top prize, and then losing her marriage.

Ethan lifted his head and leveled his gaze on her. "You did good."

"Thanks. I think what really bothers me is people think the TV show and living in New York City was the best time of my life and I somehow settled by coming back home. I didn't settle. I'm here because I want to be here."

"Would you do the show over again?"

She shrugged. "I'm not sure."

"Honest answer."

She didn't want to think any more about her time on the Culinary Channel or her divorce or the end of her publishing career. "I have a full day. After Audrey's garden tour, I have errands and I have to bake for the library's bake sale." Every year since she was a little girl, she'd baked dozens of cookies for the annual fund-raiser. Spending the afternoon baking wasn't a hardship and it also provided content for her blog. Bake sales would be popping up all over the place, and she had a series planned on the perfect treats plus tips on presentation and pricing. The first recipe she planned on making was the double-chocolate raspberry bar she'd been dreaming about for weeks. The first run-through delivered the cookie of her dreams. But since she'd promised her readers she would test a recipe three times before posting it, she had two more batches of the bars to make. Luckily her friends and family were willing to be her taste testers.

"What about you? What's on tap for you besides fighting crime?"

Ethan chuckled. "With Jefferson being named as one of the safest towns in the state, there isn't much crime to fight. I have a meeting up in Hartford this morning. Then I was thinking we could have dinner."

"That sounds good. I'll whip something up and we'll have cookies for dessert." Hope glanced at her watch. "Shoot. I've gotta get going. I haven't done the barn chores yet." She ate the last bit of the cinnamon bun, wiped her mouth on a napkin, then stood. Grabbing her plate and mug, she deposited both in the sink.

"Why don't you hire someone to help you around here?"

"There isn't that much work. I can handle it for now. Oh, there's more coffee. Help yourself. Call me later." She dashed out of the kitchen and grabbed a jacket from the mudroom before heading out to the barn. Closing the door behind her, she felt a twinge of satisfaction knowing that if she turned and went back inside, Ethan would be waiting for her. That little feeling put a spring in her step. And the little extra boost would come in handy as she collected eggs from her hens.

Holidays always brought a smile to Hope, and when the day revolved around her favorite cookie, she could barely contain herself. She knew that National Chocolate Chip Cookie Day wasn't a holiday that closed schools and the post office, but that was clearly an oversight. To celebrate the day, she would share five of her favorite recipes on her blog. She wanted to serve up a traditional cookie where it was all about the dough and the chocolate chip, but she also wanted to incorporate two hot trends in the foodie world—caramel and salt.

"Good morning."

Hope looked up from her laptop as her part-time assistant, Vanessa Jordan, walked into the kitchen. She'd set up at the table, which was convenient for recipe testing. Still, she needed a proper office, and she planned to do a series for the blog on the project. Off the kitchen, there was a small room being converted into her office. There was enough space for a desk, a nice span of wall for bookshelves, and enough light for her photography.

Vanessa removed her jacket and draped it over a chair then dropped her purse on the table. All of five feet, she was a small powerhouse of organization who ran a tight ship, working for both Hope and her friend Audrey Bloom. Meeting the energetic thirty-something through Audrey was the best thing that had happened to Hope in months.

Vanessa eagerly took on the tasks that ate up valuable time for Hope, freeing her to create more content and focus on developing e-products to sell on her website. Though Hope wondered how long she and Audrey could continue to split Vanessa's time.

"Today is crazy. I have to be over at Audrey's house in a couple of hours." Vanessa moved over to the coffeemaker and poured a cup.

"Well, there are only a few things you need to do here. Then you can head out." Hope returned to the post she was writing about her love for chocolate chip cookies. Her fingers tapped on the keys, and her mind drifted as she wrote about her first attempt at baking the cookie.

Utter. Failure. Overbaked, overbrowned, and hard enough to use as hockey pucks. She smiled as she remembered her parents ate them with tall glasses of milk and praised their youngest daughter's baking. She was only ten, and she fell in love with baking.

"I saw Peaches McCoy putting up the For Sale sign at your neighbor's house." Vanessa settled down at the table and turned on her laptop.

"Hmm." Hope looked up. "You saw Peaches?"

Vanessa nodded.

"Gilbert mentioned something about selling his house now that Mitzi has broken her hip. The place is too big for them to maintain."

Vanessa's heart-shaped face pinched with annoyance. "He had to select her as his agent? Really? What about Claire?"

Hope shrugged. She wasn't privy to Gilbert Madison's decision-making when it came to hiring a real estate agent. "I'm sure he had his reasons for hiring her. We have a lot to get done before Audrey's garden tour." She wanted to get Vanessa's focus on work, not Jefferson's newest real estate agent. Though the woman seemed to have everyone talking for one reason or another.

"Audrey was a bundle of nerves last night. I assured her today would be fine. She's worried about Elaine coming because Sally has her granny panties in a twist."

"That sounds more like you than Audrey," Hope said.

Vanessa nodded. "Guilty. But, what's the big deal? The garden club voted Elaine president. It's not like they didn't know what they were getting."

Hope's assistant did have a point, but she probably shouldn't share it with Sally Merrifield. As a founding member of the Jefferson Garden Club, Sally felt a responsibility to the club, to ensure it carried on its mission to promote gardening within the community. As a retired librarian, she also believed in structure, and structure was a somewhat foreign concept to Elaine Whitcomb. Instead, Elaine was outgoing, flirtatious, and slightly scattered, but her husband's wealth helped people look past her flaws.

"It's difficult for Sally to accept Jefferson didn't make the top twenty-five community gardens in the state. She's worked hard over the past ten years to make sure our town green and smaller gardens throughout town were recognized by *Connecticut Living* magazine," Hope said. While living in New York City, her friends and coworkers thought their lives were complicated living in a big city. They had no clue what happened in small-town New England. Maybe she should forget her blog and write a novel.

Vanessa shrugged. "It's time to get over it and move on. Hopefully with spring now blooming all around us, Sally will forget all this nonsense. God knows, those three acres she has should keep her occupied."

"Speaking of gardens, we both have to be out of here soon."

"Right." Vanessa turned her attention to her computer and, for a few moments, she was silent. "Hey, have you checked your stats?"

"Not today."

"Holy cow! Did you see the spike in traffic already? And look at how many downloads of your spring cleaning worksheet. Wow, low bounce rates, too."

Low bounce rate. Three little words every blogger loved. The visitors to "Hope at Home" stayed around to check out a lot of her posts. They also signed up for her mailing list, which meant she could promote her blog and products to them. "At least something good came out of that interview."

"Come on, it was a good interview, even though Morning Pete was kind of a jerk. He could have framed his question about *The Sweet Taste of Success* a little better."

Hope shrugged. She agreed with Vanessa, but she also realized what Morning Pete dished out came with the territory and if she was going to build a career on a public platform like a blog, she needed to toughen up. She would be forever the runner-up winner of *The Sweet Taste of Success*.

"Well, seeing these numbers, if you have the opportunity go on Morning Pete's show again, you should. Do you think Audrey would make a good guest?"

"Morning Pete didn't strike me as a gardening kind of guy."

"I keep telling Audrey she needs to keep her blog updated on her website. I'm trying to get her into the twenty-first century. It's like pulling teeth."

"Really?"

"She doesn't even own a tablet. Who doesn't own a tablet nowadays? It's like my grandparents. Newspaper clippings. Ugh, I can't stand it. You know, Meg even offered to write the posts for her."

"I didn't know Meg was a writer," Hope said.

Meg Griffin was full of surprises, just like she was in high school. Back then there wasn't a word to describe Hope and Meg's relationship but now there was—frenemy. After being away for so long, Hope thought things would be different between them. They weren't. You could take the girl out of high school but you couldn't take the high school out of the girl.

"She's not a writer. But I guess she has a lot of skills. She's even set up a Facebook page for the preservation society. She's like a mini-me of Audrey with tech skills." Vanessa laughed.

"It's good Audrey has someone to help her with the group. It's a lot of work."

"And speaking of work . . ." Vanessa smiled. "I'm sorry. I guess I'm a little nervous about the garden tour. There's so much that can go wrong, and I don't want that for Audrey."

"It's going to be a lovely day. A walk around a beautiful garden, some refreshments, and a book signing." Hope turned back to her work. "What could possibly go wrong?"

"Pffft."

"You're not going to turn Audrey's garden tour into a fiasco." Hope aimed her key fob at her vehicle and clicked it.

"What do you think she and her stupid preservation group are doing to Jefferson?" Claire snipped. "The Society to Protect Jefferson. Ha! More like the society to keep Jefferson in the Dark Ages."

Hope began to walk, passing by Sally Merrifield's sensible station wagon. A lifelong gardener, Sally would never miss a gardening event. Each year she held a garden party at her family's business, The Merrifield Inn, to showcase her hard work all year long and to celebrate her love of plants and flowers. Hope noticed Meg Griffin's sporty SUV. She sighed. Yet another opportunity to travel back to high school. "Looks like a few people have already arrived. I hope Audrey is all prepared."

"We're just going to be walking around a garden full of dead stuff. What can go wrong?"

"I don't have time to make a list."

"You know, if I can convince Audrey to let me list her house, I'd get a hefty commission." Claire followed her sister along the herringbone-patterned brick path to the Federal period house.

"You'll do no such thing. Besides, you know she'll never sell this house."

Claire rolled her pale blue eyes. "*Loves it.* I know. Like old homes aren't a dime a dozen in Connecticut."

Hope reached the red front door and pressed the doorbell. "It's more than just an old house. It's her grandmother's house. And the material for her gardening books."

A few seconds passed before the door opened and Audrey greeted them.

"Good morning." Audrey's unsteady smile vanished when her gaze passed over Hope's shoulder and found Claire. "I thought you'd change your mind about coming."

"Like I said last night, she's not going to cause any trouble," Hope reassured her friend. When they spoke, she found that nerves combined with frustration made a wicked combination. Audrey was frustrated by the town council's recent approval of Whitcomb's proposed development plan. But she'd promised Hope TSPJ wasn't going to back down, they were looking at other legal options. Hope had considered not telling Audrey of Claire's intention to attend the event. But she'd decided her friend should know. Forewarned was forearmed.

"Whatever." Audrey opened the door wider for her guests to enter.

Hope and Claire entered the spacious antique-filled foyer. Overhead a crystal chandelier glistened in the early-afternoon sun. A fleur-de-lis-stenciled chair rail and a treasured Persian rug finished off the elegant space.

"That mutt of yours isn't loose, is he?" Claire glanced around.

Audrey exhaled a deep breath. "His name is Bigelow and he's out in the garage for the tour."

"Great. Is there coffee yet?" Claire asked as she took off for the kitchen.

"Help yourself." Audrey gestured for Hope's coat and then hung it in the closet. "I heard this morning Whitcomb intends to break ground in two weeks."

"He's not wasting any time moving forward."

"Thank goodness you're here, Hope." Sally Merrifield approached from the living room. The former librarian, a close friend of Hope's mother, had a deep frown on her face.

"What's wrong?" Hope asked.

"I simply cannot understand why Elaine was sent an invitation to attend this wonderful tour," Sally said.

"She's the garden club's president. How could I not invite her?" Audrey asked in a tight voice.

"What's the problem?" Hope asked.

Elaine Whitcomb wasn't the most popular person in Jefferson, especially for those with husbands, because of her flirtatious nature. But Hope didn't understand why Sally was so upset while Audrey had put their differences aside for the day.

Sally's frown deepened. "Because of her, we didn't even rank in the top twenty-five community gardens in the state."

"This isn't the time or the place to discuss this. Elaine has been invited. If she shows up, we'll just have to deal with it," Audrey said.

"Letting the inmates run the asylum," Sally muttered as she marched back to the living room.

Audrey turned her attention back to Hope. "I need your help. The girls I hired from the high school haven't shown up yet, and I'm shorthanded in the kitchen."

Hope smiled. "Don't worry. I'll take care of everything." The students from the culinary program at the high school were usually reliable and prompt, and she expected they would show up any minute. Until then, she'd lend a hand.

Audrey glanced at her watch. "Great. I can't believe how late it's getting. There's a tray of pastries on the island, could you put it on the server for me?"

Before Hope could respond, her friend was already halfway up the staircase.

"You're a lifesaver." Audrey dashed up the remaining steps and disappeared into her bedroom.

Hope headed to the kitchen. Claire was seated on a stool at the island, checking her lipstick in her designer compact.

"Nicely done, Sis. She never saw it coming." Claire took one final look in the mirror. "You know you have a serious problem."

"I don't know what you're talking about." Hope lifted the tray of pastries off the granite countertop.

"She just asked you to help, didn't she? Fess up. What did you do with the high school kids she hired?"

Hope shook her head. "Don't be ridiculous. I'm just lending a hand."

"Is that all you're doing? My guess is right now you're thinking about rearranging the pastries, aren't you?" Claire pointed to the silver tray.

Hope bit her lower lip. She was thinking about rearranging the tray. The napoleons should have been placed in the center, flanked by the mini-cream puffs and éclairs. Exercising restraint to prove her sister wrong, she stepped into the dining area without touching one pastry.

Pure hell. But she resisted.

Decorated in yellows and blues, with white accents, the room was bright and cheery. The scent of vanilla floated in the air from candles arranged throughout the room. White-painted French doors overlooked a flagstone patio, where a collection of potted dwarf evergreens was displayed. The assorted cedars, spruces, and junipers were neatly groomed and were the perfect entry out to Audrey's early spring garden.

Hope set the tray down on the server and stepped back to admire the buffet set with silver pots, floral plates, and heirloom flatware. "It's beautiful."

Claire snatched a strawberry from the fruit tray. "But is it perfect yet?"

"No." Hope readjusted the ivory sateen napkins so they cascaded toward the edge of the server, rather than just being lumped in a pile. "Now it's perfect."

"Yeah, the napkins make all the difference."

Hope cleared her throat. "So far, so good. Despite you showing up."

"You worry too much. And worrying will only deepen your lines," Claire said before snatching another strawberry and biting into it.

"Be careful, Sis. You're about to exceed your caloric intake for the day." Hope turned and went to the refrigerator. She had pulled out a carton of milk and filled a crystal creamer when she remembered what she'd left in the car. "I forgot my camera."

"Just use your phone."

"I prefer the camera since I'm writing a post about the tour for the blog. I'll be right back." Her fancy digital camera cost a small fortune, but since her blog was photo rich and her readers loved seeing images, it was worth the investment. Just as she began to hurry out of the kitchen, she heard Claire squeal.

Hope spun around and found Claire looking out the window over the sink. "What's wrong?"

"The dog is loose out in the garden," Claire answered.

Jeez.

Hope turned and rushed to her sister and peered out the window. Bigelow was digging in the garden.

"I'll be right back." She sprinted through the mudroom to get outside to the backyard. For a moment, she paused and looked around in awe. Audrey's garden had good bones. Stone walls in the distance ran along the property, while evergreens stood tall and decorative urns were strategically placed. Distinctive edging skirted fluid borders, and a Japanese maple spilled over a corner garden bed. A sea of early daffodils popped the landscape with color and the hope of warmer days to come.

A playful bark drew Hope back to her mission—corral Bigelow before Audrey realized he was loose. She reached the rectangular patch where Bigelow dug. The medium-sized dog raced toward Hope and then bounced back to the hole he was digging.

"You're supposed to be in the garage," she said, but the dog ignored her and continued to dig.

"Is the tour beginning?"

Hope glanced over her shoulder. Some of the guests emerged from the house. Leading the group were Claire and Meg. Claire already looked bored and cold while her companion exuded enthusiasm.

Trailing behind them was Drew Adams, a local reporter and one of Hope's closest friends, with camera in hand. He was his usual J. Crew self from head to toe. His chinos were perfectly pressed, and he held a notepad and pen. Hope didn't recognize the three women walking with him, but they might be the gardening editors and writers.

And finally a sour-looking Maretta Kingston marched behind them. It was hard to believe she was a member of the Jefferson Garden Club by her less-than-enthusiastic appearance.

Sally and Jane Merrifield were soon ushered out of the house. The sisters-in-law were cheerful in nature and smiled. A little bit of cold didn't dampen their spirits.

Elaine Whitcomb lagged behind them. *So she did show up.* No doubt those three-inch heels she wore gave her problems with traction.

But where was the hostess?

The back door swung open again and Audrey appeared with a few more guests behind her. She hurried to catch up with everyone.

Hope grabbed Bigelow, who'd settled next to her legs, by the collar and walked him to the garage, where she would give him a chew toy to keep him busy. With any luck, that would keep him occupied until the tour was over.

When she joined the group on the patio, Audrey had eased into her role as host. She shared tips, techniques, and advice with grace and poise.

Hope listened to Audrey's tips for pruning. "Every tree needs to be assessed, and the rule of thumb is . . ." Or at least she tried to listen until she got elbowed in the ribs.

"Ouch." Hope glared at her sister, the assailant.

"Sssh," Maretta hissed.

Hope rubbed her side. "You have bony elbows."

Claire nodded for her sister to turn around. Hope

did and couldn't believe her eyes. Peaches McCoy. What the heck was she doing at the tour? Shocked, Hope could only stare.

Dressed warmly for the day, Peaches wore a navy jacket over a pair of dark jeans and a beige sweater. Her long strawberry-blond hair blew in the wind and her hands were buried deep in her coat pockets. She approached the group with no sign of hesitation or concern that she was unwelcome. It was that confidence that made Peaches such a successful real estate agent.

Meg turned around. A cold glare revealed she wasn't happy. "Why on earth would Audrey invite her? She, along with Whitcomb, are trying to destroy this town."

"They're trying to improve Jefferson," Claire countered.

Meg shook her head. "How? By destroying farmland for subdivisions? My family has been here for over one hundred years and I'll do whatever it takes to stop them both. Any outsider who thinks they can stroll into town and buy and sell like it's some board game will have a battle, I promise you." Meg held Claire's gaze for a moment before she marched forward to keep up with the rest of the group.

Hope turned and gave her sister a warning look to let Meg go. They didn't need to engage in a spirited debate on the pros and cons of development at that moment.

"I can't believe she had the nerve to show up here. She's nothing but trouble." Maretta Kingston came to a stop next to Hope and Claire.

"She's probably just here to dig up trouble," Claire said.

"Yes, that's the only thing she'd ever dig for. Trust me, she's no gardener," Maretta said.

"Sssh," Hope hissed that time. "You'll distract Audrey."

"Like she won't?" Claire gestured at Peaches, who was just a few feet away from them.

"Enough," Hope warned.

"Humph." Maretta crossed her arms in protest. Quiet descended.

If Audrey had noticed Peaches' arrival, and Hope didn't see how she could have missed it, she never let it show.

"I use leaves I've raked up in autumn and pile them around each rose plant." Audrey stood in front of her expansive rose garden. "Then I wrap them in burlap, and as you can see, there's been very little, if any, damage to them."

Out of the corner of her eye, Hope noticed Peaches had caught up with them and stood dead silent behind them.

"Hope, everything seems to be going well. Doesn't it?" Vanessa asked as she entered the kitchen. Her long paisley skirt fluttered as she moved along the buffet. "Despite *that* woman showing up. Do you know why she came?"

"I was going to ask you the same question." Hope grabbed a handful of stirrers and empty sugar packets off the buffet and deposited them in the trash container. She'd returned to the kitchen to check on things and ended up tidying up.

"I have no idea. I'm dying to ask Audrey if she invited her at the last minute. But why, I have no idea." Vanessa poured a cup of coffee from the urn.

Hope wiped her hands on a clean dish towel. "Maybe Audrey decided it was a good idea to not be enemies with Peaches since she's considering running for mayor."

Vanessa shrugged. "Possibly. That would be a smart thing to do, but they're on such opposite sides of the development issue in town. I can't see Peaches supporting Audrey's run for mayor." She set her cup on the table and glanced at her watch. "It's almost time to start the book signing." She scooted out of the kitchen, brushing by Claire.

"What was that all about?" Claire asked.

"Book signing." Hope pulled open the door of the dishwasher and loaded it with plates, coffee cups and saucers.

"Didn't those girls show up?"

"I'm just helping out." Hope lifted the door and shut it.

"You have a serious problem."

"Did you enjoy the walk around the garden?" Hope wiped down the counter. Her last act of tidying up. She promised herself.

"Forget about the tour. We have to find out why Peaches is here."

When Peaches arrived in Jefferson a year ago, she turned the real estate agency Claire worked at upside down. The small firm wasn't used to her aggressive selling tactics, but the agency owner, Alfred Kingston, didn't complain about the profits.

"She might hear you. Besides, she can't be all that bad."

Claire glanced over her shoulder. "See for yourself." She sidestepped to allow her sister full access to the real estate agent.

Peaches strode into the kitchen with purpose and paused for a nanosecond to look around. Either she was impressed with Audrey's decorating or she was calculating the market value of the space. Hope guessed it was the latter.

"Is there something you need?" Hope stepped forward, away from her sister.

The rest of the guests weren't going out of their way to make Peaches feel welcome. So she decided she would attempt to do so. Peaches frowned then glanced to the cup she held. That was when Hope saw a brownish stain on her sweater. She recognized it immediately. A coffee stain.

"Someone bumped into me and I spilled my coffee." Peaches discarded the cup with a thump on the counter.

"What a shame," Claire said.

Hearing a faint note of pleasure in her sister's voice, Hope glanced at her sister. Claire struggled not to smile.

"I can help." Hope dashed across the kitchen to the table where her purse was and whipped out a spot-removal stick.

"No, you don't need to go to any trouble," Peaches said.

As Hope turned to head back to Peaches, her sister cozied up to her and quietly said, "Seriously, you carry around a stain-removal stick? I'm still baffled we share the same DNA."

Hope ignored Claire. "It's no trouble." Snatching a towel off the counter, she was prepared to treat the stain before it fully set into the sweater. "First, we need to blot away any excess." She pressed the towel onto the sweater for a few moments.

"You seem to know about this kind of stuff," Peaches said warily.

"You should see her with a clothing steamer," Claire said.

Hope shot her sister a warning look. "Okay, it looks like we got most of the excess off your sweater, which, by the way, is very pretty."

"Thank you." Peaches' tone was cool and distant.

Hope tossed the towel back on the counter and then picked up the stain-remover stick and pulled off the cap. "I'm going to rub this onto the stain."

"And this will get the stain out?" Peaches asked.

Hope pressed the tip onto the stain several times to release the stain remover solution. "It's an on-the-go solution which should keep the stain from setting in. You'll need to treat it at home before putting it in the laundry. I can text you the instructions." She gently rubbed the tip across the stain.

"I think it's going to be a lot easier just to toss the sweater." Peaches pulled back from Hope and her stain-remover stick.

"Don't be silly, I'm sure the stain will come right out and it'll be as good as new."

Peaches raised her hands, clearly indicating for Hope to stop. "I don't have time to remove stains with a little stick or anything else. I have a life." She brushed past Hope and walked out of the kitchen, all the while shaking her head.

Claire stepped forward. "I warned you about her."

Hope's brows furrowed in confusion. "Why wouldn't she want to remove a stain?" After returning the stick to its pouch, Hope set it in her organized bag.

Claire rolled her eyes. "Would you forget about the sweater? We have a bigger problem."

"Like what?"

"Like the fact she's here." Claire pointed her index finger in the direction of the hallway, where Peaches had disappeared into. "What is she up to?"

"The event is almost over so I don't think we have to worry. Nothing has happened and I'm sure nothing will," Hope said with confidence.

Vanessa popped into the kitchen. "We're ready to start the book signing." She disappeared just as fast as she'd appeared.

"Let's go." Hope walked out of the kitchen with her sister. In the hall, Meg stood at the coat closet, and Hope motioned to Claire to go ahead without her. But before she could reach Meg, Jane Merrifield intercepted her.

"Dear," the elderly woman said as she rested a hand on Hope's forearm.

Hope paused and smiled at the white-haired woman who wore a floral dress and her bright pink signature lipstick.

"Are you enjoying yourself, Jane?"

"Oh, yes, immensely. Do you have any idea why Miss McCoy came today? She's causing quite a stir."

Without question, the focus of the event had been shifted from Audrey and her garden to Peaches. That was probably the reason Peaches had shown up. She wanted to ruin Audrey's big day. But why? They were on opposite sides of a hot-button topic, but showing up at Audrey's home during a private event seemed to be taking their disagreement a little too far. Peaches had definitely crossed a line.

"I'm sure she'll be leaving soon," Hope said.

Jane leaned closer and in a quieter voice she said, "Sounds like a classic mystery, starting off with an uninvited guest. There's a story here, dear."

Chapter Three

Hope shook her head. "I'm sure there isn't a story here today."

Jane's mind always seemed to be concocting murders, which left Hope wondering why the older woman stopped writing murder mysteries. It had been over forty years since Jane wrote her last book, but her imagination still seemed very fertile. Perhaps that was the reason Jane was the perfect organizer for the library's mystery book group. A club Hope belonged to on and off since high school.

Vanessa popped out of the dining room. Her eyes narrowed and a deep line creased between her brows.

"Is there a problem?" Vanessa ran a tight ship and she detested veering off schedule.

"You better go in there. I'll be right behind you." Hope sent Jane on her way and turned her attention back to Meg. "You're leaving?"

Meg yanked her coat off a hanger then shut the door a little louder than she probably wanted to. "I have to leave." She jammed her arms into the coat sleeves.

"Are you okay?"

Meg zipped up her coat. "I've stayed long enough with that woman here."

"I know it's easy to blame Peaches for the development defeat."

"If you only knew." Meg stopped talking and took a breath. "I have to go."

Hope closed the door behind Meg and tried to make sense out of the day, which was more of a circus than Morning Pete's show. Guests showing up uninvited, guests storming out, and guests demanding other guests not be in attendance. Sally was right, the inmates were running the asylum.

Hope made a quick mental note to never host an event that revolved around the Jefferson Garden Club.

"Hope!" Vanessa called out from the dining room. "We're starting."

Hope hurried into the dining room to join everyone and get her copy of Audrey's brand-spanking-new gardening book, the third in a planned five-book series about the seasons of gardening. Audrey beamed happiness and pride as she signed each book with a personal note. She had worked hard over the years to build her brand, which started when she was in high school. She was the youngest member of the garden club and regularly published in their newsletter. By the time she graduated college, she had a gardening column for a local newspaper and was writing for magazines. Within a few years, she got her first book deal and then the Audrey Bloom brand took off with regular appearances on daytime television providing gardening advice.

Hope was next up for her book. "How are you holding up?"

"Okay, I think. It's just been so hectic. Everyone has been so wonderful today. I'm truly blessed." Audrey finished writing her note in Hope's book.

"I'm sorry, I have to ask. Did you invite Peaches?" Hope's curiosity was killing her. She had to know. Taking the book from Audrey, she opened the cover and read the inscription.

Hope, you're one of my dearest friends and I am forever grateful to have you in my life.

She choked with emotion. She closed the book and blinked a few times to hold back the tears.

"Right back at you," Hope said with a big smile.

"No, I didn't invite Peaches. I have no idea why she showed up, but I didn't want to cause a scene by throwing her out. That would be rude. But I will have a word with her later."

"Of course you will." It was time to shift the focus from Peaches back to the reason everyone was at Audrey's house. "I can't wait to read this." Hope held the book close to her chest. "I need so much help with my gardens. I don't know where to start."

"Let me know if I can help."

Hope nodded then stepped away so Sally could get her copy of the book. She moved over to a window and paused to flip through the book. Page after page, there were color photographs and advice on creating a lush, plentiful garden. While inspiration practically jumped off the page, it took hours of dedication and hard work to maintain a garden like Audrey's. Hours Hope didn't have to spare.

"Isn't it a beautiful book?"

Hope looked up. Calista Davenport, Audrey's book editor, stood in front of her holding a copy of *Seasons in the Garden.*

"Yes, it is. You and Audrey did a great job."

"We did," Calista said.

"It's your modesty I admire most about you." Hope closed her book and gave Calista a hug. Hope had met Calista years ago at some function in New York and, while they weren't friends, they remained friendly acquaintances. When Audrey was looking for a new publisher, it was Calista who signed her and edited the seasonal gardening books.

"How's it feel to be back up in the woods?" Calista set her book on the sideboard.

The ultimate urban girl, Calista had traded in her uniform of black leggings, black tunic, and a black leather jacket for dark green skinny jeans topped with a caramel-colored turtleneck and tweed jacket. Her black hair was cut in a severe bob that accentuated her large blue eyes and full lips.

"It feels good. You should try it."

"No thanks. I'll stay in the city. To me, Brooklyn is the suburbs, and that's as far I think I'll ever move. But I have to admit, you and Audrey live in a great town. It's so . . . cozy . . . quaint." Calista seemed to struggle to find a non-offensive description of Jefferson.

"You make us sound like a greeting card." Hope looked around the room, and it was filled with people she'd known for years, with a few exceptions. Maybe Jefferson was like a greeting card. Was that a bad thing?

Calista shrugged. "I guess we all can't live in the city. It's kind of like a calling. Either you have it or you don't."

Hope considered for a moment. As a teenager, all she'd wanted was to live in the city. To have an apartment in a tall building and ride the subway and have a hamburger at any time of the day. *Silly teenage dreams.* The apartment she got in a tall building came with staff that required fat holiday bonuses to ensure her packages were accepted, the subway was dirty, and hamburgers in the middle of night added ten pounds to her lean frame.

"Audrey is one of my best authors. She's driven and she knows exactly what she wants and she gets it. What about you? Was walking away from the magazine what you really wanted?"

Hope's answer was on the tip of her tongue. It was well-rehearsed because she'd been asked that question a bazillion times by everybody in the world. Okay, maybe not the world, but a lot of people. She couldn't very well tell them the truth that she was scared out of her mind when she resigned from her position or that, while there was a brief moment she wanted to return to the magazine, they wouldn't hire her back. No, staying on message was the way to go. But there was always that nagging question of what her life would have been like if she'd stayed in Jefferson like Audrey did. But since her life wasn't a two-hour made-for-television dramatic movie, she wouldn't be transported back in time to see how another life choice would have turned out.

"No regrets," Hope said simply.

Calista held Hope's gaze for a moment then nodded, seemingly approving of Hope's life choice.

"There you are." Audrey swooped in and linked arms with Calista. "I must steal you away for a moment."

Hope stepped aside and let the two women pass her and then disappear into the adjoining living room. She then caught a glimpse of Vanessa waving to her, and she knew it was time to stop thinking about the what-ifs. Vanessa gestured to the patio door, where Hope saw a group gathered outside. Time to rejoin the festivities.

Hope helped herself to another cup of punch and mingled with the other guests. The topic of conversation was naturally gardening but there was a lot of curiosity about her blog. Most people didn't understand what being a blogger entailed, and they certainly didn't understand how much hard work it took to earn a living as a blogger. Analytics, SEO, and ad networks were definitely buzz-kills, so Hope just talked about the bright and shiny stuff of blogging—photography, recipe testing, and free stuff. She wandered back into the dining room and found an empty tray on the sideboard. She lifted it and began gathering discarded items.

"Did Peaches leave?" Claire joined Hope as she exited the dining room.

"Probably. I haven't seen her since Audrey signed a book for her." Hope carried a tray of empty cups, plates, and utensils. She couldn't help herself. Her sister was right. She had a problem. Too bad there wasn't a support group for obsessive housekeepers. Then again, maybe that was a good thing. Because of her disorder, she had plenty of content for her blog.

"Looks like all she came for was a free book. Talk about cheap. I'm going to get some tea." Claire broke away from Hope and headed for the kitchen.

"I'm leaving." Drew approached Hope. He'd zipped his jacket and his camera was safely stored in a carrying case. "For a moment I thought I'd have a real story when Peaches showed up. Now I just have another gardening story."

Hope smiled at her friend and knew nothing she said would make him feel better. No, it was better to let him pout and get it out of his system until the next crisis in his life. And there would be another one. There always was. "I'm sure you'll write a fabulous article like you always do."

"It'll be just another gardening piece."

Sally ambled out of the living room and stopped. "I'm glad this event is over. I can't believe how bossy Vanessa's been. She acts like this is her home and this was her tour."

Hope juggled the tray as she reached for a discarded cup on the table. "She was just trying to help Audrey. It's her job."

"Well, it did turn out to be nice, despite Miss McCoy showing up. Do you need a hand, dear?"

"No, I've got it covered. Why don't you go and get another cream puff? They're your favorite." Hope liked to spoil Sally, even though she griped a lot.

"I had one too many, I'm afraid." Drew patted his slim midsection.

"I shouldn't, but I can't resist them." Sally turned and headed to the kitchen.

"Has she been complaining all day?" Drew asked.

"No, not really." Hope continued down the hallway and stopped at the closed study door. She twisted the doorknob then entered with Drew behind her. A wall of floor-to-ceiling bookcases greeted them, along with the faint smell of cigars. Leather furniture, dark wood, and a massive desk left no question the room belonged to Audrey's husband, Harrison.

Hope's gaze narrowed on three half-empty glasses left coasterless on the end table. She swiped them up with precision, setting them on the tray, and was pleased to see no rings on the hardwood. A visual search of the room found no other unattended glasses, but it did turn up a messy situation over by the desk.

"Look at this mess. I can't imagine Harrison leaving his study like this."

Papers were scattered on top of the impressive desk that gleamed from regular polishing. Her gaze traveled downward, where she saw more papers and folders scattered on the floor. It was as if someone had been searching for something.

"My career is going nowhere." Drew's head dipped down and he tapped on his cell phone. He was always checking his messages for the next big story.

"That's not true and you know it." Hope knew a thing or two about a career going nowhere and was even more intimately familiar with a career that had crashed and burned. She inched cautiously toward the desk. Something felt off, but she couldn't put her finger on what it was. She froze in place. A shudder zipped through her body and her muscles tensed as she looked down.

Peaches McCoy's body was sprawled, facedown, on the carpet, and a pool of blood puddled along the side of her head.

Hope gasped.

The tray fell from her hands. The china cups and glasses shattered against the hardwood floor. The tray landed with a loud clank.

"Find a scratch on the floor?" Drew peered over Hope's shoulder. Then he gasped. "Holy crap! Is she dead?"

Chapter Four

Peaches was dead all right. For lack of an official cause of death, it appeared Peaches had been bashed in the back of her head with the bloodied rock next to her body. The ruthless real estate agent had more enemies than friends in Jefferson. Many of them were gathered on Audrey's patio.

The police officers who arrived first on the scene had moved each person outside and then, one by one, interviewed them. While they waited, Hope tried to serve beverages, but an officer denied her access to the kitchen. She could only sit and wait with the rest of them. Did they feel as helpless as she did?

Sally and Jane sat together on the cushioned wicker sofa in front of the outdoor fireplace. Audrey had spared no expense when she installed the curved flagstone patio and managed to balance good taste with functionality. Hope noticed Jane's blue eyes were wide with curiosity. No doubt her mind was racing to solve the murder. In sharp contrast, Sally sat stoically. She was born and bred a Yankee who'd weathered many storms, and this one would be no different.

Elaine Whitcomb sat on the edge of the love seat and avoided eye contact with anyone. She shifted in her seat and fidgeted her hands. She and Peaches had one thing in common. They both had difficulty making friends. Though it looked like Peaches did make a deadly enemy.

Hope's sister stood with her arms crossed over her chest and her brow furrowed deeply.

Her focus was on the garden. She hadn't moved since they were shuffled outside, other than to complain that the police officer had the nerve to take down her birthdate. It was common for her to shave a few years off her age, and she probably would have preferred to confess to murder than to actually say her birth year.

Maretta Kingston sat alone at the long dining table. The middle-aged woman sat very straight with her hands clasped on the table. Her gaze was fixed on the lawn, and she hadn't uttered a word since she squawked about being detained and that the mayor would hear about the police's abuse of power.

The remaining guests were scattered throughout the patio. Audrey had created the perfect entertaining space, and Hope bet her friend never expected the space to be used for witness detention. The police had requested they not discuss any part of the investigation. Hope wondered if the police knew they were up against a difficult crowd. The gossip chain was alive and well in Jefferson, with many of its active participants right there on the patio.

One of the French doors swung open and Drew stepped onto the patio. The fact he was the only reporter on the scene allowed him limited access to the investigation. This advantage gave him what he'd been dying for—an exclusive. He made a beeline for Hope and leaned in close.

"Peaches was texting when she was murdered," he whispered into Hope's ear.

She looked at him and mouthed, "What?"

He grabbed her by the arm and they moved onto the lawn to continue their conversation without having to use sign language.

"How do you know that? The police told you?" Hope asked.

"While you were busy calling the police, I took a look around and found her phone. You must have missed it."

Having never found a dead body before, Hope had been too distracted to search the study. "Someone had to call for help. Did you read the message?"

Drew nodded. "She didn't complete the message before she died."

"What did it say?"

"It was to someone named Matt and she confirmed their meeting tomorrow."

Hope shrugged. "Probably just a client."

"I don't think so. She texted that she didn't find what they needed."

"What was she looking for?"

"Don't know."

"So that's why she came here today. Not for the tour but to search Harrison's study."

"Maybe she thought with everyone busy with the tour and the book signing, no one would notice that she had slipped away to search the room."

Hope took a sweeping look across the patio. "Maybe Jane was right. Maybe this garden tour was destined to end with murder."

"I just have a few questions for you, Ms. Early," Detective Sam Reid said.

"I understand." Hope seated herself across from him at the dining-room table.

The detective wasn't a physically imposing man. His slight, thin build didn't hint at the fact he'd been a police officer for over ten years. His thick eyebrows cast a shadow over his dark, narrow eyes that seemed capable of pinpointing deception a mile away with precision.

"You were cleaning up when you discovered Ms. McCoy's body, is that correct, Ms. Early?"

Hope nodded. "Yes, that's correct."

"Didn't Mrs. Bloom hire people to do that?"

Hope nodded again. "Yes. I was just helping. You know what they say, many hands make light work." She paused because she was on the verge of rambling.

Reid studied her for a moment. The brief instant of silence was deafening for Hope. What was he thinking? Did he think she killed Peaches? That was ridiculous. But one of the guests had to be the killer.

"What did you see when you entered the room?"

Hope filled him in on what happened from the moment she entered the study to the moment she found Peaches' body. How many more times would she have to tell the tale?

"Prior to the incident, had you spoken with the deceased?"

"Briefly when she came into the kitchen. She had a coffee stain on her sweater, and I tried to pre-treat it for her so she'd be able to get the stain out later, but she didn't want to be bothered doing that. She said she had 'a life.'" Hope realized what she'd just said in her rambling. "Oh, guess she was wrong."

Detective Reid jotted down some notes. "To your knowledge, Ms. McCoy wasn't invited to today's event?"

"No, she wasn't."

"Did Ms. McCoy indicate why she showed up today?"

"Not to me."

"Do you know if she spoke to anyone today?"

Hope shrugged. "I didn't notice. I was busy."

"Helping out?"

Hope nodded.

"Why would Ms. McCoy not have been invited today?"

"You'll have to ask Audrey. This was her event. And she made the decision on the guest list."

"Your sister, Claire Dixon, wasn't on the guest list. She also showed up uninvited."

"She came as my guest."

"Why wasn't your sister invited?"

"She's not a gardener."

Reid frowned. "She's a real estate agent who is pro-development in town. Which Mrs. Bloom is fighting against, so it makes sense she wouldn't be invited to a social event hosted by Mrs. Bloom."

Hope shifted in her seat. Why was he asking about Claire? He needed to focus on finding the killer. She locked in on his steely gaze, and a pit formed in her stomach. Detective Reid was focusing on finding the killer by asking about Claire.

"Your sister and Ms. McCoy worked at the same real estate agency, and by nature real estate agents are competitive."

"Claire is a smart businesswoman."

"I'm sure she is. Is it true Ms. McCoy was chosen as the listing agent for Lionel Whitcomb's new development over your sister?"

"Why are you asking? Do you think my sister had something to do with the murder?"

"I'm just asking a few questions, trying to gather the facts."

"Well, let me save you some time. Claire isn't your murderer. From what I know, Peaches didn't have many friends here in Jefferson. Perhaps you should be asking some other questions."

"Thank you, but I don't need assistance with my time management."

"Are we finished? I'd like to go home."

"Yes, we're finished . . . for now. Everyone will be permitted to leave shortly. We do apologize for the inconvenience."

Hope stood to walk away. Her feet speed walked toward the closed door. She wanted to put a lot of distance between herself and the detective. She didn't like the questions he asked about her sister and her relationship with Peaches.

"Oh, one more thing, Ms. Early."

Hope cringed. She wasn't fast enough. She stopped and turned to face the detective, bracing herself.

"The fact that you are a close, personal friend with the chief won't keep me from doing my job."

Hope stiffened. *Personal?* The way he said the word made her relationship with Ethan sound dirty, almost bad. Was she supposed to feel ashamed for being friends with him, caring about him or for thinking of him as *sweet and delicious?* Okay, the last part might be a little embarrassing to admit out loud. But who was Detective Reid to cast judgment on their relationship, whatever it was?

"I wouldn't expect that it would. Now, if there's nothing else, it's been a long day, as you know." Hope walked out of the dining room, closing the door behind her. For a moment she stood motionless as her frayed nerves settled. She should have never agreed to bring Claire with her to the garden tour because now she was a murder suspect.

Chapter Five

Hope knocked on Audrey's bedroom door and waited for a response. Audrey had been allowed to go to her room to pack a bag for herself and Harrison since the police informed them the house was a crime scene and they couldn't stay there. An officer permitted Hope to go upstairs and help Audrey. Hope knocked on the door again.

"Audrey, it's me." Hope tried to gather her thoughts. What did you say to a friend whose house was a crime scene because of a murder? Everything that came to mind was just lame. It was probably best to listen. Yes, she'd give Audrey a sympathetic ear and a shoulder to cry on, if necessary.

Footsteps approached the other side of the door, and the door opened slowly. Audrey gestured for her to enter.

"I'm so glad it's you. This is just awful." Audrey turned and walked back to her chaise lounge, where there were two large overnight bags surrounded by neatly folded clothing.

Hope entered the elegant room, where antique and reproduction furnishings mixed together effortlessly. Placed in the center of the room was a four-poster bed piled high with luxury pillows. Between two windows, which offered magnificent views of the garden, a skirted vanity stood. Beloved objects were grouped together on top of a mirrored tray. Among them was Audrey's most treasured possession, her grandmother's jewelry box. Her life seemed as manicured as her perfect gardens.

Except on that day. There was a corpse in her study.

Hope closed the door behind her. "How are you holding up?"

"This doesn't make sense. Why did she even come here today?" Audrey looked at Hope, her red, swollen eyes searching for an answer. She'd removed her makeup, leaving her face pale and tired. Her image of fine living had disappeared and was replaced by exhaustion and fear. Audrey had every right to be fearful. A woman she despised was murdered under her roof.

"What could she have wanted? For God's sake, why did she have to die here?"

"I doubt she planned to die," Hope said.

"Well, if she hadn't come here, she wouldn't be dead downstairs." Tears streamed down Audrey's face. She tried in vain to wipe them away with her hands.

Hope snatched a tissue from the vanity and handed it to her friend. She returned to the vanity and sat on the petite chair. For a brief moment, she felt like a princess. A princess caught in a murder.

"Could she have come here hoping to use the tour as a distraction to look for something? The desk looked like it had been searched," Hope said.

"That's impossible. What on earth could she have been looking for?" Audrey had wiped away her tears and began packing both bags. The police had said they should have their investigation within the house completed by tomorrow and the Blooms could return home.

"What does Harrison keep in his study? In his desk?"

"Financial papers, work documents. I'm not sure. When he gets home I'm sure he'll tell the police." Audrey zipped one bag and then walked into her closet and came out with a pair of jeans she placed into her bag.

As Audrey continued packing, Hope tried to figure out what Peaches had been looking for and who she would have been sharing that information with. Harrison worked for Northwest CT Bank, which had branches throughout the state. Most likely any work documents he had were kept on his computer and not in a desk drawer. A knock at the door pulled Hope out of her thoughts.

"Mrs. Bloom, it's Chief Cahill."

Hope's head swung around. Ethan's deep, steady voice was exactly what she needed to hear. She needed the reassurance that everything was going to be okay. She glanced back at Audrey, who gestured for her to open the door for Ethan.

Hope crossed the room and opened the door.

In uniform, there was no mistaking Ethan Cahill's solid broadness, which slipped by her earlier in the morning because she'd been distracted by the pastry bag. What she would have given to be back at her kitchen table eating cinnamon buns with Ethan.

His strong hands rested on his hips and a flash of annoyance flickered in his dark espresso eyes. Maybe that could have been due to the fact that everyone was supposed to have remained outside and she knew the newbie officer had made an exception for her by allowing her upstairs.

"I'd like a word with you," Ethan said.

Uh-oh. Hope faintly smiled at Audrey "I'll be right back." Unless she got escorted off the property or arrested for interfering in a police investigation. Either way, it wouldn't be good. Still, she closed the door behind her as she stepped out into the hall.

"What can I do for you?" she asked softly.

The flicker of annoyance in Ethan's eyes deepened and his jaw tightened. "You can tell me what you're doing up here. This house is a crime scene now."

Even though he was clearly displeased with Hope at the moment, his nearness calmed her. He was her rock. An angry rock at the moment, though.

"I wanted to check on Audrey. Help her pack since Harrison isn't home so she could get out of the house faster, leaving your officers free to do their jobs without anyone interfering." Her ex-producer, Corey Lucas, would have been proud of the spin she put on disobeying a police directive.

"I spoke with Harrison a little while ago. He's

on his way home." With his hand, Ethan guided Hope away from the bedroom door.

His touch on the small of her back sparked a surprising sensation of warmth through her body. She tried to focus on what Ethan had just said and not the tingling in her body, at what was the most inappropriate time.

"You'd think he'd be here by now, considering what has happened."

"I talked with Reid. You said you only spoke with Ms. McCoy once today." Ethan pulled out a pen and a small pad from his jacket pocket.

"Briefly. She came into the kitchen and I tried to remove a coffee stain from her sweater."

Ethan grinned. "Of course you did."

Hope chose to ignore his little dig, even though it was all in good fun. "She was only in the kitchen for a few minutes."

"What did she say?"

"Not much. She didn't say why she was here, if that's what you're asking."

A slamming door interrupted them. Hope suspected Harrison had arrived home. She was right. Heavy footsteps ascended the staircase and she caught a glimpse of his silver hair.

"Chief Cahill." Harrison reached the top of the landing.

Ethan crammed his notepad into his jacket pocket and said to Hope, "Excuse me."

Hope couldn't miss the stern look on Harrison's face, his mouth drawn tight and his forehead furrowed. She thanked her stars she didn't have to deal with him. The two men exchanged words and neither looked pleased with the other.

"This is my house . . ." Harrison's voice boomed in the hall. "I want your people gone." Not waiting for a response, he brushed past Ethan and headed toward his bedroom.

Hope braced herself. She wouldn't be able to get out of his way fast enough. His stride was long and it took only seconds, really nanoseconds, before he reached her.

She'd never seen him look so angry. At six feet, he towered over her. His nostrils flared and his steel blue eyes bore down on her. He was beyond angry. He was furious.

"You look terrible. You should go home and get some rest." He opened his bedroom door and closed it behind him.

"He's right." Ethan approached Hope.

Her brows arched. "That I look terrible?"

"That you should go home and get some rest."

"Do you have any suspects?"

"You know I can't comment."

"Can't or won't?"

"Rest assured we will complete a thorough investigation. This is a police matter. Do you understand?"

"Yes." What Hope understood was that Detective Reid was interested in Claire and, considering his job was to arrest someone for murder, that wasn't a good thing.

Two doors down, Maretta appeared from the hall bathroom. "Chief Cahill, may we leave now?"

"Has everyone disregarded police instructions?" Ethan asked.

"If you must know, I needed to use the facilities and the one downstairs was occupied and you have seen fit to block off access to the kitchen, so I couldn't use the one in that area of the house. What was I supposed to do, go in the woods?"

Hope shot Ethan a "glad you asked?" look.

He cleared his throat. "We're doing the best we can, given the circumstances."

"If you didn't realize, the library is setting up for its annual bake sale and it takes many hands to do that. May I leave or am I still under house arrest or patio arrest? Really, keeping us outside like pet dogs. You should be ashamed of yourself."

The bake sale. Hope cringed. She'd forgotten, but Maretta hadn't. While she saw Peaches death as a tragedy, Maretta viewed it as an inconvenience.

"You haven't been under house arrest, Mrs. Kingston," Ethan corrected her.

"That's your perspective." Maretta directed her gaze to Hope. "I saw you signed up to volunteer after several years of not participating."

Maretta would expect Hope to drop everything in her life while living in New York City to come back to Jefferson to sell cookies at the library.

"I'm baking extra cookies this year, too," Hope said. Maybe that would appease the older woman.

Maretta stiffened. "I see."

No appeasement.

With a huff, Maretta turned and walked to the staircase. Her bony hand held tightly onto the banister as if she needed help with her balance. She descended the carpeted stairs slowly.

"Shall we?" Ethan stepped aside to allow Hope to follow Maretta down the stairs.

"Everyone can go home now. And I mean go home."

*   *   *

The early afternoon sun streamed through the windows of the foyer and backlit Jane Merrifield as she opened the hall closet.

"Do you need any help?" Hope offered as she came off the last step of the staircase. Apparently the guests were allowed back into the entry hall to gather their personal belongings as an officer stood watch.

Jane pulled her coat out of the closet and slipped it on. "Today has been dreadful. You know, a cup of chamomile tea will make you feel better," she advised.

"I'm okay," Hope lied.

Jane was a worrier, a nurturer, and wouldn't think twice about taking over Hope's home to care for her. She'd show up with her box of teas, her cure-all chicken soup, and her knitting.

"Who would have thought there would have been a murder here in Jefferson?" Jane motioned for Hope to move closer to her. "I admit it's all very exciting." Her eyes sparkled. "You've got yourself quite a mystery."

"I have?"

"Yes, dear. You were my most enthusiastic Mystery Book Club member. You always figured out who did it before anyone else."

The Mystery Book Club. When she was a teenager, Hope joined a handful of other kids once a month to read and discuss mystery novels. Jane was the group leader and chief sleuth. Together they worked through the puzzles and discussed the whys and hows of murder. Hope's mother thought it unseemly for her teenage daughter to be discussing murder as

an extracurricular activity. But Hope found it fasci-
nating and never missed a meeting. She often fan-
tasized about being one of the sleuths finding the
victim and solving the crime. A chill snaked through
her as Peaches' bloodied body flashed in her mind.
Most fantasies didn't live up to their expectations.

"They were books. And I'm not a police detective."

The older woman waved away the objection. "Neither was Barbara Neal. But that never stopped her."

Great. Hope was being compared to Jane's fictional college coed sleuth.

"The obvious suspects are Audrey and Harrison.
She would be my first choice. She and Peaches
were divided on the future of this town. Audrey is
very passionate about keeping Jefferson the way it
is, and sometimes passion can lead to a deadly mistake."

"I can't believe Audrey would do such a thing,
not even in the heat of the moment."

Jane nodded. "I know, dear. You see, what I realized is the French doors in the study lead out onto
the garden and anyone could have entered through
them while we were walking around the property."

Hope hadn't thought of that. Someone who
wasn't attending the event could have entered the
house. Could Peaches have been looking for the
powder room and mistakenly entered the study?
Was it possible Peaches was killed simply because
she was in the wrong place at the wrong time?

"Did you happen to notice if the doors were unlocked or damaged from someone breaking in?"

Hope shook her head. "I didn't notice."

"Tsk. Tsk. But no need to worry, dear." Jane patted Hope's hand. "I'm sure you'll have another opportunity to look around the crime scene."

Hope didn't have the heart or energy to tell Jane she had no desire to ever enter that room again. "I'm sure the police will do a thorough job investigating Peaches' death."

"They'll do their best, dear. But they'll need some help. They always do."

Chapter Six

"Couldn't this wait until tomorrow?" Hope glanced over to Claire, who was seated in the passenger seat of her SUV.

Claire let out a dramatic, exasperated sigh. "Are you kidding? This is the break I've been waiting for. Do you know how big Whitcomb's business is? He's putting developments up and down the East Coast."

"A woman was just murdered." Hope's gaze shifted back to the road. Winding, narrow roads made up the majority of the northwest hills of Connecticut and it was common to have squirrels or chipmunks dart out in the blink of an eye. In a few hours, as the sun set, deer would be added to that list.

"It wasn't me and besides, I didn't like the woman, so I'm not going to waste time fake mourning for her."

"Fake mourning?" Hope shook her head. Her foot eased off the accelerator pedal as she approached a stop sign. What on earth was Claire talking about?

"You know, when you say all nice things about someone who just died or you cancel a social event out of respect or sign a condolence card with some sappy one-liner."

"Sappy one-liner?"

"Like 'I'm sorry for your loss, you're in my prayers.' Seriously, who really does that?"

"Someone who is polite."

"Well, then they wouldn't be fake mourning." Claire didn't say it, but the implied "duh" was very clear.

Hope shook her head. She opted not to continue with that conversation thread and to continue through the intersection. When the police had released all of the guests, Hope found Claire on her cell phone arranging a meeting at the real estate office with her boss, Alfred Kingston, and developer Lionel Whitcomb.

"Look, it's horrible she was murdered and that it happened on Audrey's big day, but I have a business to run, a mortgage to pay, and two kids to put through college. If it'll make you feel better, I'll wear black tomorrow."

"This isn't about me."

"Then who is this about? Me?"

"Yes. Taking over her listing just hours after her murder could shine an unfavorable light on you."

"What the heck are you talking about?"

Hope flicked on her turn signal and made a left

onto Main Street. The Jefferson Town Real Estate office was just ahead. "You could have a motive for murder."

"Says who?"

"Detective Reid."

"He said that?"

"Well, not in so many words. He implied it."

"Ridiculous. I didn't murder anyone."

"I know." Hope pulled into a space outside the row of brick buildings. The center one was where Claire worked. The window was cluttered with printouts of available homes in town and the surrounding area.

"Then why are we talking about this?"

Hope let out a deep sigh. To continue the conversation was pointless. Claire had no intention of canceling the meeting. Being the big sister, she always knew what was right. Well, at least she liked to think she did. "Here we are. Go to your meeting."

"Thanks for the lift. I'll have someone give me a ride home afterwards."

"Good. I wasn't planning on coming back for you."

Claire flashed a grin. "Love you, too, Sis." She eased out of the car and closed the door behind her.

Hope watched her sister enter the building. When the door closed behind Claire, Hope saw Wallace Green approach her car. He owned a landscaping business in town and knew most of the residents either from his mowing services or his award-winning hardscape design work. He'd been on Hope's list of calls to make since she bought her house. He had a deep frown etched on his face. He'd heard already and, by dinnertime, the news would be all over Jefferson. She pressed the button to lower the passenger-side window.

"Is it true?" Wallace leaned in after removing his baseball cap that had the logo of his company embroidered on it. He ran his fingers through his thinning brown hair. "Peaches was murdered?"

Hope nodded. "I'm sorry."

"My word, how is this possible? Murdered in Audrey's house? I can't wrap my brain around it."

"Tell me about it. Seeing her there . . ." Hope's words trailed off as her throat tightened. Peaches' body flashed in her mind.

"You saw her?"

Hope nodded again because she couldn't form the simple word yes.

"That must have been horrible."

Wallace's devastated look forced Hope to pull herself together. Everybody in town was going to feel awful, whether they liked Peaches or not. Hope couldn't think of one person who wouldn't be saddened or horrified by a murder. Her friend was grieving and she needed to be strong for him. "I'll be fine."

"Do the police have any idea of who did it?"

"No one was arrested. I don't know what kind of leads they have."

"I hope they catch the killer and throw away the key."

"Did you know Peaches?"

"No, not really. Only met her a few times. She was a client. We mowed her lawn. Are you playing detective, Hope? Did Jane Merrifield put you up to this?"

"I . . . I don't know what you're talking about?"

Wallace grinned. "You were the shining star in our mystery reading group. Don't think I've forgotten that. You always figured out who did it before anyone else. You probably should have become a cop instead of a blogger. I better get back to the office. I'll call you later." Wallace pushed off of the car door and walked to the curb, then crossed when there was no traffic. If she was a cop, Hope would have given Wallace a ticket for jaywalking. He was right, she was a blogger, not a sleuth, and besides, she didn't have time to go digging into a murder investigation. She had full confidence in Ethan's police department to conduct a thorough investigation that would prove Claire had no part in the murder. Claire was innocent.

The back door of Hope's kitchen swung open and Claire burst in, waving the *North Country Gazette*, the daily newspaper serving Litchfield County.

"Peaches McCoy is dead." Claire slammed the door shut.

Good thing Hope was baking cookies and not a soufflé.

"We already know that. And it made the paper already?" Hope continued scooping spoonfuls of oatmeal cookie dough onto prepared baking sheets.

"No! But there was an article on Whitcomb's development on the front page." Claire's voice held a hint of mirth.

Hope shook her head. After she returned home from the garden tour, she'd spent a couple of hours in a funk. She wasn't sure what to do first. E-mails, barn chores, bake cookies, or just collapse on the sofa and watch mindless television. She chose to put on her apron and bake.

The soothing hum of the stand mixer, the productive whizzing of the food processor, and the satisfying tick of the timer put everything right in Hope's world. At least for a little while.

"I'm certain Peaches manipulated, lied, and probably seduced Lionel Whitcomb to get the listing for the Hunting Hills development."

With one subdivision under way and another ambitious one just approved, developer Lionel Whitcomb's name was on everyone's lips those days. Though what usually followed wasn't very flattering, at least from those opposed to new building in Jefferson.

"Ah," Hope acknowledged, with careful neutrality. "Is that what you plan to do?"

"God, no! I can't imagine how she could have slept with that slob. Obviously, she didn't have standards. Besides, I'm married." Claire tossed the newspaper on the island countertop.

Hope didn't want to discuss anyone's sex life. The day had been too brutal, and she hadn't had enough coffee. "What happened to talking about the weather?"

"The weather? My career is going down the toilet and you want to talk about the weather? Well, maybe not completely down the toilet. With Miz Pits gone, Whitcomb is seriously considering me to be the exclusive agent for Hunting Hills. I impressed him at our meeting, and I just happen to be the agency's number one agent now, since Miz Pits bit the dust."

"Stop it! You do realize you just admitted you have a motive for killing her? You don't want to repeat any of what you just said to anyone. Got it?"

Claire nodded, and Hope prayed she understood the gravity of her words. "Okay, I get it. I just need a listing like this."

"Hunting Hills won't be the last subdivision in town. Unfortunately."

"Not you, too? For goodness sakes, wake up and smell the dollar per square foot. That land is a desirable location. How could it not be developed?" Claire reached for a cookie and broke it in half.

Hope sighed. "Desirable location? You know how much I hate that phrase." She looked out the window over her soapstone sink and scanned the towering trees that rose out of the thawing ground. Nearly every day she saw glimpses of deer grazing, wild rabbits hopping about, or that big old woodchuck ambling across her property. In her heart, that was what made property valuable.

"It's a fact of life."

"It's a curse."

"Oh, please. You're starting to sound like some tree hugger."

Hope looked sharply over her shoulder. "Maybe I should become more active in the fight to protect and preserve my hometown. Lord knows you won't."

Claire began to open her cookie-filled mouth to

protest, but Hope raised her hand and continued, "I don't have time to debate the pros and cons of development."

"Good, because that's not why I'm here."

"I have a ton of things to do. And on top of everything else, I'm working the bake sale." She shouldn't have volunteered, but she wanted to be a part of the community again. All she'd been doing since trading New York City for Jefferson was working. Her days were filled with writing content for her blog, promoting her blog through social media, and settling into her newly purchased home. But she loved every hardworking minute of it.

Hope picked up one of the chocolate chip cookies off the rack and bit into it. The warm, dark morsels melted and swirled together with the comforting richness of butter and fresh eggs from her hens. She'd found heaven again, despite the not-so-angelic blonde sitting in her kitchen.

She slid a couple of cookie sheets into the bottom oven of her two wall ovens and set the timer. "Can we please talk about something other than Peaches McCoy and the deadly garden tour?" Hope had planned on keeping busy to distract her from thinking about the gruesome day. What she hadn't planned on was her sister revisiting it.

Claire cocked her head sideways. "Okay. How's the dating going? Seeing anybody?"

Hope should have been clearer. Conversations about Peaches, the state of the economy, or her nonexistent love life were off limits. Every few weeks her sister brought up the topic of her not dating, which was followed by Drew and then by everyone else in her life. If she didn't know better, she would have thought her family and friends had rotations scheduled.

"Ethan's been hanging around a lot more lately. Has he spent the night yet?"

The doorbell chimed, interrupting Claire's inquiring, much to Hope's delight. She was too confused by her feelings to explain them to someone else. Even her sister.

"I'm not expecting anyone," Hope said.

"I'll go see." Claire hurried out of the kitchen and moments later returned. "You have a visitor."

Hope looked up from her baking sheet of cookies. Calista Davenport was standing next to her sister. She was the last person she'd expected to show up, since she wasn't the drop-by-for-a-quick-visit kind of woman. Calista's life, scheduled down to the minute, was managed by a calendar app on her smartphone, and Hope doubted she was a to-do item on that calendar. Calista's gait was long as she made her way across the wide pumpkin pine floorboards. She glanced at the spots where the flooring creaked.

"It's over a hundred years old." Hope found the salvage flooring in Vermont. Since buying her house, she'd gone on hunts for doorknobs to floors to light fixtures. Some of the excursions resulted in fantastic finds like the pumpkin pine floorboards while others were busts, but she and Drew had some fun road trips.

Calista smiled. "How charming."

Hope had heard that compliment often, and was very proud of the home she loved. The kitchen and family room of the farmhouse seamed together into one large space, creating the keeping room. Without question, it was her favorite part of the house. A cooking hearth, original to the house, stood solid at the end of the room. Twelve over twelve paned windows lined the south side of the room and looked out over her expansive gardens and her classic red barn.

"I wasn't expecting a visit from you." Hope cleaned her hands on a towel.

"I apologize for just dropping by, but I'd like to speak with you." Calista glanced over to Claire. "Privately."

"Oh, I see. Okay. I'll check my messages." Taking her cue, Claire turned and walked out of the kitchen.

"What can I do for you?"

"You can help me try and save what's left of Audrey's career."

"What are you talking about? I thought the book had good pre-orders and she mentioned she got good merchandising in all of the retailers."

"Yes, but that was before today. What happened at her house is all over the Web."

"Oh, I see. Would you like a cup of coffee?" Hope moved over to the coffeemaker and grabbed two mugs from a cabinet.

"Yes, thank you." Calista stepped to the island and sat on a stool. "We should have stopped Audrey from getting involved with the development battle in town. We thought the controversy would be good for her brand, which is home and hearth, and her taking on a big developer and the town government to protect her town . . . well, that was good PR."

"Until it wasn't." Hope pulled out a milk carton from the refrigerator.

Calista took a long drink of her coffee. "Correct. The woman who was murdered is the woman Audrey went head-to-head with at the town council meeting. From what I heard, they got into a nasty argument."

"Don't scandals sell books?"

"In some cases. And believe me, this isn't one of those cases. My boss isn't happy."

"You said you want me to help. How can I do that?"

"You have a very prominent social media presence. You're an influencer. I need you to pledge your support for Audrey. She had the misfortune of being tangentially involved with a tragic death."

Hope swung her head up, almost choking on her sip of coffee. Calista Davenport, editor of countless bestselling books and maker of dozens of authors' careers, was asking for her help. She wanted Hope to use her small piece of the Internet to preempt the negative publicity that would swell due to the murder. She set her mug down on the soapstone countertop.

"Your publishing house has a publicity department. Can't they do what you're asking?"

"Of course they can, but it won't mean anything because it's coming from her publisher. You, on the other hand, are a friend, longtime friend, right? You've known Audrey since high school. You knew her parents and her grandmother. You know how hard she's worked and what she's sacrificed to get where she is today. Your followers will know whatever you say about her comes from the heart and not from a profit-and-loss statement. Which means they'll click on the share button and share with their friends and so on."

"Yes, I've known Audrey a very long time, and I know there's no way she's capable of murder, but I don't feel comfortable with what you're proposing."

"I see." Calista pushed her mug away and shook her head. "I clearly have wasted your time."

"No, you haven't. I'll think about it. I promise."

"Don't think too long. We don't have a large window of time before Audrey's career crashes and burns. You know how that feels, right?" Calista stood. "I'll show myself out."

"You do that." Hope swiped Calista's mug off the counter and dumped it into the sink. She would do anything for a friend, but before she made a decision, she needed to talk to Audrey.

Night settled over Jefferson with a deft hand. After Calista left, Claire remained and Hope prepared a light supper for them. Neither had much of an appetite. All afternoon Hope saw flashes of Peaches' body, bloodied and lifeless on the floor of Harrison's study. She hadn't realized it was possible to have nightmares during the day. Then Reid's insinuations that Claire could have had a motive for murder fired her up. How could anyone think her sister could be a cold-blooded killer?

Sure, Claire was a shark when it came to business, but she was also a loving sister, wife, and mother.

She'd hoped making dinner would ease her anxiety. Some people meditated, Hope cooked. The slicing of vegetables and sizzle of chicken cutlets on the grill pan should have calmed her and eased the tension in her neck, but instead, she found herself chopping the carrots a little too hard.

Claire left just after they finished dinner because she had to pick up her son, Logan, from baseball practice. She hesitated, not wanting to leave her sister to clean up by herself, but Hope insisted she'd be fine. Some quiet time would be good. Before she took care of the dishes, Hope packed up all the cookies for the bake sale the next day. With the cookies taken care of, she turned her attention to the kitchen, and when she looked at the clock, it was only seven thirty.

She knew from experience she'd have a difficult time falling asleep. She desperately needed something to exhaust her physically or else her mind would keep her tossing and turning until morning. A run. The sun had set and she wasn't a fan of night running, but she didn't have a choice.

It took only a few minutes for her to change into her running clothes, and out the door she went for a quick, intense run. She made her way down her driveway, past the hedge of boxwoods that lined her property, and onto the sidewalk. She'd head to the center of town, loop around and, she hoped, by then be tired enough to get a few hours of sleep.

Hope quickened her pace. Her sneakers slapped

the asphalt as her arms pumped and she began to
get into the zone. The night air was cold and still.
The silence settled her nerves, which she didn't realize were on edge. She slowed as she approached
Gilbert Madison's colonial house and saw Gilbert
approaching his property with his golden retriever,
Buddy.

"Kinda late for a run." Gilbert came to a halt,
Buddy joining him.

Hope stopped and reached down to Buddy to
pet him. "It probably is too late, but I needed to
run." She straightened and caught sight of the For
Sale sign on his front lawn.

"Peaches put the sign up today. And now she's
dead. Terrible thing." Gilbert shook his head.
Nearing seventy, he was a small man with thin
white hair and sparkling blue eyes. But that night,
his eyes were somber and his normally big smile
was missing.

"Where are you planning on going?" Hope
asked.

"A retirement community, Cobb Hill Estates.
It's not far. This place is too big for us to take care
of." He glanced over his shoulder.

"You must have just signed the contract with
Peaches."

Gilbert nodded. "Yesterday afternoon. She told
me the house would sell fast. These days, fast is important. I'm not a kid anymore, I can't wait
around for things to happen."

"Is that why you went with her? Because she told
you she could sell your house fast?"

Gilbert's head dipped slightly. Maybe he felt

guilty for not signing with Claire. "You're not upset I didn't hire your sister, are you?"

"No, no, of course not." Hope waved away the silly thought. He had every right to choose the agent he wanted to work with.

"Good. Because having one of you angry at me is enough."

"Claire's angry with you?"

"That would be an understatement. I spoke with her about listing the house, but then Peaches showed up the next day with a detailed marketing plan. I made tea, and she told me how she planned on selling my house. I must admit, she is . . . was . . . a pretty girl. Not that Claire isn't. Peaches was charming. I have a feeling she got men to do a lot of things for her. But, boy, was Claire upset. You know she showed up at my house demanding to know why I chose Peaches."

"I doubt Claire was that upset." Hope prayed Gilbert would revisit his statement. The last thing Claire needed was for him to repeat that to the police.

"You know how she gets. There was no reasoning with her. She just stormed off. But I guess now I'll list with her. I need someone to sell this place. Your sister is quick to anger, but she's good at what she does."

Buddy whined and nudged Gilbert's thigh with his snout.

Gilbert looked down and patted Buddy on the head. "I better get inside. There's a show on barn pickers in a few minutes. It's amazing what great finds they turn up in barns that are barely standing. Have a good night." Gilbert turned, tugged on Buddy's leash, and headed to his front door.

Hope dragged in a deep breath. So much for a relaxing run. There was no way she'd be sleeping through the night. Not with her sister becoming more and more the primary person of interest in a murder.

Chapter Seven

Hope didn't know what was worse—the incessant beep of the alarm clock or the nasal voice punctuated with drama at five thirty in the morning.

"What is going on up there in Mayberry? Murder?" Corey Lucas demanded over the telephone from his New York City loft. The reality television producer had kept her number and used it at the most inconvenient times. A creature of his morning ritual, Corey was on his treadmill, which was situated between a mega-screen TV and a wall of windows that looked out to the city skyline. No surprise he chose the TV for his view. The sound of a news anchor filtered through the line. "What happened? Did you see the body? Are you doing interviews?" Her ex-producer's rapid succession of questions snapped Hope out of her sleep fog.

Wide awake and irritated, she knew the only way to get off the phone was to give him a recap of yesterday's events. After ten minutes, she managed to get him off the phone and she got out of bed. She'd spent most of the night tossing and turning, caused by nightmare after nightmare. She flung off her covers and dragged her reluctant, exhausted body off her ultra-comfortable featherbed to start her day.

She plunged into her normal morning routine in hopes of keeping her mind off of the day before. She headed out to the barn to feed the chickens and collect their eggs. After a quick cleanup and with the basket filled, she twisted the knob on the back door and padded through the mudroom to the kitchen and found someone in her kitchen.

"You should lock your doors." Ethan looked up from his plate of chocolate chip cookies. "See you held some from the bake sale."

Hope set the basket of colorful eggs from her Araucana hens and speckled eggs from her Guinea hens on the countertop. She liked using the brown eggs for her baking because of their rich yolk.

"They were a part of my recipe testing." She shrugged off her barn jacket. The mornings, like the evenings, were still cool, and she didn't expect any significant warmth until mid-May, so having a jacket at the back door was a must.

"You need a recipe for chocolate chip cookies?"

Hope laughed as she moved closer to him. "Of course you do. There are different types of chocolate chip cookies."

"Is that so?" Ethan held up a cookie and inspected it.

"Yes, that's so." She turned and rested her hand on her hip. "I prefer the soft, chewy chocolate chip cookie. Logan prefers a cakey chocolate chip cookie and you, Ethan Cahill . . ." She studied him.

His dark eyes were fixed on her, a glint of playfulness flicked and a slight grin tugged at his lips.

"What do I prefer?" His voice deepened as he inched forward.

Hope cleared her throat. They were still talking about chocolate chip cookies, right? "You . . . you like crispier chocolate chip cookies."

He smiled broadly. "You do know me."

A zing of warmth shot through her. She liked knowing what he liked and she liked that he knew that. She gave herself a mental shake because she was reading too much into their conversation about a cookie.

"I should. I've known you since high school."

Ethan's younger sister was one of her closest friends, and she spent countless afternoons after school and weekends at the Cahill house.

Ethan was like the big brother she'd never had but always wanted. He played football, drove a Camaro, and dated a cheerleader. Yeah, Ethan was way cool back then. Too cool for a Goody Two-shoes like Hope Early, who spent her free time baking for any fund-raiser, discussing murder mysteries at the library, and running for school government offices. Not much had changed over the years. Hope was still baking, she still enjoyed a good book, and she was focused entirely on her career while Ethan chased after bad guys and carried a gun. Yeah, he was still too cool for her.

"I see you made coffee. I can use two or three cups," she said.

"Rough night, huh?" Ethan finished the last cookie and set the plate in the sink. He slipped by her and walked to the table with his mug of coffee, then sat at the table. Hope walked over to the coffeemaker and opened the upper cabinet. She pushed aside her *The Sweet Taste of Success* mug, a souvenir from a time in her life she still couldn't decide if she should regret or not, and reached for her oversized FAVORITE AUNT mug. For a birthday, Logan filled the mug with a bag of coffee beans and slapped a bow on it. A simple, thoughtful gift she appreciated very much at that moment. She filled the mug to the rim, leaving very little room for milk.

"Corey called first thing this morning." She took a long drink of the hot beverage. Perfection. Ethan had brewed a pot of coffee just as good as she did. The man had many talents.

"What did he want?"

She shrugged. "He probably wants to develop a reality show based on the murder." She'd met the twenty-something producer through his life partner, Wilson, who worked with Hope at the cooking magazine, *Meals in Minutes*. Corey was casting a baking competition show and Wilson thought it would be a great opportunity for Hope. And so did she. After an introduction to Corey and an audition tape, Hope was selected as a competitor. She was naïve to think the show was all about baking skill because her producer couldn't have cared less about the perfect crème brûlée. He wanted high ratings, and pitting competitor against competitor created conflict and drove ratings. By the end of the first week, she realized what she'd signed up for was a repeat of high school. Mean girls, jocks, and geeks all rolled into one hour of prime time with a side of brownies.

Hope pulled out a mixing bowl and then the flour canister. "While I make pancakes, you can tell me what I owe this visit to."

Ethan grinned. "I'm just checking up on you."

She smiled. "Why?"

"It's my sworn duty to protect all of the citizens of Jefferson."

"Is that what I am to you? Another job duty?" She arched an eyebrow and waited for his response.

Ethan shifted in his seat and before he could answer, the back door swung open and Drew rushed in, coming to a halt when he saw Ethan. A part of her was relieved Ethan wouldn't be answering the question because she wasn't sure what she wanted to be to him.

"My sources tell me there were no fingerprints found on the murder weapon." Drew shrugged off his jacket and draped it over a chair at the table. He wasn't wasting any time getting to the point.

"Your sources? Whom might they be?" Ethan asked.

Drew cocked his head sideways. "I'm sorry, I'm not at liberty to reveal them. Coffee?" He turned to Hope.

"Help yourself." She gestured to the coffeepot.

As Drew poured his coffee, she glanced at the clock on the wall ovens.

"Need to be somewhere?" Ethan asked.

"No. Vanessa was supposed to be here by now. She's never late." Hope crossed the kitchen to the seating area and dug through her purse for her cell phone. There were a dozen text messages and one was from Vanessa. "Oh, she's not coming in today. I guess it's understandable." She barely got out of bed herself, and if it weren't for her hens, she probably would have stayed under the covers.

"Are you whipping up pancakes?" Drew peered into the mixing bowl.

"Yes." Hope returned to her mixing bowl and shoved him out of her way with a smile.

"So, either the killer wore gloves or the rock was wiped off after striking Peaches on the back of the head, but since there was still blood on the rock, it seems unlikely the killer wiped it," Drew speculated.

"No comment." When it came to work, Ethan was tight-lipped and Drew knew that.

But that didn't stop Drew from digging, so Hope just watched them do their little dance of police procedure versus the people's right to know.

"Either it was premediated or we have a murderer who had enough presence of mind to remove his or her fingerprints," Drew said as he joined Ethan at the table. "Which do you think it is, Ethan?"

"No comment."

"Peaches and Audrey had a tumultuous relationship, and she had access to garden gloves at her house. It's all very tidy, isn't it?" Drew grinned, clearly pleased with his deductive reasoning.

"I should be going." Ethan stood.

"No comment for the press?" Drew asked.

"No."

"You can't stonewall me."

"I'm not trying to. Just make sure you get your facts straight." Ethan turned to Hope. "I'll see you later." He grabbed his uniform jacket off the back of the chair and paused. "It wasn't because of my sworn duty," he said to Hope in a low, husky voice.

The unexpected comment took Hope's breath away. "Okay," she barely managed to say.

"Any time." Ethan nodded then exited through the mudroom.

Okay?

What kind of answer was that? He just told her he came to check on her because he cared for her, not because it was his duty. *Whoa.* They were friends. Of course he'd check on her. She found a dead body yesterday. She shouldn't go reading more into it than there was.

Drew's head swung around so he had Hope in full view. "What was that all about?"

Hope shrugged before she ladled pancake batter onto the grill pan. The sizzle confirmed the buttered pan was the right temperature and within minutes she'd have a stack of golden buttermilk pancakes.

"That!" Drew gestured in the direction of the back door. "I'm not blind. What just happened?"

"I don't know what you're talking about." Hope wanted to avoid the impending discussion because she knew exactly what Drew was talking about. Ethan had been spending more time at her house and they'd shared more meals together. It was a reasonable conclusion to make that their friendship was developing into something more, something bigger.

"Did he spend the night?"

"No." She flipped the six pancakes and smiled with satisfaction. Perfectly golden brown.

"Just asking." Drew took a drink of his coffee. "You could do a lot worse."

"We don't have that kind of relationship."

"Too bad," Drew said with a frown.

Hope had had enough. Now wasn't the time in her life to pursue a romantic relationship. A distraction was needed to get Drew off of Hope's nonexistent love life. She clicked on the television, which was tucked into a corner, and switched to the local morning news channel. As she returned to the pancakes, a Barbie clone read the morning headlines.

"There was a murder in Jefferson yesterday during the book signing of gardening book author Audrey Bloom."

Hope's head jerked up just in time to see Audrey's headshot from her publicity packet. That wasn't the distraction she was looking for. "Good grief."

"Following a tour of Ms. Bloom's garden to promote her new book, the body of local real estate agent Peaches McCoy was found. The cause of death has not been released."

"She got her head bashed in," Drew said to the television in a tone that mimicked a five-year-old who knew something the adults didn't.

Hope moved closer to the television, holding a spatula, ignoring Drew.

"The police and Ms. Bloom had no comment. Also in attendance at the event was Hope Early,

Connecticut's own season-one finalist on the reality show *The Sweet Taste of Success* and blogger. She hasn't been reached for comment."

"That's the way I want to keep it." She pointed her spatula at the television screen. "I'm surprised they released her name already. Has her family been notified?"

Drew shook his head. "She doesn't have any. Her dad died when she was a baby and her mother was killed eleven years ago by a hit-and-run driver."

"She had no one." Hope's heart ached for the dead woman. She couldn't imagine not having a family, no one to notify if anything happened to her.

Hope turned her attention back to the pancakes. Perfectly golden and ready to be served. She stacked them onto a plate and set it on the table.

"You make the best pancakes." Drew smothered them with butter and maple syrup then took a bite. "I finally have an exclusive. I thought that would never happen here in Dullsville."

"What do you have so far?" Hope retrieved her mug then sat down at the table across from Drew.

"Well, I discovered the body."

"We," Hope corrected.

Drew shrugged at the minor detail. "Whatever. I have a partial text message to an unknown person. I also have photos of the crime scene."

"Photos? You took photos?"

"I did. While you were calling the police, I snapped a few photos with my phone. Wanna see?"

"What do you think? Show me."

Drew pulled out his phone and tapped on the

photo app. He handed her the phone, and Hope swiped through the photos. She cringed at the bloody scene. She'd hoped she would forget what Peaches looked like at that moment. Now she'd have to start all over again.

"It looks like Peaches was searching for something. A couple of the desk drawers were pulled open and the file cabinet in the credenza was opened. It doesn't look like a very precise search. It looks like Peaches had no idea of where to look."

"What were all those papers?" Hope asked.

"Personal and household papers. None of it seemed important." Drew took another mouthful of pancakes.

Hope handed Drew his phone back. "I doubt Harrison kept business files in his home office. Everything is on a tablet or computer or a flash drive nowadays."

"When you spoke with Audrey before we left, did you ask her why Peaches showed up?"

Hope nodded. "She said she had no idea."

"So she shows up uninvited and then is murdered. Who did it?" Drew asked.

Hope helped herself to the two remaining pancakes and drizzled maple syrup over them, then took a bite. As she chewed, she ran a mental list of who was in attendance yesterday. She never thought she'd be making up a list of possible murder suspects from the people who lived in her hometown. The names belonged on a Christmas card list, not a most-likely-to-commit-murder list. But remembering her interview with Detective

Reid yesterday afternoon, any hesitation she had vanished. Of all the guests, Claire had been the most vocal about her dislike for Peaches. Hope wasn't going to let her sister get railroaded for a crime she didn't commit.

"Maretta was there yesterday. What motive could she have had? Maybe since Peaches didn't volunteer at the bake sale."

"Or, how about if she felt her marriage was threatened?" Drew asked.

"What? Alfred and Peaches?" Hope couldn't hold back her laughter. The sixty-plus balding Realtor had hairy ears and a belly that hung over his increasing belt size. Not quite stud material. "Are you serious? He's as sexy as an elf."

Drew gave her a sideways glance. "What do you have against elves?"

Hope shook her head. "Never mind."

"Sally was also there."

"No. If Elaine had been the victim, then I would consider her a suspect. Sally only cared about the garden club. She didn't have anything against Peaches. Unlike Audrey," Hope said.

"What about Elaine?"

Hope shrugged. "She does come across as a woman who could be jealous of other women who are around her husband. Lionel and Peaches had to have spent a lot of time together."

"Jealousy. Yes. A rage like that could have been enough to make her pick up a rock and smash it into Peaches' head."

Hope shivered at the visual. Discussing a cold-blooded murder over pancakes seemed surreal.

Who had conversations like that? Ethan, since he was a cop. Jane, since she was a mystery writer years ago. But not Hope. She was a blogger.

"Or Claire."

"Drew!"

"I'm sorry, hon. I'm a journalist and I need to remain objective."

"Why does everyone think Claire killed Peaches?"

"Well, duh, she wanted the new subdivision listing, the one Audrey was fighting against, right? It would have been a nice commission check for her. With Peaches out of the way, she'd have no opposition."

That was exactly what Claire had said yesterday. And probably what Detective Reid thought. Hope chewed on her lower lip. In a matter of twenty-four hours, she went from baking cookies to finding a woman dead to friends and family becoming murder suspects.

"So, what you are you going to do? You know you have to do something," Drew said.

"Why me?"

"You were Jane's most enthusiastic member of the mystery reading group when we were kids. You always knew who the killer was before any of us. You realize, you were very annoying back then." Drew grinned. He liked teasing Hope.

Hope smiled. She remembered all those weekly meetings at the library. Jane led the discussions while Sally kept an eye on all of them to make sure the library's rules were being enforced. The two sisters-in-laws couldn't have been more different. Hope kept a black-and-white composition notebook for each book they read, and she made meticulous notes, which allowed her to solve the mysteries before anyone else in the reading group. And much to her dismay, Drew had a point. She couldn't very well stand by and do nothing. Besides, what harm could asking a few questions do?

Chapter Eight

By noon business was brisk at the bake sale. Patrons and volunteers filled the Jefferson Public Library's community room. The large space hadn't changed since Hope was a little girl. Paintings from local artists hung on the walls, a tall bookcase held editions of books authored by local writers, including Jane Merrifield's handful of novels, and opposite the bookcase was a fireplace that was used solely for ambiance. Dozens of people milled around, checking out all the treats for sale, sampling and buying until their pastry boxes were stuffed. Tucked in a back corner, there were cloth-covered round tables where customers could sit and enjoy their baked goods. Hope had to give Maretta credit. It was a genius idea. They ate what they'd purchased and then had to buy more to take home.

Hope stood behind her assigned table. She was selling out fast. She'd baked dozens of three varieties and provided her own stainless-steel trays, along with pastel napkins. Tucked under her table were the containers she'd transported the cookies in. Like always, they'd go home empty. She'd almost sold out when Meg stopped by to check in with her.

"Oh, my, you don't have many cookies left." Meg surveyed the table. "I think you'll be the first one to be officially sold out."

"Well, this isn't a competition." Hope waved away Meg's comment.

Meg tilted her head, and she smiled a little too sweetly. "Too bad, you'd win this one."

Hope forced a smile because she'd learned, since being on the *Sweet Taste of Success*, there were three types of people. The first group was impressed by her fifteen minutes of fame. The second group was jealous of her fifteen minutes of fame. The final group had no idea she'd had fifteen minutes of fame, and once they found out, they didn't care. Meg fell into the second group. Hope realized early those people just weren't worth her effort of engaging with them. She simply smiled, stepped away, and carried on with her life. But she couldn't step away at the moment because she had cookies to sell.

"Hope should have won *The Sweet Taste of Success*. She was the best baker on that show." Jane came to Hope's defense.

"Of course she was. I absolutely adore her cookies." Meg swept back her bangs. Her pixie haircut complemented her round face, though her smile looked frozen and about to crack.

"Thank you." Hope dipped down and reappeared

with a stack of smaller trays. She swiftly moved the remaining cookies onto the trays while Meg and Jane looked on curiously. "Oh, downsizing the platters make the cookies look more abundant and that way more appealing." She discarded the larger trays and then tidied up the cookies.

"These look absolutely delicious." A woman approached the table. "I'll take a half dozen of each." She handed Hope a pastry box.

"Half dozen it is." Hope filled up the box and then accepted the payment. The happy customer walked away, making her way along the long line of tables.

"Very nice, dear." Jane handed Hope a dollar and snatched two chocolate chip cookies. "Keep the change. Have either one of you spoken with Audrey yet?"

"No," Meg answered.

"Same here. I've left a couple of voice mails for her."

"Where did she go last night?"

"To a hotel. She and Harrison are going to stay there a couple of days," Hope said.

"Smart move. What happened yesterday was all over the news this morning. I can't imagine being in Audrey's situation right now. Leave it to Peaches McCoy to get herself killed in a place she wasn't supposed to be in the first place." Meg looked away quickly.

Hope wasn't sure if she was embarrassed by what she'd just said or if she was surveying the bake sale. She was one of the volunteer coordinators and she answered to Maretta, so Hope didn't have any doubt Meg wanted everything to go perfectly.

"I doubt that was her plan for yesterday," Hope said.

"Though it does raise the question as to why Peaches was there. Had someone invited her? Why?" Jane asked.

"I didn't understand the woman when she was alive, and I have no interest in understanding her now that she's dead. I have to get back to work." Meg walked away.

Meg stopped at several tables before disappearing into the back room, which normally served as a storeroom and was turned into command central for the bake sale. Since early the day before, boxes and trays of desserts had been dropped off, as well as the supplies for the sale. Every now and then Hope saw one of Maretta's inner-circle volunteers scurry back there to replenish supplies. At the opposite end of the community room, near the elevator, a beverage table was set up. Coffee, tea, or a tall glass of milk were available for a nominal fee. Maretta knew how to squeeze every penny from the supporters of the library. But nobody seemed to mind because traffic had been steady since the doors opened at ten.

"Now that she's gone, tell me everything you know so far." Jane leaned over the table.

"I don't know anything more than I did yesterday." Hope took a sip from her bottled water. With business being brisk, she hadn't taken a break. She was thirsty, hungry, and her feet hurt, even though she'd had the foresight to wear very sensible shoes. It would be a long day, so the right footwear was important. She'd pulled her long, brunette hair up into a loose ponytail to keep it off her face as she sold dozens of cookies.

Jane waved her hand, dismissing Hope's response. "You mean you haven't spoken with Ethan since yesterday at Audrey's house?"

"Yes, I have, but he hasn't shared anything about the murder."

Jane straightened up and joined Hope behind the table. "I guess that's to be expected. We need to review everything we know up to this point."

"It's not going to be much." All Hope had was conjecture from her breakfast with Drew. She had no concrete evidence that pointed to anyone and as much as she hated to admit it, Claire was the only person with a strong motive to kill Peaches.

Her stomach knotted at the discomfiting truth.

"Tsk. Tsk." Jane wagged her index finger in Hope's direction. "I know this is difficult, having your own flesh and blood a murder suspect, but you must remain strong. At this time, it appears no one had more of a motive than Claire."

Hope put up her palm, signaling to Jane to stop talking. She'd already heard that from Drew earlier and didn't want to hear it again. It could be some kind of bad karma thing. Say something enough times and it comes true.

"It's no surprise the police are focused on her." Jane ignored Hope's obvious signal to stop talking. "That's why we will find the killer."

"We?"

Jane patted Hope on the forearm. "Perhaps we

can have dinner this evening and identify others who would have had a motive for murdering Peaches."

Hope took another swig of her water while Jane added a few more cookies to her box. She didn't have any plans for dinner so she might as well work on the murder. Her cell phone rang and she pulled it out of her purse. Her nephew's name came up on the display. No doubt he wanted a box full of cookies. Glancing at the table, she'd have to pack him up the leftover cookies she had at home.

"Logan, what's up?" She stepped back from the table as a familiar woman approached with two little girls.

"That police detective took Mom to the police station. He said it was for questioning."

"What?" The question came out louder than she expected, and the woman and the little girls looked up, startled. Hope mouthed "sorry" to her customers and stepped farther away from the table to continue the conversation with Logan. "Where are you?" She stomped down the panic rising. She needed a clear head to talk to the twelve-year-old. He might have considered himself the man of the house since his dad was away on business, but he was only a kid and no doubt scared his mom left with a police officer. Heck, she was scared.

"Home. Evelyn was still here and she told Mom she'd stay until she got home."

Hope was relieved Claire's housekeeper had remained at the house. Logan and his younger sister, Hannah, were taken care of, so she could head over to the police station and find out what was going on."

"Good. You and Hannah stay home and listen to

Evelyn. I'm going to see your mom. Everything is going to be okay."

"Sure it is. It's kinda cool the police hauled Mom away." Logan chuckled.

"No, it's not cool. I have to go. Love you." Hope clicked off her phone and looked up to see Jane making change for the woman with the little girls. She was grateful Jane stepped in and covered for her. She couldn't possibly impose on Jane to stay for the remainder of the bake sale, though. Could she?

"What's happened?"

"Detective Reid took Claire in for questioning. She's at the police station now." This was not good. The knot in her stomach constricted.

Without saying another word, Jane placed her hand on her arm and squeezed gently. "Go. I'll man the table until closing time. I don't have to be at the Inn today."

"Are you sure? Thank you." Hope gathered up her purse and cardigan. Before Jane could change her mind, Hope was already at the top of the flight of stairs and on her way out of the library.

As she made her away through a crowd of people climbing the stairs to the library's front entrance, Hope's cell phone buzzed again. Smiling to neighbors and friends, she pulled the phone out of her purse and saw Corey Lucas's name.

"Now's not a good time." She reached the bottom of the brick stairs that descended from the front entrance of the library. She headed in the direction of the police department.

"There's never a bad time for a great opportunity," he said.

"Not interested."

"You will be. I'm pitching this afternoon. Food blogger solves murder mysteries. This is perfect for you. Those culinary, cozy mystery novels or whatever they're called, are hot, and this reality show will make you a household name. You'll be at the top of reality TV."

Hope came to a stop. "Corey, a woman is dead. I'm not going to become a household name by stepping over dead bodies." Rather, she'd work hard to build her brand through her blog.

"Just finding them seems to be working fine."

"This conversation is over." She clicked off her phone and shoved it back into her purse. Not only hadn't she won *The Sweet Taste of Success*, she was stuck with the producer who believed he could make her a star. She wasn't sure how to get Corey out of her life. He didn't take "no" for an answer and she wasn't about to go onto another reality show.

And at that moment, reality was all too scary. Claire was in the police station because Detective Reid suspected she was a killer. Her pace quickened, her heart pumped with anticipation, and the shops she passed on Main Street were a blur because her eyes were watering. Terror seized her and every possible scenario played out in just the few minutes it took her to walk from the library to the police station. Claire could be arrested. She could be convicted of murder. She could be sent to prison. What would happen to her children? What would happen to Hope without her big sister?

Hope wiped away the tears that streamed down

her cheeks. No, she wouldn't let any of that happen. She pushed away those thoughts because they would distract her from what needed to be done.

Hope arrived at the Jefferson Police Department, a one-story brick building on the border of the historical section of Main Street with simple landscaping and a wide concrete path that led to the glass doors. She passed a curved granite bench anchored on either side by potted flowers. The flowers were bright and cheery. Too bad her mood hadn't let her enjoy the sight of them. She pulled open one of the doors and entered the building. Behind protective glass, she was greeted by the dispatcher, but before she could ask to see Ethan, she was intercepted.

"Ms. Early, what brings you here?" Detective Reid approached.

She squared her shoulders. "I came to see Ethan and bring my sister home."

"The chief is busy right now."

"I'll wait." Hope headed to a row of plastic chairs lined up against a wall. She'd sit and wait as long as it took to see Ethan and her sister.

"Well, while you wait, why don't we have a talk?"

Chapter Nine

An interrogation room?

"Have a seat, Ms. Early." Detective Reid seated himself across the table from Hope.

She did as requested and then took a moment to regroup. They were probably in the nondescript room because he didn't have a private office. Just because it looked something like an interrogation room she'd seen on numerous television shows didn't mean he was about to interrogate her. The explanation seemed logical. Right? Besides, the room seemed brighter and cleaner than the ones in those fictional police stations.

The detective rested his hands on the table and laced his thin fingers. "I know from personal experience that sisters are very close. So close, they'd do anything for each other."

Hope tilted her head sideways. "You want to talk to me about sisters?" While he looked very much at ease, her spine felt so rigid she feared it would snap into pieces if she tried to unwind.

"When one sister is in trouble, the other will do whatever is needed to help."

"Are you saying Claire is in trouble?"

"Your sister is in a lot of trouble, Ms. Early."

Hope's heart nearly plummeted to the ground. Official confirmation. "You've arrested her?" She bounded from her chair and headed for the door. She had to see Claire.

"We haven't arrested her. Please . . ." Detective Reid gestured to the chair.

Hope inhaled several relieved breaths as she returned to her chair. "Then what are you talking about? Tell me what is going on here." She returned to her seat.

"What do you know about your sister's financial situation?"

Alarm bells went off, and she heard the warning shouts of "danger!" from far off in the distance. Well, okay, nobody was actually yelling "danger," but she still heard it from every fiber of her body. She chewed on her lower lip. No doubt he'd twist whatever she said about Claire. But if she said nothing, how would that reflect on Claire?

"I really don't think I should answer that question. Not without a lawyer."

"You're not under arrest, Ms. Early."

"I understand. Which means I don't have to answer your question." She'd read enough mystery novels and watched more than her share of crime dramas to know she wasn't obligated to answer any questions.

Detective Reid eased back into his chair. If he

was angry at her refusal to answer his question, he didn't show it. Then again, being a police officer, he knew how to control his facial expressions so they remained neutral, never giving away what he was thinking. But Hope guessed he wasn't very pleased with her at the moment.

"She's in serious financial debt."

Hope remained silent.

"She needed to get the exclusive listing for Lionel Whitcomb's subdivision. She needed to get rid of the competition."

"That's crazy. My sister didn't kill her. There are plenty of other people who didn't like Peaches."

"Is that so?" Detective Reid shifted in his seat as he jotted down a note on a legal pad.

"Elaine Whitcomb was jealous of Peaches."

"Was she?"

Hope nodded. "There are others. Meg Griffin had some beef with her. She left abruptly just before the book signing. I'm sure there were others at the garden tour yesterday who disliked Peaches."

Detective Reid leaned back in his chair and grinned. "Are you adding sleuthing to your blogging career?"

"I'm keeping an open mind."

"Ms. Early, I have an open mind. I want to arrest the killer of Peaches McCoy. And if that person happens to be your sister, I won't be stopped in making my collar regardless of your relationship with Chief Cahill."

"This is the second time you've brought up my friendship with Eth . . . ah . . . Chief Cahill. Do you have a problem with it?"

"Only if it interferes with me doing my job. Just

like I'd have a problem with an amateur sleuth inserting herself into my murder investigation."

"I'm doing no such thing. I can't help it if I know things. Things that could help you solve your case."

His brows arched, giving her a questioning look. Before he could say something, his cell phone buzzed and he glanced at his belt, where the phone was holstered. "We're done for now."

"Really?"

"I have work to do, and I'm sure you have something to blog about. Just one more thing, Ms. Early."

"And what would that be?"

"If you come across any information, I expect you'll bring it directly to me and you won't withhold anything that could lead to you facing an obstruction-of-justice charge."

With that warning, Hope stood, then positioned herself behind the chair. "I'd like to see Claire now."

"She left already after refusing to answer any questions."

Inwardly, Hope seethed. Why didn't he tell her that when he found her out in the reception area? She slung her purse over her shoulder and walked to the door.

"Have a nice day," Reid said as she exited the interview room.

Have a nice day.

Like that was possible after dealing with Detective Reid. Up until finding Peaches dead, Hope hadn't had the opportunity to meet the man. And now she wished she'd never met him.

As the main door of the police department closed behind her, she checked her phone for messages.

The first message was from Jane. She would pack up all of Hope's supplies from the bake sale and return them later. The second message was from Claire. She'd arrived home and was going to soak in her tub to relax. Hope shook her head. Leave it to her sister to be able to close the door and sink down into a bath while her whole world was about to crash down around her.

After leaving a message for Claire to come over for dinner, she shoved her phone back into her purse and zipped up her jacket. The day had turned chilly, and the wind had picked up. The meteorologist on the morning news said a line of severe thunderstorms would be making their way through the state later in the day. Glancing up to the graying sky, Hope thought it looked like he was right.

She crossed the street and passed a row of antique shops. Jefferson was known for its abundance of antique shops that lined Main Street and dotted the side streets. Those shops were often destinations for new and seasoned antique collectors. A display of Wedgwood china, the delicate floral pattern Hope loved, drew her closer to the front window of the Red House Antiques shop. Set atop a nineteenth-century mahogany breakfast table, the scene was warm, welcoming, and inviting. There was no hint of the ugliness that had swept down on Jefferson the day before. Murder. The word was ugly. She shook her head in disbelief. She took in a sweeping view of her town and wondered if she'd ever see it in the same way she had just twenty-four hours ago.

"Hope!"

She glanced over her shoulder. Ethan was approaching. Good. They needed to talk.

"I just heard you stopped by to see me. Is everything okay?"

Hope turned around and squared her shoulders. "No, everything isn't okay. Claire was dragged out of her home in front of her children by your ace detective, Reid. Then I was interviewed by him. He shared with me Claire has a motive and she had an opportunity to murder Peaches."

Ethan's forehead crinkled. "I'm sorry about that."

"Not as sorry as me."

"He's just rattling a few cages to see what shakes out. That's the way he works."

"By accusing innocent people?"

Ethan reached out and touched Hope's arm. "Please, don't be upset. He's just doing his job. And, trust me, it's not a pretty one."

"I'm not going to let Claire be arrested. Just because she's having some financial difficulty doesn't make her guilty of murder."

Ethan's eyes shifted. "There's more."

"What?"

"We found text messages between her and Peaches."

"That's not unusual. They were professional colleagues."

"It appears the day before the murder there was an exchange between them over Gilbert Madison's house. Claire accused Peaches of stealing the listing and texted her she was a dead woman."

"What? No, I don't believe it."

"I saw Peaches' cell phone. Look, I don't want you involved in this."

"That's what Reid said just before he told me I must have a blog post to write." The man's dismissive attitude irritated her. Like most people, Reid had a dim view of blogging. While she couldn't blame him, she worked hard at establishing herself in the blogosphere and getting the attention of brands. She started her blog two years before appearing on *The Sweet Taste of Success* as a way to share her love for housekeeping, DIY, and cooking. She slowly built a readership, and her reality show stint helped boost her blog. Now she was able to earn a decent income from a career she loved. And it was a career, even if the likes of Detective Sam Reid didn't see it that way.

Ethan nodded to a couple of residents as they passed by. "Reid doesn't have good people skills. But he is a good detective. I'll handle him. Please, stay out of this."

Hope wanted to consider his request, but knew she was all in now and there wasn't anything he or Reid could say to change her mind. "Do you want to come over for dinner tonight?" A vegetable lasagna could lead to a little pumping of information. She wanted to know everything the police knew since her sister was now a "person of interest."

"Thanks, but it's going to be a long night."

She shrugged. "If you change your mind, you know where to find me and the lasagna." She knew dangling a thick, cheesy dish in front of him would catch his attention. He loved anything combined with pasta, cheese, and sauce. Confident her last-minute plan was in full gear, she crossed the street and headed to the general store. One of the perks of living near Main Street, just north of the historic district, was all the shops were in walking distance. She needed a few items for a recipe she wanted to test for her blog. As she grabbed hold of the paper bag of groceries, she was surprised to find Maretta stalking her with a deep scowl.

"I cannot believe that man," she huffed. "The nerve of Chief Cahill. He didn't have the time to see me? Who does he think he is? Where does he think his salary comes from? I will not be treated like that by anybody."

"But you were." Hope knew she shouldn't poke a bear, but she couldn't resist. She was tired, frustrated, and scared, so the last thing she wanted to do was to coddle Maretta Kingston.

Maretta straightened and let out a huff.

"I noticed you left the bake sale early." Maretta changed the subject.

"Family emergency."

Maretta's brows arched. "Yes, having a relative arrested for murder is a family emergency."

Hope exhaled an exasperated sigh. The last thing she wanted was for Maretta to go around town repeating that statement. "Claire was not arrested. Just interviewed."

"Oh, the catfights she and Peaches had in the office were horrible."

"Claire is not a murderer."

Maretta harrumphed.

"I have to go." Hope stepped around Maretta. The bag was getting heavier in her arms, and her patience was getting shorter.

"Well, whoever did it did us all a favor."

"That's a terrible thing to say."

"The woman was shameless. Whenever she got the chance, she flirted with Alfred."

"You saw her do that?"

Maretta's nostrils flared, and her dark eyes widened with irritation. "I caught her several times in the office trying to entice my husband. I'd gotten to the end of my rope with that hussy."

Hope didn't miss the anger in Maretta's voice. She also detected bitterness with a hint of impatience, which was what the uptight, self-righteous woman usually spewed out. But anger? Rarely. So Hope couldn't help but wonder if Drew had been right.

Could Maretta have murdered Peaches?

"Your cookies sold out at the bake sale," Maretta said as if she just hadn't accused Hope's sister of murder or declared Peaches McCoy's murder a public service.

Hope smiled weakly and took the olive branch. "I'm glad to have helped."

"Well, we did have to scramble to find someone to take your table, after all. Jane wasn't able to manage on her own."

So much for an olive branch.

Hope exited the general store with her groceries and the intention of heading home but as she walked along Main Street, she passed the Jefferson Town Realty office, where Peaches had been employed and where other possible suspects could be found. Claire couldn't have been the only agent who had a motive. Right? She stopped and looked at the front door of the brick building. If she went in, she would officially be ignoring Ethan's warning about staying out of the murder investigation. She weighed the consequences and decided it would be better to apologize to him than to let her sister be arrested. She turned the doorknob and pushed open the door.

The open first-floor office was full of dark wood furniture and tasteful artwork hung on the walls. A staircase led to the private offices of Alfred and the top agents upstairs. Claire's office was located up there, right across from Peaches' office. Hope imagined that made for some awkward moments in the hallway.

"Hi." Hope approached the front desk.

"If you're looking for Claire, she's not here." Amy Phelan, the agency's secretary was walking back to her desk holding a stack of files.

"I'm not here to see her."

Amy sat down. "Then you must be here to talk about Peaches. Everybody is today." She gestured to the chair beside her desk.

Hope sat, setting her grocery bag on the carpeted floor. "That's not surprising."

"I can't remember the last murder in Jefferson. Can you?"

Hope shook her head. She couldn't. Too bad she'd never be able to say that again. "How well did Peaches get along with the other agents?"

Amy leaned forward and, even though it was just the two of them in the office, she spoke in a low voice. "Peaches didn't play well with others."

"How so?"

Amy reclined and tidied up the papers on her

desk. "She poached some clients, like Gilbert Madison, for example."

Hope cringed. "Who else did that happen to?" If Claire wasn't the only agent who had a client stolen by Peaches, then Reid would have to investigate.

"Kent Wilder. He lost Annabel Layton's listing to Peaches. Oh, what a beautiful Victorian. The gingerbread trim, the sweeping front porch. She's closing in a week. I don't know who will be handling it. Maybe Kent."

Getting the listing back could have been a motive for murder. Hope wanted to talk to Kent and find out where he was yesterday afternoon.

"You're asking the same questions as the police. What's up, Hope? Doing a little sleuthing on your own?"

Hope chewed on her lower lip. "No, no. I'm just curious. How was the relationship between Lionel Whitcomb and Peaches?"

Amy gave Hope a suspicious look, then smiled. She seemed to believe Hope's answer. "Peaches pursued Lionel Whitcomb relentlessly to get the listing to Hunting Hills. She began acting weird. She kind of lost interest. It was almost like she enjoyed the chase more than the actual victory." Amy shrugged. "To be honest, I never understood her."

"When did she begin to act weird?"

"I'm not sure. A couple of weeks ago."

"Thanks for your time."

Back outside, Hope headed to the Coffee Clique, her favorite coffee shop in all northwestern Connecticut. She loved the coffee and the fact the shop was opened by four girlfriends who ditched the rat race for coffee and scones. With the grocery bag in one hand and a mocha latte in the other, she headed home.

As she made her way along the brick sidewalk, her home came into view. The two-story white farmhouse, with its deep roots in Jefferson, was in disrepair when Hope put in her offer fifteen months ago. With a lot of hard work and long hours, the outside of the home was now classic and crisp, with a white picket fence and a front lawn coming to life after a harsh winter. Soon she should be setting out potted containers filled with bright annuals and planting perennials and shrubs that would bloom year after year. As she juggled her coffee and grocery bag to open the front gate, a list of things she needed to get done ran through her mind. Dinner. Painting. A blog post to write. She fumbled a little, but she maneuvered her hand to open the latch on the gate.

She let out a relieved sigh and preceded to step forward, but a hand grabbed her shoulder and jerked her back. Surprised, Hope dropped her bag of groceries and her latte and screamed.

Chapter Ten

The groceries hit the walkway, followed in a split second by the nearly full cup of latte, and Hope's legs were instantly soaked in coffee.

"Oh! My! Goodness!" a female voice squealed.

Hope swung around, her heart pounding. Elaine Whitcomb, of all people, was standing behind her.

"What are you thinking sneaking up on me like that?" Hope bent down to gather her groceries. "Just great," she mumbled as she picked up her empty cup from the puddle of coffee. "My latte is gone."

Elaine bent down to join Hope. "I guess we're all a little jumpy these days. I still can't believe there was a murder yesterday and I was right there. One minute we were having coffee and the next minute the police were carrying a body bag out of the house. *Shivers.*"

Hope remembered how Elaine stood on the

outskirts of the conversations yesterday. She had successfully inserted herself into the garden club and other local organizations because of Lionel's generous donations and connections. But she couldn't buy friendships. Either the women distrusted her because of her constant flirting and her excessive cleavage or they opposed her husband's developments in town.

"Leave it to Peaches to upstage the hostess. She was always so dramatic, right?" Elaine tilted her head sideways. Her forehead was line free, while her face was expressionless.

And there was the other reason Elaine didn't have any friends. She had no filter.

"Why are you here?" Hope gathered her groceries back into the bag. Luckily the brown paper bag hadn't ripped and she didn't have anything breakable in the bag.

"Are you going to school?" Elaine stood, holding a composition notebook and two cans of whole tomatoes.

Hope snatched the notebook from Elaine's hand. She wasn't about to explain how she intended to use the notebook. When she was a member of the mystery book club, she used a notebook to jot down clues and her thoughts on a story. She was going to use the notebook she just purchased at the general store for the real-life murder mystery unfolding around her. "Thank you for your help."

"No problem. You should be more careful. If you'd had eggs in the bag, you'd have a total mess." Elaine smiled, yet her face still remained expressionless.

Hope had seen that before in New York City. Models, trophy wives, aging executives. Fillers and injectables were as common as wearing black among the women hustling to survive in the concrete jungle. If she'd stayed in the city or won *The Sweet Taste of Success* and gotten her own television show, would she have succumbed to the pressure to look young?

Hope bit back her reply. She wasn't clumsy, she was startled because Elaine snuck up behind her. "Again, why are you here?"

"I came to ask a favor. I need you to give me a cooking lesson."

"I'm not a cooking instructor."

"You teach cooking on your blog. Your recipes, tips, and techniques."

"You can read my blog." Hope hoped Elaine would take the hint.

"I don't have time to do that. And reading really isn't my thing." Elaine set the two cans of tomatoes into the grocery bag.

"Of course it isn't. I do have a lot to do today." Hope turned. She walked along the brick path to the front porch that ran the length of her house. She'd stripped and stained the wood floorboards over the weekend, hung new light fixtures and set out a round café table in the corner with three chairs. In a few weeks, she'd hang baskets of flowers and add more seating and tackle the landscaping around the porch. Ever since she had been a little girl, she'd dreamed of having a front porch. Her parents' colonial had a simple front step, and her New York City condo had a small terrace. Now she could spend warm days with a cup of iced coffee and a good book. Where she could wave to neighbors as they walked by and where she could hand out candy on Halloween to trick-or-treaters. Elaine's footsteps followed her. Clearly, getting rid of her wasn't going to be easy.

"Hope, I really need your help. I have to learn how to cook."

Hope reached the steps of the porch. She looked over her shoulder. "Why do you have to learn how to cook?"

"Because . . . yesterday . . ." Her eyes watered.

Was Elaine going to cry? Hope prayed she wouldn't. Did the woman need a hug? A tissue? A mood stabilizer? "What's wrong?" If she was lucky, Elaine would gloss over her sudden display of emotion.

"Yesterday reminded me how unpredictable life is. It may seem like a little thing, especially to a woman like yourself, but to be able to make dinner for my husband after he comes home from a hard day of work would mean the world to me. Please." Elaine grabbed hold of Hope's forearm and held tightly. Her large green eyes begged Hope to help.

Hope wanted to turn Elaine away, but there was a small chance a few hours spent with Elaine could lead to some information that might help prove Claire didn't kill Peaches. From Hope's experience, she guessed Lionel couldn't have been happy with a wife who batted her eyelashes at every man she met and liked to flaunt her surgically enhanced assets. If true, that meant Elaine could have believed her marriage was in trouble and she could have been jealous of Peaches. Peaches was professional, smart, and wore modest blouses keeping her assets private. Jealousy was a powerful emotion.

"I'll think about it."

Elaine smiled a triumphant smile. "Great. Call me." She turned and hurried down the brick path to the road, where she slid into her luxury car and drove off.

Hope continued to her front door and entered her house. Just a few minutes earlier she'd promised Ethan she'd stay out of the murder investigation. Now she was actively inserting herself into the investigation against his wishes. She pushed away the thoughts of what would happen when he found out she'd lied to him. How would their friendship be affected? The thing that was going on between them, which was still a big unknown and unnamed, was going to be changed. It had to be if he couldn't trust her to keep her word. Whatever that thing was, she wasn't sure she wanted to lose it.

Hope put away the groceries in record time so she could jot down some notes about the murder and she began with Elaine. Elaine's unexpected and surprising visit was still fresh in her mind so the notes came quickly. Hope had a couple of theories of why Elaine could have murdered Peaches.

Number one. Elaine could have been jealous of Peaches and wanted to get rid of a threat to her marriage. Elaine might come off as a bimbo, but Hope would put money on the fact Elaine was a smart woman and she could have easily lured Peaches to Audrey's house under false pretenses. Hope stared at the rest of the lined page in the composition notebook, waiting for theory number two, but nothing came. Then an idea sparked. Number two. Perhaps Peaches was cheating on Lionel somehow in their business arrangement and he and Elaine planned together to kill Peaches. Elaine led Peaches into the study and Lionel entered from the garden and hit her on the head, killing her.

Pleased with herself for coming up with two viable motives for murder, Hope set the notebook aside because she needed to prepare dinner. The few minutes she focused on Elaine kept her mind from churning over what Detective Reid had said about Claire. She tied on her apron and began chopping vegetables. The mundane job settled her mind, and by the time she rinsed off her chef's knife, she had bowls of zucchini, peppers, mushrooms, and a couple of minced garlic cloves ready to go when the lasagna noodles were *al dente* and her thoughts about Claire's financial situation calmed down. She was confident that when her sister arrived for dinner, she wouldn't lose her cool and make things worse. She needed Claire to open up in order to help her.

The more she thought about Reid's claim that Claire had money problems, the more impossible it seemed. Just two weeks ago they had hit a string of stores in Manhattan's trendy Meatpacking District and Claire shopped without a care in the world. Hope shook her head as she recalled all the receipts her sister stuffed into her purse. Not once did she hint at the fact she didn't have the money to pay for all the clothes and shoes. Her sister couldn't be that irresponsible? Could she?

Once the noodles were cooked and cooled to

the touch, she assembled the lasagna, layer on top of layer, in a large rectangular stoneware dish. She'd made her vegetable lasagna a hundred times. She loved the familiarity of the recipe and the surprise it provided each time she made it because of the different ingredients she used. She selected what was in season or what she craved.

Hope popped the completed lasagna into the oven and set the timer. While the lasagna baked, she responded to new comments on her recent post about spring cleaning. The trend of commenting on posts was down across the blogosphere, so she was grateful for every comment left and made it a priority to reply to each one. She wanted a relationship with her readers because blogging was a lonely job. When she worked at the magazine, her days were filled with meetings, conference calls, and a little water-cooler conversation. Now she was working alone in her kitchen most days. Vanessa came and went throughout the week, depending upon how much work Hope had for her and how much work Audrey had for Vanessa. Most days Hope enjoyed the solitude, the ability to focus without any interruption, but some days she missed having coworkers, missed having a reason to delay a specific task because of a sudden emergency. There were moments now when Hope looked back at those good old days and wondered if she'd made the right choice in leaving her publishing career, her Upper West Side condo, and her favorite coffee shop to come back to Jefferson.

The oven timer dinged, and she hurried to pull the dish out and set it on a cooling rack. The lasagna took her breath away. Utter deliciousness. The mozzarella cheese topping was lightly browned, bubbling hot, and melted to perfection.

As she admired the lasagna, she realized only time would tell if she'd made the right decision by moving back home.

Speaking of time, Hope glanced at the clock on the wall oven. Claire should be arriving any minute.

Right on time, the back door swung open and Claire entered, looking as if she hadn't a care in the world and that it wasn't raining outside. Her long blond hair bounced with soft curls and her makeup was subtle and flawless, while her shift dress exuded professionalism without being severe.

Hope glanced at her outfit of the day, which was a pair of slim khaki pants with a chambray shirt. Good thing she chose not to write a fashion blog.

"Today has been a crazy day." Claire dropped her tote bag on the island.

"That's an understatement." Hope opened the refrigerator and took out a pitcher of iced tea, then filled two glasses.

"You seem stressed." Claire took a glass and then a long drink. "Something smells really good."

"I made a vegetable lasagna. It needs to set for a little bit, then we can eat and you can tell me about your visit with Detective Reid. And about the text messages between you and Peaches."

"Oh" was all Claire had to say.

"Let me see your phone." Hope held out her hand. She wanted to see every one of the messages between Claire and Peaches. If she was going to help her sister, she needed to know everything.

Claire's shoulders slumped and she sighed. "They really don't mean anything." She put down her glass then reached into her sleek leather tote to pull out her phone. She handed it to Hope.

Hope swiped the phone on and tapped on the Message icon and read the most recent texts between Claire and Peaches. Her eyes widened with disbelief as she read their catfight play out with emoticons and acronyms.

"They really don't mean anything? Seriously? You told her she was a dead woman." Hope looked back up at her sister.

"It was a figure of speech."

Shaking her head, Hope handed the phone back to Claire. She didn't need to see any more of the text messages. She got the picture and so did Detective Reid.

"You need to take this seriously," Hope warned.

"I am." Claire put her phone away.

"I'm not seeing that. You know you won't be able to have Jacques color your hair if you're in prison."

Claire looked shocked.

"Good. I got your attention. Finally."

"What are we going to do?"

"Right now, we're going to have dinner." Hope pushed away from the island and began to set the table for the two of them. As Claire moved the tray of lasagna to the table and grabbed two cloth napkins from the hutch, Hope sliced a baguette. She didn't want to discuss murder while they ate, so they talked about Claire's kids and about how Hope finally decided on a color for the dining room. They agreed on a date to fly down to Florida to visit their mother.

As they cleared the table together, Hope was reminded of when they were kids. Their mom had dinner ready for them every night, and cleaning up after the meal was the responsibility of her daughters. It didn't matter if the girls were fighting; they had a job to do and their mother expected them to do it without any drama. Two girls and no drama was a tall order.

"Detective Reid told me you're having financial difficulty. Why didn't you tell me?" Hope carried the dishes to the counter.

"It's not a big deal." Claire followed with the lasagna.

"Maybe you should work for Corey. You have a gift for putting a spin on a terrible situation. You could make a fortune in reality TV."

"It's not a spin."

"You're right. It's a denial. And it's more than a little problem. Or else Detective Reid wouldn't think you had a motive for murder.

"It's not that bad, really. Since Andy and I are both self-employed, cash flow is always a challenge. We didn't go unscathed during the recession. Both of our industries took a hard hit, but it's better now. Reid is blowing this all out of proportion."

Hope let out a sigh of relief. "So you didn't need Peaches to die in order to pay off any of your bills?"

"No. Sure, she got the Hunting Hills listing, but there's a new condo development in the works, and it has more units than Whitcomb's stupid subdivision. And I have an *in* with the developer. I'm good." She winked.

"I'm so happy to hear that."

Claire wrapped an arm around Hope's shoulder. "Look at my little sister, all worried about me."

Hope smiled. "I was."

"But do you really think I'd be so irresponsible? My finances just don't affect me. Andy and I have two children. I would never do anything to hurt them. I'd sell all my shoes for those kids."

"I know how much you love your shoes."

"I love my kids," Claire assured her sister.

"I'm sorry. He just sounded . . ."

"So certain?"

"Yes. And that's what I'm worried about. It doesn't seem like he's looking anywhere else for a suspect."

"What are we going to do?"

"Find the killer." Easier said than done. Hope knew she couldn't investigate under the radar. Her ten years in New York City she enjoyed the anonymity that came with living in a place with over eight million people, which made reentry into Jefferson challenging.

"I better get going. The storm is getting worse. I'll call you tomorrow." Claire hugged Hope. "Don't think I didn't notice your new composition notebook on the coffee table."

Hope smiled. Her sister knew her well. She let go of Claire and watched her leave the kitchen. As she filled the dishwasher, the mudroom door closed. She glanced over to the coffee table. The notebook called to her, but she needed to do something first.

With a deep breath, she grabbed her phone and punched in Elaine's phone number. While she was preparing the lasagna, she'd brainstormed a simple menu for Elaine's lesson. Simplicity was key because she had no idea of Elaine's skill level in the kitchen. A Parmesan chicken cutlet with risotto and asparagus would be a good meal for Elaine to cook. Though, considering Elaine's attention span may be too short to make risotto, rice pilaf would be a better choice.

After a few minutes on the phone with a very excited Elaine, they set the cooking lesson for the next day. Hope stepped back from the windows in her family room. The storm had ratcheted up in intensity. The antique glass rattled, and the cold penetrated, sending shivers down her spine.

As she set the phone back into its base, she wondered if she would be giving a cooking lesson to a killer.

Chapter Eleven

A gust of wind whipped outside, tossing branches across Hope's yard and dragging her from her thoughts. She needed to do something besides speculate on suspects and motives for murder.

The perfect project to keep her mind out of the murder investigation was painting. She'd finally decided on the paint color for the dining room after weeks of paint swatches on the walls. She'd studied each color to see how it changed throughout the day. Some colors were discarded because they were too light, others were too intense for the room, others didn't feel right to her with the decorating scheme she had planned for the room.

The winning color was Vanilla Cream, aka off-white, and it was a Frye-Lily paint. The company had provided her with the paint and paid her a fee to write a series of posts on the painting projects in her new home. Sponsored posts were a large part of her income from her blog and admittedly the most difficult aspect of blogging because she needed to find the balance between promoting the product and being authentic to her readers. So far, she believed she was doing okay because she was pleased with Frye-Lily paints, and her posts reflected her enthusiasm for the products. A win-win for the paint company, her, and her readers.

With the roller by her side, Hope stepped back from the interior wall of the dining room and marveled at the improvement a couple coats of paint made. The wall had been dingy and dirty after years of neglect, and now a fresh warmth spread across the expanse of the wall. She'd refinished an antique hutch that would fit perfectly there. It was in the living room waiting to be moved to its new location. A stack of boxes waited in the center of the dining room to be unpacked. Inside was her grandmother's Wedgwood china she treasured and couldn't wait to display. She still needed to purchase a table and chairs, along with a chandelier. Good thing she planned on hitting the flea market over the weekend.

"Hope!"

She looked over her shoulder, in the direction of the kitchen. Ethan. She set the roller in the tray and hurried into the kitchen.

"Hi." She crossed the space to Ethan.

His hair was damp and rain dripped from his uniform shirt collar.

"I made vegetable lasagna for dinner. Let me reheat a plate for you." She moved toward the refrigerator and pulled open the door.

"Thanks, but I grabbed a sandwich earlier."

She shut the door and turned around. "Oh.

Would you like some dessert? I stashed some cookies I baked for the library, and I can put on the kettle."

"Don't go through any more trouble. I just wanted to check on you. I really don't like the way we left things earlier."

"Neither do I. I was angry and scared, and I felt a little unsettled. I've never found a dead body before."

He walked forward and reached out to her, and she extended her hand to him. "I'm sorry you had to experience that."

She glanced down. Her hand fit nicely into his, and his tight squeeze was reassuring. A smile tugged at her lips. She felt safe with him. Her gaze lifted, and she found him staring at her. Was he thinking about kissing her? Nerves and anticipation shimmied through her. She leaned forward, and he leaned forward. She was going to kiss Ethan.

A thunderous crackle exploded outside. Hope jumped while Ethan ran to the window over the kitchen sink.

"Darn storm," Hope muttered.

"Doesn't look like anything is down." Ethan turned back to Hope. "Do you think you should be alone?"

The question caught Hope off guard. Was he thinking he should stay the night? If he was, he'd be sleeping on the sofa. Right?

Hope shrugged. "It's just a storm. Besides, I wasn't alone tonight. Claire was here for dinner. I'm actually tired. It's been a long day and I didn't sleep well last night. Plus the painting." She yawned, covering her mouth.

"Sure. I need to get back to the station. Call me if you need anything, okay?"

She followed him to the mudroom and locked the door behind him. She was tired, but she wasn't ready to go to bed just yet, and she needed to clean up her painting supplies. But first, a cup of tea. She set the teakettle on the stove and pulled out a large mug from an upper cabinet. When the kettle whistled, she poured the hot water into the mug and let the tea bag steep. She took her mug over to one of the chairs by the fireplace, where a sweater waited to be finished. She reached into the basket and pulled out the turquoise partially knitted sweater and began working the needles. The turtleneck sweater was going to be a birthday gift for Claire's daughter, a fashionista in the making. Hannah loved clothes and she loved the boho look. The sweater could be paired with a flowy skirt and worn with boots in the fall. Hope was a few rows into the sleeve when the telephone rang. She set aside the sweater and walked over to the counter, where her cordless phone was. The caller ID told her it was Vanessa.

"Hi, Vanessa. How are you doing?"

"I have to talk to you. It's important. Very important," Vanessa said in a rushed breath.

"Okay. I was just doing a little knitting. But I can talk and knit at the same time." Most of the time she could if she wasn't involved in a complicated pattern. Luckily the sweater she was working on was a simple pattern, and she could juggle Vanessa and the center back of the sweater.

"No, not over the telephone."

"Tomorrow morning?"

"No," Vanessa said quickly. "It's too important. I really have to talk to you tonight. Now. I've been piecing this thing together, and I want to show you what I have so far. I may be completely off the mark, and that's why I need your opinion. It's about the murder. Can you come over now?"

Hope glanced at the clock on the wall oven. Nine thirty. Just a few months ago in New York City her night was beginning at nine thirty. Now, in Jefferson, her night was winding down. Oh, how things changed.

"I can come over. I'll be there soon."

"Thank you," Vanessa said gratefully, then the line went silent.

Hope clicked off her phone. A few minutes later she was in her mudroom, grabbing her rain jacket and umbrella and heading out to see Vanessa. Had Vanessa been doing a little sleuthing of her own?

The moonless night draped Old Village Road. With no street lamps, the headlights of Hope's SUV lit the way to Maretta Kingston's house, where Vanessa rented a small cottage. The whooshing of bare tree limbs filled the night air as gusts of wind assaulted everything in their path.

Hope slowly drove up the driveway and turned off the ignition. Maretta's quaint colonial stood equally as dark as the night and eerily quiet. On any given day, it was a little scary to approach her house, but that night the scary factor significantly increased. Maybe the first murder in Jefferson's recent history, coupled with a fierce storm, had something to do with it or it could have been at-

tributed to the fact Hope had no idea what Vanessa
was about to tell her.

Her call was cryptic. What had she discovered
about the murder? A chill rippled through Hope.

Hope popped open the glove compartment and
grabbed her flashlight. She pushed the door open
and struggled to get out. The wind was ferocious
and cold and fighting against her. Using an umbrella
would be useless. It would be no match against the
wind. She pulled the hood of her jacket up over her
head and hoped to not get completely drenched
by the time she made it to the carriage house. Clearing the main house, the small white cottage in the
distance came into view. A flagstone path cut
through the lawn to the front porch. The cottage
was built for Maretta's mother-in-law. Hope remembered the late Mrs. Kingston as being as ami-
able as her son, and she had taken an enormous
amount of grief from her daughter-in-law. Hope,
along with most of the town, considered the woman
to be a saint.

As Hope got closer to the cottage, she noticed
the front door was ajar. She stepped forward cautiously and pushed the door open.

"Vanessa," she called out.

There was no answer. She shone the flashlight
into the small living room. Nothing.

She lowered her hand slightly and swept the
light from one side of the room to the other.

Her hand froze in mid-sweep.

The beam of light discovered Vanessa Jordan's
body, sprawled out on the carpet with a pool of
blood around her head.

Chapter Twelve

"So you came out in the middle of the night to talk to Vanessa about the murder?" Ethan pulled off his JPD baseball cap and dragged his fingers through his dark hair. "Couldn't it have waited until morning?"

Hope stood just inches away from him in the center of Maretta Kingston's living room and was disconnected from everything and everyone around her. She barely heard his question. Her eyes darted around the room. Minutes earlier an officer had deposited her there after she led the police to Vanessa's body. Her house was modest in size, and most of the furnishings had been passed down from Maretta's parents, except for the walnut armoire. That treasured piece belonged to Alfred's mother, the Saint. A newly purchased oriental rug in jewel tones kept the room from looking too "secondhand," while lace doilies, family photographs, and needlepoint pillows were scattered throughout the room. Those little touches kept Maretta's stiffness at bay.

"You have no idea how I wish it could have waited."

"Do you know the potential danger you put yourself in tonight?"

"How? The murderer wasn't there when I arrived."

Concern creased Ethan's forehead. "What if the murderer was still in the cottage when you arrived? What then?"

A lump caught in Hope's throat, nearly choking her. Ethan was right.

She swallowed hard. "I hadn't thought of that."

"Well, I have and I don't like it." Ethan shook his head. "I'm so angry right now that you put yourself in this situation." He reached out for her and pulled her into his arms.

The embrace startled her, but she recovered quickly and easily in his arms. She didn't miss her ex-husband, Tim, very often, but when she was scared or weak, she missed having someone to lean on. She thought by now she'd be a stronger person and not need to rely on any man for comfort. But she'd just found a second dead body, and she was scared.

"I'm grateful you're safe," he said in a low voice for only her to hear.

"Are we interrupting?" Maretta's tight voice filled the room.

Yes, you are. But it was probably for the best. Hope pulled herself out of Ethan's arms and turned to face Maretta, who wasn't alone. Alfred stood beside her. Both wore robes over their nightclothes and neither looked pleased by the evening's deadly events.

"I'd like for Hope to wait in here a little while longer until we're finished," Ethan said to the Kingstons.

Maretta's scowl deepened. "That would be preferable to her skulking around outside."

"I wasn't skulking," Hope snapped.

"I stand corrected," Maretta said sharply. "You were merely trespassing."

"Vanessa invited me." Hope took a deep breath. She was too exhausted for Maretta's nonsense. She looked back to Ethan. "I can wait in my car until you're done."

"That won't be necessary," Alfred Kingston said. "Please, sit down." He gestured to the sofa.

"Thank you." Hope eased onto the beige sofa. The plump cushions felt good as she leaned back and allowed her body to completely relax, as much as was possible in Maretta's home.

"Did either of you hear anything tonight?" Ethan asked.

"Police sirens," Maretta said.

Hope rolled her eyes. Maretta seemed determined to make the interview more painful than the actual murder. She tried to remember a time when Maretta wasn't difficult and came up empty. Maretta never made anything easy. Why should questioning her about a murder be any different?

"Before the sirens," Ethan said.

"No. We didn't even hear Hope arrive," Maretta said.

"Do you both always go to bed so early?" Ethan asked.

Maretta stiffened. She fixed her gaze on Ethan and arched her brows. Hope wondered if he'd ever encountered a more formidable witness. "I really don't see how our sleeping habits would be a concern for the police department."

Ethan looked up from his notepad. "We could do this here or at the station. Which would you prefer?"

Maretta blinked. "I had a headache so I turned in early." Her demeanor knocked down a notch.

Impressive. Ethan handled her perfectly. When he took the job as the police chief of the normally sleepy town, he probably thought it would be a piece of cake compared to his years on the Hartford police force. Little did he understand the dynamics of a small town when he moved to Jefferson. From what she'd just witnessed, it looked like he had fully acclimated to life in a small town.

"I had a long day at the office," Alfred added.

"Thank you. I'll be back shortly." Ethan walked out of the room, leaving Hope at the mercy of her reluctant hostess.

Maretta glared sharply at Hope as she lifted her chin and shoved her hands into the pockets of her rose robe. "I guess I'll put the kettle on."

"Please don't go to any trouble on my account," Hope said.

"You should have thought of that before you came over here tonight." Maretta swung around and headed out of the living room.

Tears threatened to flow, and Hope's hands were shaking. She clasped them together in her lap in hopes of stopping the trembling. Hope looked at

Alfred. "She's acting as if I found a dead body just to disrupt her sleep."

"You know how she gets." With his index finger, Alfred pushed his wire-rimmed glasses up past the bridge of his nose. "Don't let her upset you."

"While we wait, could you tell me about Peaches? Why did she irritate Maretta so much?"

Alfred gently shook his head. "She really had no reason to dislike Peaches so much."

"So why did she?"

"Peaches flattered me." A tinge of redness tipped his cheeks. "I guess Maretta was jealous."

Hope hesitated to ask the next question right on the tip of her tongue. But she had to ask. "Is that all Peaches did?" She quickly said a silent prayer the answer would be "yes" and she wouldn't have to hear any awkward confessions. *Please, please, please, say yes.*

Alfred padded over to the sideboard and lifted a crystal decanter off the sterling silver tray. He pulled out the stopper and poured two glasses of sherry.

Oh, goodness, he needed alcohol for his answer. Hope braced herself for a whole lot of awkwardness.

"Peaches flirted with me. But it wasn't what Maretta thought it was." He lifted the two cut-lead crystal glasses and turned to Hope.

He offered her a glass. Sherry normally didn't appeal to her. She would have preferred something stronger, like an espresso, but it was liquor. Not sure of what Alfred was going to say next, she downed the drink and set the glass on the coffee table.

Alfred gave her a puzzled look. She guessed Maretta sipped her sherry.

"What was it then?" she asked.

"Peaches was trying to convince me to sell the agency to Lionel Whitcomb."

"He's a developer."

Alfred sipped his sherry. "He's a very successful businessman. He owns several businesses, including a few appraisal businesses."

Hope didn't have thorough insight into the world of real estate, other than what Claire shared and what she'd gleaned from watching the reality show *Millionaire Agents of NYC*. Watching reality TV was still a guilty pleasure, but now when she watched, she knew the dark side, the side the camera didn't reveal. The shows were like train wrecks. You couldn't look away, and she admittedly didn't.

"I had no idea. Were you going to sell?"

"No, I wasn't."

"It seems Peaches had a closer relationship with Lionel Whitcomb than just being his listing agent."

"I'm sure they did. But I wasn't aware of that until Lionel chose Peaches to be the listing agent for Hunting Hills. I suggested Claire."

"Did you check his past?"

"Yes. The best I could and found no reason not to do business with him."

"Does Maretta know he wanted to buy you out?"

"No, and it's better to leave it that way for now."

For the first time, Hope heard Alfred sounding assertive. When Maretta wasn't around, he obviously wore the pants.

"Leave what?" Maretta entered the room carrying a serving tray with three filled teacups.

Alfred's head swung around, and Hope swore she saw him change right in front of her eyes. Gone was the confident businessman and back was the dutiful husband. "This murder investigation is best left to the police."

"It is their job." Maretta set the tray on the coffee table, then swiped the crystal glass off the table and placed it on the tray. "I made herbal tea. I can safely say we've had enough excitement for this evening."

"Here, let me serve." Alfred moved closer to the tray. "Hope, do you have any idea how much longer the chief will be?"

Before Hope could answer, the doorbell chimed.

"Are they going to be traipsing in and out all night?" Maretta stomped out of the room only to return moments later with Drew. "I suppose I'll have to get another cup."

"Let me, dear." Alfred set down his cup and left the living room.

"Maretta, would you mind giving us a moment?" Drew asked bravely.

Maretta huffed. "I'm sorry if I'm in the way in my own house." She turned and stomped out of the room, again.

"How did you get in?" Hope expected the officer posted at the front door of the house to keep him out since he was a reporter for the *Gazette.*

Not waiting for Maretta to return with another cup, Drew helped himself to one of the cups of tea on the tray, he added a drop of milk, and stirred. He appeared to have been savoring the moment of kicking Maretta out of her living room. Normally, Hope would have let him have his moment, but not that night. "How did you get past the cop?"

After he swallowed his drink of tea, he settled on the sofa next to her. Even in the middle of a stormy night, Drew looked pulled together, casually dressed in a gray T-shirt, white jeans, gray tassel loafers, and a tailored navy wool jacket. She glanced at herself. She'd left her house in her black fleece pants and pink sweatshirt hoodie, and her hair was damp from the rain.

"Officer Roberts knows we're friends, and I'm here as your friend." He set his cup and saucer on the coffee table and then held his arms wide open. "Where else would I be at a time like this?"

Tears streamed down Hope's face, too many to wipe away. She'd found a friend murdered. She fell into Drew's open arms and cried. His hold tightened around her, making her feel safe. Their friendship went back to elementary school and never wavered, even when they both left Jefferson for college and she decided to remain in New York City. He was one of the few people in her life she could always count on.

"There. There. Let it all out. Don't hold anything back." His voice was gentle and caring.

Hope nodded. It was a like a dam burst. All of the sadness, fear, and anger spilled out. She hadn't had a moment like that since she'd discovered Tim cheated on her. Then, she didn't have Drew or anyone to turn to for comfort, for reassurance. It was nice not to be alone anymore.

"Good girl. I can't believe you came out in this storm."

Hope shrugged. It really wasn't a big deal. She

often went out way past ten down in the city, even in bad weather. Out and about on her own was something she was used to. Though, she'd never found a dead body in New York City but two so far in Jefferson. That gave her pause for consideration. Was the little town tucked away in northwestern Connecticut really safer than the melting pot of New York?

Drew patted her back gently. "And finding Vanessa, dead. Murdered in her own home moments after talking to you on the phone."

Hope shivered. Had the storm not been so severe, she might have arrived a few minutes earlier. Would she have come face-to-face with the killer? Ethan was right. She'd put her life in danger. *Stupid, stupid, stupid.*

"Then bravely calling the police. By the way, while you waited for the police to arrive, did you happen to take a look around her cottage or Maretta's garden shed?"

Hope shook her head. When the beam of light from her flashlight shone on Vanessa's body, she froze. It took a few minutes for her to process what she'd just found. She lifted the beam of light and swept the room again, looking for someone. The house was empty, except for Hope and Vanessa's body. Satisfied the killer was gone, she retraced her steps back to her car to call for help.

Whoa. Garden shed?

Hope exhaled a deep breath. So much for comfort. She pulled herself out of Drew's hold, reached to the tray for a napkin and dried her face.

"I waited in my car." She crumpled up the napkin and tossed it on the tray.

Drew rolled his eyes. "Making a reporter out of you is going to be tougher than I thought." He picked up his teacup and took a drink. "Now the police will find the bloodied blunt object before us."

"What bloodied blunt object?"

"Duh. The one that killed Vanessa."

"You think Maretta killed Vanessa?

Drew shrugged. "Maybe it's in her purse. She's hidden the murder weapon in her purse."

"I doubt it."

"It's big enough to fit the whole freakin' shed in it. I bet Maretta killed Peaches and then Vanessa found out and that's why Maretta killed her."

"You really need to be careful not to hurt yourself." Hope reached for her cup of tea and took a sip. She really needed something stronger.

"Hurt myself how?"

"Jumping to all those conclusions."

"Ha ha. You know very well I could be right."

Hope gave him a pointed stare. "Did you do any real journalist work today?"

"Yes, I did. I found out Peaches McCoy was born and raised in New Jersey and moved to our fair state when she was a teenager with her mother."

"Hope, are you up to driving home? I'll follow you." Ethan entered the room, interrupting Hope's conversation with Drew.

Hope looked over to the doorway and nodded. She could drive. Slowly, but she could drive. "Yes, let's go." It took all of the energy she could muster to stand. And that must have shown because Drew reached out to her and grabbed hold of her arm to assist her. She flashed an appreciative smile, then walked toward Ethan.

All three headed to the front door. They were almost in the clear.

"It's about time. But I have no idea how I'll be able to go back to sleep," Maretta said from down the hall.

Hope should have just continued out of the house, gotten in the car, and driven home, but she stopped and turned around. She'd had enough of Maretta's selfish behavior. "Do you ever think of anybody but yourself? Ever?"

Maretta lifted her chin and glared at Hope but said nothing. A hand wrapped around Hope's arm and gently tugged her to the door. She glanced over her shoulder. Ethan was shuffling her out of the house. She threw one more look back at Maretta before walking out of the house. The woman had no shame. Maybe Drew's theory that the cranky old woman was the murderer wasn't completely off-base.

Chapter Thirteen

Hope descended the staircase, her eyes blurry and puffy from too much crying last night, and padded through the hallway to the family room. She surveyed the space. Her knitting was left out on the chair and a cup of half-finished tea remained on the end table. She picked up the cup and headed to the kitchen. What was she thinking the night before to rush out with no one knowing where she was going? She hadn't thought logically—instead, she'd acted impulsively and could have been murdered as a result.

But the thought of leaving Vanessa's body to lay there all night, alone and with no one knowing she'd been killed, stabbed at Hope's heart. She closed her eyes tightly. No, even with all that could have gone wrong, she had done the right thing.

She turned on the faucet and rinsed the cup. The day-old tea swirled down the drain. *Gone.* If she could only wash the past few days down the drain.

She pushed herself away from the sink and moved toward the fireplace. Her stomach constricted as she stopped midstride. She barely knew Peaches, and her friendship with Vanessa was new, yet she felt intimately connected to them.

Of course she would. She found their bodies.

The mudroom door opened. "Morning."

She swung around. Ethan entered the kitchen in his uniform, gun holstered at his side, carrying a basket of eggs.

Who'd have thought a guy could look sexy holding a basket of eggs? She gave herself a mental shake. She was exhausted and not thinking clearly. And given that two women were dead, this wasn't the time to indulge in silly schoolgirl behavior.

"You collected the eggs for me." Every morning she trekked out to the barn where the chicken coop was located and filled up the basket. Otherwise there was a risk the chickens would eat the eggs and once that started, she could kiss the eggs good-bye because the habit was nearly impossible to break.

"I did. But I didn't clean them." Ethan grinned. He set the basket on the island and then washed his hands. "I also fed them."

"I can't believe you did this for me. Especially since some of the girls can be difficult. Helga is very high-strung." Hope did a quick inspection of the eggs. Yeah, some needed a little bit more cleaning than others. She'd take care of that later.

"So that's her name. I could collar her for assaulting a police officer." Ethan turned around, drying his hand with a paper towel.

Hope laughed. "She'd resist arrest."

"Are you going for a run this morning?" He eyed her pajamas.

She shrugged. "Maybe later." She needed coffee first. She turned to the counter and found the coffeepot filled. He'd made coffee, too. She took out a mug from an upper cabinet and poured a full cup.

"You're taking such good care of me."

"That's what friends do." He grabbed a mug and filled it.

Friends. They'd been friends since high school, and, for the past few weeks, she hadn't been sure if they were still just friends. She'd sensed a change. A change in herself and a change in Ethan, but she wasn't certain, so saying something seemed risky. What happened if she was wrong? If nothing had changed for him, would their friendship be ruined? Just the thought of losing Ethan as a friend made her sad. So, whatever was causing her stomach to flutter when she thought of him or her pulse to pick up its pace when he said her name would have to stop. True friendship was far too valuable to risk for something as uncertain as love. She'd already tried that once and ended up divorced.

And given the events of the past few days, she would be smart not to make any assumptions or make any moves that could be embarrassing.

Gosh, she was feeling like an adolescent girl. She shook off her romantic thoughts and saw the worry in Ethan's dark eyes.

"How long did you stay at the Kingstons' house? You didn't get much sleep last night, did you?"

He stifled a yawn. His expression became more serious. "I'm fine. I'm concerned about you."

She shook her head. "Don't be. I'm okay. I just don't know why Vanessa didn't call me earlier. She obviously knew something about Peaches' murder. Why didn't she just tell me when she called?" She took another drink of coffee as she headed to the table.

"I thought I told you to stay out of the investigation." The seriousness on his face turned a shade darker. Bye-bye worry, now anger flickered in his eyes.

Hope squared her shoulders. She didn't appreciate the deepening tone of Ethan's voice or the fact he believed he could tell her what to do.

She set her mug down on the table with a thump and squared her shoulders. "The last time I checked, I was an adult who didn't need to be told what to do." She headed toward the hall. Whether she liked it or not, she had a full day. She planned on visiting Audrey, and she had the cooking lesson with Elaine and was already way behind.

"Where are you going?"

She stopped midstride and looked over her shoulder. "To take a shower. If that's okay with you."

"Don't be like that. You're exhausted, upset."

"Then maybe you should leave." She turned and continued out of the kitchen. By the time she'd reached the staircase, the back door closed. She inhaled a jagged breath. Had Ethan crossed the line by telling her what to do, again? Or had she overreacted to his obvious concern? Given she was exhausted and still in shock from finding two women murdered, she probably overreacted. She grabbed hold of the banister and made the climb up to the second floor. An apology was definitely in order, and she'd be giving it soon. Right after she gave Elaine her cooking lesson.

Showered and ready to begin her day, she opened her closet, flicked on the light switch, and winced as the soft light flooded the space. The previous owners had carved out a space for a walk-in closet but only inserted basic rods with one lone shelf up high for storage. Since there were bigger projects to tackle, the closet would have to wait.

She stepped over last season's suede boots—three pairs and all in black. To think, she accused her sister of being the fashionista. Bending over, she pushed three shopping bags full of clothes out of her path. What wasn't in bags was hung tightly on the rods while shoeboxes were piled and sweaters were crammed on the shelf, with scarves and belts draped over everything and anything. She really needed to raise the priority on the closet organization.

With temperatures predicted to be in the high fifties, she grabbed a V-neck sweater and a pair of twill pants. She slipped on a pair of ankle boots and headed back downstairs. She'd finally gotten a message from Audrey and planned on stopping by before going to Elaine's cooking lesson. She also decided to visit Gilbert Madison and ask him some questions about his meeting with Peaches a few days ago. She couldn't very well show up empty-handed at either house, so she had some baking to do before she left. The morning hours flew by as she baked, and as both treats cooled on a rack, she was confident the coffee cake would be a gift of comfort to Audrey and the loaf of apple bread would be a tasty little bribe to get Gilbert to open up about his conversation with Peaches. At her first stop of the day, Hope made her way up the flagstone path to Gilbert's tidy gray colonial house with white trim with the warm loaf of apple bread. His wife, Mitzi, was an avid gardener and Gilbert did his best to keep the landscaping and gardens up to her high standards while she recovered from a hip fracture. Early spring flowers dotted the front yard in the curved garden beds, while large branches were scattered throughout, reminders of the storm last night.

"Good morning, Hope." Gilbert came around from the side of the house with an armful of branches. "Nasty storm last night."

"Yes, it was. Did you have any damage?"

"No. Just a bunch of branches down. I guess it's good exercise picking them up, right?" His dog, Buddy, trotted over to his owner with a stick in his mouth. The golden retriever looked so proud.

"My little helper," Gilbert juggled the branches in one arm so he could pat Buddy on the head.

"It's always good to have help."

"Terrible thing that happened last night."

"Yes, it was."

"Do the police have any idea of who murdered Ms. Jordan?"

"No."

Gilbert shook his head. "I've lived here my whole life. Nothing like this has ever happened. But you, living down in New York City for a few years, must be used to all this crime."

"Actually, I'm not. And it's different here. We knew these women. They weren't strangers." Hope followed Gilbert as he walked to a pile of branches.

Gilbert dropped his armful of branches on top of the pile he'd already collected. It looked like he'd been working for a while. Buddy joined them and he shoved his nose up under Hope's hands, sniffing the loaf pan she held.

Hope laughed. Buddy wasn't shy. He was lovable and knew he could get away with such bold behavior.

"This isn't for you." Hope gently moved Buddy's head from the bread. "I baked it this morning. It's cinnamon apple bread." She handed the wrapped loaf pan to Gilbert.

His blue eyes twinkled. "Thank you. I do enjoy your baking. Come on inside. I'll put the kettle on for a cup of tea."

Hope smiled and followed Gilbert and Buddy inside the house. Gilbert busied himself making tea and finally sat at the table and eagerly cut into the bread. He served up two slices.

Gilbert took a bite and savored the tart Granny Smith apples blended with spices and topped with a nutty streusel. "This is delicious. I have to admit I was worried you wouldn't bring me any more treats after what happened with Claire."

Hope waved away his concern. "You told the truth to the police. There are no hard feelings. But I do have a couple of questions." She cut another slice of bread and plated it for Gilbert.

Gilbert broke off a piece of bread and popped it in his mouth. He smiled his appreciation and chewed. Hope never tired of seeing the joy her baking brought to people. That was why she signed on for *The Sweet Taste of Success*. She envisioned sharing her passion and enthusiasm for baking with America. Looking back, she realized how naïve she was for a thirtysomething. America didn't want her enthusiasm or recipes, neither did the network. They wanted conflict and drama, which made for good television. But right there in Gilbert's kitchen, he just wanted to enjoy her bread.

She wanted answers to her questions.

He swallowed his bite of bread. "What kind of questions?"

"When you last saw Peaches, did she seem out of sorts?"

Gilbert seemed to be deep in thought for a moment. "I really can't say. I didn't know her well. She was very direct and competent. She had the marketing plan for my house all in place, ready for me to read. She told me this kitchen and the bathrooms were the challenges. Guess everybody wants stainless and white cabinets." He glanced around his traditional oak kitchen with black appliances.

"Yes, they do." Cookie-cutter kitchens were all the rage and exactly what Hope decided would not be in her home. She enjoyed modern appliances for their efficiency and sleekness but character had charm. She'd chosen a white porcelain farm sink instead of a stainless sink and soapstone countertops rather than granite. They added charm to her twenty-first-century kitchen.

"I didn't have the wherewithal to do any remodeling, so we agreed on a price and I signed the contract."

"What happened after that?"

"We enjoyed a cup of coffee and chatted for a few minutes. That's what I miss the most about not having Mitzi here. There's no one to sit and chat with."

Hope's heart broke for the elderly man, and she mentally chided herself for not realizing he was lonely and for having an ulterior motive that prompted her visit.

"It must be very difficult for you, and I'm sorry for that."

"There's no reason to be sorry. Mitzi will be home soon from the rehab center. Life isn't supposed to be easy. That's what I told Peaches, too. And she agreed. She'd gone through loss in her life. She understood."

"She did?"

"Yes. Her father died when she was a baby. Then her mother was hit by a car and killed. She started to tear up so she didn't want to talk about the details. But she said she was finally going to have closure."

"Closure? Did she say how?"

Gilbert shook his head. "No, and I didn't pry." He took another bite of the bread. After swallowing, he said, "You know, I haven't had the chance to tell you, but I really think you should have won the competition. You are the best baker, Hope Early." Gilbert finished the rest of his bread.

A nudge at her arm brought Hope's attention to Buddy. With his snout, he lifted her arm and slid his head onto her lap and his big brown eyes looked up to her. He knew how to work her. She broke off a piece of her bread and fed it to the dog.

"That's all you get." She patted his head.

"Buddy's a bit spoiled," Gilbert said.

"There's nothing wrong with a little spoiling." Hope would remember that, and the next time she visited Gilbert, there would be no secret agenda.

Chapter Fourteen

Hope drummed her fingertips on the steering wheel of her SUV as she waited for the traffic light to change. She left Gilbert's house with more questions than she had when she arrived with the loaf of apple cinnamon bread. Gilbert didn't know much more about Peaches than Hope did, but he did know she was looking for closure with her mother's death. How so? Usually closure came when something had been resolved. Did this mean the person who was driving the car that killed Peaches' mother was never arrested? Was Peaches doing a little sleuthing of her own?

An OPEN HOUSE sign caught Hope's attention at the corner of Chestnut Road. The real estate agent hosting the open house was Kent Wilder. He'd lost a client to Peaches, and Amy had said he wasn't happy about it.

Hope made a right turn onto Chestnut Road and drove down the dead-end street until she came to

the blue Cape Cod house with a steep roof and attached garage. By the number of cars in the driveway, it looked like Kent had a full house. She
parked on the street and walked up the driveway
to the brick path to the front door.

She pulled open the screen door and entered
the small entry hall. The home was modest in size
but big on brightness, thanks to its soft white walls
and bare windows that let light in.

Directly in front of her was the staircase to upstairs and to her right was the living room with a
minimally decorated fireplace and cozy furnishings. To her left was the formal dining room set for
an intimate dinner party and Kent Wilder talking
square footage with a potential buyer.

"Hope." Kent broke away from the potential
buyer and made his way over to her. "I didn't realize you were in the market. Tired of your new
home already?"

"No, nothing like that." Hope walked toward
Kent.

Kent laughed. He was the consummate salesman.
Bright, white teeth, tanned skin, and an expensive
suit with a logo watch and shiny black leather shoes.
He knew how to make small talk turn into a binding
agreement and he knew how to gloss over flaws in
a home and focus attention on the positives, no
matter how small they might be. Hope knew first-
hand how good Kent could be. Just before she
bought her farmhouse, he'd shown her another
fixer-upper that would have landed her in the
poorhouse with all of its problems.

He shoved his hands into his pants pockets.
"Then what can I do for you today?"

"You've heard about Peaches McCoy, right?"

"Everybody has. Good news travels fast," he said in a low voice, leaning forward.

"Good news? Is that how you see her murder?"

Kent shrugged. "Well, let's just say I'm not mourning. I'm too busy to do that. Her clients need a new agent."

"Like Annabel Layton? I heard you lost her listing to Peaches."

The cocky look on Kent's face morphed into confusion. "What exactly do you want?"

"Where were you when Peaches was killed?"

Kent pulled his hands out of his pockets and grinned. "I don't believe this. You're asking me for an alibi? Look, I didn't kill Peaches. Sure, she came into town all full of herself, stealing clients and depositing big commission checks, but over the past few weeks, we'd all gotten to see the real Peaches. Sloppy."

"How so?"

"Calls not returned, contracts not signed. It was only a matter of time before Alfred and Lionel Whitcomb kicked her to the curb."

"Did she appear distracted?"

Kent shrugged again. "Don't know, didn't care. I was just going to let her crash and burn." His attention was diverted to a young couple who entered the dining room. The woman pointed to a wall and whispered while the man took out a tape measure. "If there's nothing else, I really need to sell this house."

"Actually, you didn't answer my question. Where were you when Peaches was killed?"

"I have nothing to hide. I was here finalizing the

details for the open house and then I picked my kid up from school. Have a nice day, Hope." Kent turned and headed to the young couple, greeting them with a big smile.

Hope made her way out of the house, leaving Kent to make his sale. His comments about Peaches' sudden change in work ethic seemed to coincide with when Peaches found closure about her mother's death. Hope was certain Peaches had been looking for the person driving the car that hit and killed her mother. Hope needed to find out more about the accident. She was so lost in thought she almost missed Meg Griffin power walking toward her.

"Good morning, Meg."

Meg came to a stop. She glanced at the Cape Cod house and then back to Hope.

"Looking to move?"

"No. I just stopped by to talk to Kent. I'm glad we ran into each other." Hope had wanted to find out why Meg abruptly left Audrey's house just before the book signing. Now seemed like a good opportunity.

"Sorry. I have to keep my heart rate up." Meg glanced at her fitness band.

"This won't take long."

Meg sighed as she rested her hands on her hips. "Make it quick, okay?"

"You left Audrey's house before the book signing because you couldn't stand to be in the same house as Peaches. Why?"

"I don't have to answer your questions. Besides, it's none of your business."

"You're right on both counts. I guess you'll just

have to answer Detective Reid's questions. Thanks for your time." Hope took a step back. It was time to go.

"Wait." Meg reached out. "I was afraid if I stood there, I would do something I would have regretted."

"And that would be what?"

"I don't know . . . like . . . slap Peaches. Okay, I wanted to slap her. There I've said it." Meg lifted her hand and pointed her index finger at Hope. "But I did not kill her. I was gone before she was murdered."

"How are you so certain?"

"Because when you tried to stop me from leaving, I saw Peaches walk out of the living room and down the hall toward the study."

"You did? Did you see anyone follow her?"

Meg shook her head. "No."

"How about anyone heading in that direction a few moments earlier?"

"I'm not sure. Everyone was everywhere. I just noticed her."

"What was going on between you two?"

Meg sighed again. "A couple of weeks ago she tried to strong-arm my Aunt Peggy into listing her house"

"How so?"

"She showed up one afternoon with a sales pitch and a marketing plan. She barged in and told Aunt Peggy it was in her best interest to sell now rather than later. She rattled off all the problems with the house. For goodness sake, the house is over a hundred of years old, so it has problems.

My aunt was so upset, she called me crying. She loves her home."

"I know she does." Peggy Olson lived a few houses down from Hope, and she admired how well Peggy took care of her Victorian house, even though she was getting older. Hope hadn't realized just how aggressive Peaches was in her real estate dealings. Maybe she shouldn't just be looking at agents for possible suspects. "Once I calmed Aunt Peggy down, I called Peaches and told her never to approach my aunt again or she'd be sorry. She was looking for commissions and didn't care about anybody else."

Hope raised an eyebrow. Did Detective Reid know Meg had threatened Peaches? "When you left Audrey's house, where did you go?" While Hope saw Meg leave, she could have easily made her way around the back of the house and entered through the study since she saw Peaches walk in that direction.

"To the gym. I took a kickboxing class. Now, can I continue with my walk?"

"Yes. Thank you, Meg, for being straight with me."

"Like I had a choice? I prefer to keep my business private and that's the only reason I've told you this. Some of us don't like our dirty laundry aired in prime time." Meg strode away, pumping her arms as she reached the end of the street and turned onto Crimson Ridge.

Hope considered what Meg had just told her, and she doubted Meg had a motive for murder, but it wouldn't hurt to check her alibi. After all, her elderly aunt was bullied by Peaches.

*　*　*

Driving over to Audrey's, Hope made a detour that took her to the only fitness center in Jefferson, The Workout Fix. Shiny and new, the fitness center was a big improvement over the previous gym that had occupied the space. Hope pushed open the front door and entered the lobby and was greeted by a perky receptionist wearing a logo T-shirt promoting her employer.

"Good morning." Hope approached the desk. On the drive over she'd tried to come up with a plan because she doubted anyone would willingly give her any information on a client since she wasn't a police officer.

"How can I help you today? Are you interesting in joining? We have a new-member package promotion." The young woman reached for a clipboard loaded with a thick sheath of papers and a pen.

Beyond the reception desk was a juice bar and a small café area with tables and chairs. In the distance, Hope saw rows of exercise equipment and members working out. Classy place. Glancing at the forms, she saw just how much the classy gym cost. Yikes! No wonder there was a food court. She'd stay with her daily runs, thank you very much. "My friend, Meg Griffin, has been raving about this place. In fact, she said she loves the kickboxing class." Not exactly a lie, but Hope was definitely skirting the truth.

The receptionist's brown eyes lit up. No doubt she earned a commission on each new-member sign-up. "Oh, yeah, Meg is great, and she does love our aerobic classes."

"She said she took a kickboxing class two days ago, in the afternoon. She told me the instructor's name but I can't remember. I was just wondering how many classes that instructor does."

"Yeah, Meg was really stressed out when she came in."

"You saw her?"

The receptionist nodded. "Sure. I'm always here. I love this place. Anyway, she looked like she'd had a rough day, but an hour in Kimberly's class must have worked out all the stress because she looked so relaxed when she left. Kimberly works you out seriously. There are just a few forms to fill out and then I can give you the grand tour." The receptionist smiled.

Hope glanced at her watch. "I do need to be somewhere right now, but I'll think about that new-member promotion. Thank you." She turned and headed to the front door. She pushed the door open and walked out of the gym. Since Meg was there after she left Audrey's house, it was doubtful she killed Peaches. Relieved and disappointed at the same time, Hope could at least rule out Meg as a suspect.

"Hope!"

She stopped and turned around. Drew was chasing after her from the gym. He was dressed for a workout in shorts and a long-sleeve shirt finished with his new running shoes that cost three digits and would be replaced within six months. A good pair of shoes was essential in running, but shelling out big bucks for the flavor of the day was extreme. But appearances were important to Drew and other than his wardrobe, he was financially savvy.

"Are you thinking about joining?"

"No, I was just following up on something."

"That would be what?" He took a swig from his water bottle.

"Meg said she came here for a kickboxing class after she left Audrey's house abruptly. Turns out she did."

"Looks like you've ruled her out as a suspect. She has an alibi."

"Yeah, it feels weird."

A concerned look hovered in Drew's eyes.

"I'm relieved she has an alibi and she's not a killer, but that means Reid can still look at Claire for the murders."

Drew reached out and touched Hope's arm. "This isn't going to be pretty. It's going to be tough."

"I know." Hope swallowed. Her pity party was just getting started, but it was feeling old fast. She didn't want Drew feeling sorry for her, so she needed to snap out of it.

"I do have some news about Vanessa's murder. The cause of death was blunt force trauma to the head."

"Just like Peaches."

Drew nodded. "But unlike Peaches' murder, the murder weapon wasn't left near the body."

"I wonder where it is. Any indication of what the weapon was?"

"No, not yet. But I'll find out."

"So, the killer used a rock on Peaches and left it beside the body, but on Vanessa he or she took the murder weapon. I wonder if anything is missing from Vanessa's house."

Drew shrugged. "I don't know if the police could get an inventory of everything since Vanessa lived alone."

"Or maybe the killer had the weapon with him or her when they arrived."

"That's a possibility."

"Yes, it is. Hope said.

Drew's eyes widened. "Do you think the killer meant to kill Vanessa the day of the garden tour? She was the intended victim all along? But something went wrong and the killer had to finish the job?"

"I wonder if the police have considered that theory. Because if they haven't, they should. Claire didn't have a motive to kill Vanessa."

"I'll see what I can find out. I've gotta go. Abs need to be worked before I can head to the office." He patted his midsection. "Call me later." He broke away and jogged back to the entry of the gym.

Hope looked to her midsection. Hmmm . . . her recipe tasting was taking a toll on her once-firm abs, and running wasn't helping in that area. Maybe gym membership wouldn't be such a bad thing. She shook her head. Her abs were the least of her worries at the moment.

Chapter Fifteen

Just before Hope's index finger pushed the door-bell for a second time, the door swung open. Any doubts she had about what she'd set in motion by asking questions about the murders vanished because she was now hip-deep in her plan to find the killer.

Audrey flung her arms around Hope and embraced her. "I'm so glad to see you."

"I've been so worried about you." Hope removed herself from Audrey's embrace and quickly inspected the cake box. No damage done.

"I've been so exhausted. Between the police, our lawyer, those damn news vultures, and my publisher . . ." Audrey's puffy eyelids lowered. Her pale pink sweater and matching knit pants got her halfway put together. But her red and swollen face gave away the truth. She'd been crying a lot.

"Publisher?"

Audrey sighed. "They're not too pleased by all

of this. Come." She closed the front door and led Hope to the living room.

Hope followed, tight-lipped. She didn't think Audrey would want to hear that, while her publisher was freaking out about the murder, Hope's ex-producer was champing at the bit to pitch a reality show about it. If there was ever any doubt reality television had no boundaries, it was gone now.

Hope glanced around the room. Warm hues and a mix of florals and plaids gave the space an easy, elegant feel, while the white mantel topped with two crystal candlestick lamps and a collection of antique porcelain dogs grounded the room. Audrey collapsed onto the deep cushion of an oatmeal-colored linen chair. A contrasting cording fringed the bottom of the chair and added a touch of whimsy.

"And, now poor Vanessa," Audrey said in a low voice.

Just a few weeks ago, Audrey had looked at ease in the chair when she gathered a few friends for an impromptu meeting to discuss the future of Jefferson. She'd shared with them she considered running for mayor. She'd been upbeat, positive, and hopeful. A very stark contrast to the defeated-looking woman sitting there now.

"You heard?" Hope set the cake box and her purse on the coffee table, then slipped out of her jacket.

"I don't think there's one person in Jefferson who hasn't. Who needs the *Gazette*?"

Hope knew news, especially sensational news, spread fast anywhere. Her own split from Tim had made a New York City newspaper's infamous gossip page and, while it stung, it was fleeting, but two murders in a place like Jefferson would linger for decades.

"I baked an apple crumb cake. I know it's one of your favorites. How about I cut you a slice and pour us some coffee?" Hope scooped up the box.

"Perfect timing. Meg just made a fresh pot of decaf." Audrey seemed to relax for a moment, and Hope was reminded of how much Audrey looked like her late mother. Both women were tall, well-poised, and elegant.

Hope stopped midstep and cringed. "Meg is here?"

"She's been such a great help since . . ." Her hand raised to her mouth and she closed her eyes. She took a moment to compose herself. Her eyelids opened, and she inhaled a steadying breath. "I'm so lucky to have such good friends."

"We're all here for you." Sooner or later she'd run into Meg again, but she was kind of hoping for later. Not roughly an hour after she grilled her about an alibi for a murder they'd be having coffee and cake together. "I'll be right back with the cake and coffee." Hope walked into the kitchen.

Meg was unloading the dishwasher. Still wearing her yoga pants and hoodie, she must have power walked her way to Audrey's house. Hope hadn't seen Meg's car in the driveway when she arrived.

"Hello, Meg."

Meg glanced over her shoulder and then straightened. "Isn't this a surprise? I'm sure Audrey is happy you stopped by."

"You seem to be taking good care of her." Hope

set the cake box on the counter. With any luck, they'd fall into the social skill that thrived in suburbia—avoidance. They wouldn't discuss their earlier conversation. In fact, they would pretend it didn't happen so they could get through their visit with their mutual friend like it never happened.

Meg shrugged. "I'm doing what I can. I see you baked something. Audrey hasn't been eating much since the incident." Meg pulled out three dessert plates from the dishwasher.

So far so good.

"I was worried about that." Hope made a mental note to cook something and bring it over for dinner. Maybe a pot roast with baby red potatoes and a side of roasted carrots.

"She just picks at food." Meg opened the upper cabinet and took out three cups and saucers.

"Maybe she'll indulge in an extra-large slice of cake." Hope removed the cake from the box.

"I can't see how she could possibly resist." Meg eyed the decadent cake. "I should be watching my weight, but I think I might have to give in to temptation. After all, I can go to a kickboxing class again."

Uh-oh. Not good.

"Tell me, did you stop by the gym to check out my alibi?" Meg leaned against the counter, crossed her arms over her chest, and stared at Hope.

Hope lowered her eyelids for a moment and wished really hard she had a different answer. But she didn't. "Yes. The receptionist remembered you."

"Ha! I told you." Meg pushed herself off the counter and reached for the coffeepot. She filled the cups and then set the pot back onto the machine's base.

"Yes, you did." Three of the toughest words Hope had to say all week. While she knew she should have been above being petty, admitting Meg was right was hard to do. Their rivalry reached all the way back to elementary school when they were both up for the lead role in the school play. Hope enjoyed the acting classes. She had fun when she was pretending to be someone else, while Meg was a full-on competitor, even at the age of eight. Their first year of competing for the lead role, Hope got chosen and Meg got angry. Looking back, Hope realized Meg was her first introduction to passive-aggressive behavior.

"I'm waiting," Meg said.

"For what?"

"An apology."

"Why would I apologize to you?" Hope cut three slices of cake and plated them.

"For insinuating I murdered Peaches."

"I was just asking your whereabouts."

"Did you happen to mention your interest in my whereabouts to anyone else? Because if you have, then I might have to look into legal action. I have to protect my good name."

Hope rolled her eyes. "Seriously? Threatening me with a lawsuit? Aren't you taking this grade-school rivalry a little too far?"

Meg narrowed her eyes, locking in on Hope. "Me? No."

Both women stared at each other. They could do that for hours but Audrey needed to eat and

Hope had to get to Elaine's house for her cooking lesson. Someone needed to break the ice.

"Good to know." Hope closed the cake box then set the plates on a tray. "When was the last time you saw Peaches? I mean before the garden tour?"

"You're not going to stop this, are you?"

"No."

Meg sighed. "About a week ago. I'd just finished running a bunch of errands and I was parked in the Village Square and that's when I saw Peaches. She was talking to a man beside her car. She looked sad."

"Sad?"

Meg nodded. "He reached out and touched her arm, like he was comforting her. It was odd to see her looking so sad, given she was so serious and being all cutthroat about development."

"Do you know who the man was?"

"No, I didn't recognize him."

"Did Peaches see you?"

"I don't know. Just then my phone rang, so I didn't pay much attention to Peaches or the guy. Audrey must be wondering what's keeping us so long."

A few minutes later, Hope and Meg entered the living room. They found Audrey rearranging a vase of flowers.

"Here you go." Hope placed the tray on the coffee table. "Have you eaten anything today?"

"No. I'm not very hungry." Audrey spun the crystal vase around. She accepted a dessert plate. She broke off a piece of cake and popped it into her mouth. "This is delicious."

Hope sipped her coffee while she relayed the events of the night before. As she spoke, Audrey's eyes welled up with tears and her forehead furrowed with anguish.

"I don't believe this." With a shaky hand, Audrey set her plate on the coffee table. She stood and paced. "I feel like I'm trapped in a nightmare. Why is this happening? You know, Ethan even told us he could keep us from being here. *Our own house.* This house has been in my family for three generations. My life is unraveling. I'm glad my mother didn't live to see this. It would have destroyed her."

Hope believed Audrey was on the verge of a breakdown. She hadn't eaten, had barely slept, and her professional life was in tatters. And, as for her personal life, she'd always be the owner of the house where a woman was murdered. Compassion for Audrey overwhelmed Hope, but she couldn't let that deter her from what needed to be done. First, she needed to remind Audrey she wasn't alone. Second, she needed to find something to prove her sister didn't kill Peaches and Vanessa.

"You know you're not alone. Staying holed up here isn't going to make what happened go away. There's only one way I know how to help." Hope never liked running away from anything, and she didn't like seeing those she loved run, either.

Audrey was on the verge of more tears. "What are we going to do?" Her voice trembled, and she looked uncharacteristically scared.

"We need to find out why Peaches came here the day of the tour."

"No one seems to know why she showed up," Meg said.

"What about Vanessa? How well did they know each other?" Hope asked.

Audrey shrugged. "I really don't know."

Hope knew something had to connect them because both of them being murdered in two days wasn't a coincidence. "Did either of you see Peaches and Vanessa together the day of the garden tour?"

Both Audrey and Meg shook their heads.

"They had to run into each other. But Vanessa was so busy keeping everything on track. I don't know what I'm going to do without her," Audrey said.

"That's right. She was anxious to get over here early. Does Harrison have any idea of what Peaches could have been looking for in his study?" Hope asked.

"No. It didn't make sense the day of the murder, and it still doesn't." Audrey stood again and busied herself tidying up the china.

"Not much makes sense. Did you see Peaches in the study?" Hope asked.

"Of course not," Audrey said.

"Audrey was with her guests for the entire event." Meg shifted in her seat on the opposite sofa. Her eyes narrowed and her lips pursed. She wasn't hiding her displeasure with Hope.

"Would you mind if I looked at Harrison's study?" Hope asked.

"Whatever for?" Meg jumped up and moved toward Audrey, placing a protective hand on her shoulder.

"I'm not sure Harrison would appreciate that." Audrey patted Meg's hand and then gently removed herself from Meg's hold. She reached for the tray and lifted it.

"I won't touch anything. I just want a look around." Hope had no idea what she'd be looking for, and her stomach did a flip-flop at the thought of stepping back into that room. Would going back in there be such a good idea?

"I guess it would be okay. Please be sure not to disturb anything. He's very particular about his space." Audrey turned and walked out of the room.

"What are you up to? Snooping around people's homes? Did Jane put you up to this? She wrote a handful of murder mysteries back in the day and since then she's been looking high and low for trouble. Now she's gotten you involved in a murder investigation," Meg said in a low voice.

"Jane hasn't gotten me into anything. Would you like to join me?"

"No. I'll be in the kitchen with Audrey." Meg turned and marched out of the living room.

Hope grabbed her purse and jacket, then headed to the study. When she reached the closed door, she hesitated before twisting the doorknob and pushing the six-paneled oak door open. She stared into the generous-sized room that had a magnificent view of the gardens through the double French doors. The expanse of lawn and meandering stone walls drew Hope into the room before she realized she was standing in the exact same spot where she'd found Peaches' body. A cold chill zipped through her body as the memory of the crime scene flashed in her mind. Quickly, she sidestepped to distance herself from the area.

She looked around the room. Dark leather furniture filled the room and a chair showed wear on the arms. There was a well-used ottoman, positioned across from the flat-screen television over the fireplace. Harrison probably spent a lot of time in the room. Would he continue to do so now that a murder had occurred in there?

Don't focus on the murder. Look for something that could lead to the killer.

Hope dropped down onto the ottoman and looked around. Brass lamps, an intricately carved chess table ready for a match, an ivory-colored storage box tucked into a corner with a stack of newspapers on top, framed photographs scattered throughout the room. Hope didn't know what she expected to find. The police had searched the room thoroughly, and any evidence left by the killer had been collected by the police.

Hope tilted her head and stared at the French doors. Closed that day, she remembered they were open when she found Peaches McCoy's body. Peaches could have been surprised by someone entering the room from the garden. The whole day revolved around the garden, so no one would have looked suspicious walking around outside or even entering the study. She stood and crossed the room to the doors and pulled one open. Someone could have easily picked up a rock from the yard, slipped into the room behind Peaches, hit her on the head, and then rejoined the other guests like nothing had happened.

A chill snaked its way through Hope's body. Just imagining the coldness of such an act made the hairs on her arms stand up. How could anyone be so horrible? She stepped out onto the patio. The sun had parted the clouds, and brightness filled the early-afternoon sky. The possibility that the day could turn out nice made her smile. Perhaps the day would be better than the previous ones.

"You think the killer entered the study from out here, too."

Hope jumped, startled by Jane's appearance from around the boxwood hedge.

"Jane. What are you doing here?"

"I came to see Audrey."

"Does she know you're here?"

"She will. Once I ring the doorbell. I just wanted to take a look around first. So, I take it you searched the study?"

"I didn't search anything. I just looked around."

Jane smiled. "If you say so, dear. And what did you find when you *looked around*?"

A loud bark caught her attention and Bigelow trotted toward them. His tail wagged playfully, and his big brown eyes were filled with mischief.

"What are you two doing out here?"

Hope looked up. Harrison stood a few feet away. He wore a jacket over a pair of jeans and a flannel shirt. He'd traded his fine Italian leather shoes for brown work boots. And he held a chainsaw.

Bigelow darted over to his owner, his tail still wagging feverishly.

Harrison ignored the dog. "Checking on Audrey?"

"Yes, I am. I also brought over an apple crumb

cake." She'd known Harrison for years, so why did every fiber in her body scream "run"?

He must have noticed her intense and nervous stare at the chainsaw. "Some large branches came down last night. They needed to be cut and chipped."

Chipped? Hope recalled a murder several years ago in another town involving a husband, a wife, and a wood chipper. Why on earth did she think coming back to her home state would be safer than living in New York City?

Harrison set the tool down and pulled off his work gloves.

She breathed a small sigh of relief.

"We're both worried about Audrey," Hope said.

"She's a strong woman. She'll be fine," Harrison assured them.

"She has no idea why Peaches came over here the other day. Do you know why she did?" Jane asked.

Harrison crossed his arms over his chest. His steely gray eyes narrowed, and his jaw clenched. "You didn't come over here to check on Audrey. You're here because Claire is the number one suspect in Peaches' murder."

Hope bit back her irritation at how casually he tossed around the accusation. "My sister didn't kill anyone."

"And you two think what? That either I or Audrey killed them?"

"You both can't be ruled out as suspects. Audrey was here at the time, and you could have easily returned through this door to murder Peaches." Jane gestured to the French doors.

Harrison uncrossed his arms and took a step forward. He pointed his index finger at Jane. "Listen to me, you old busybody—"

Hope sidestepped, putting herself between Jane and Harrison. "It seems odd Peaches would have been in your study. And the room looked like it had been searched. Like someone was looking for something. What could that have been?" Hope kept her position and didn't back down.

"I would have thought Chief Cahill would have warned you to stay out of this." Harrison unfolded his arms, reached down, and picked up the chainsaw.

"I'm just trying to find the truth."

"Then talk to your sister and ask her to confess so we can all get on with our lives." He took a few steps forward before he stopped and looked over his shoulder. "Come on, Bigelow."

The dog obeyed and trotted away with his master. For a second time, Hope had been dismissed by Harrison.

"It appears Harrison is a bit rattled. He's hiding something," Jane said.

Hope looked over her shoulder at what, on the outside, appeared to be a doting elderly woman engaged in activities like gardening and knitting. But Hope knew better. "Why? Because he's angry we're snooping around his house and practically accused him and his wife of murder?"

Jane waved away that notion. "Because we're getting close to something. You're doing a fine job, dear."

"Do you want a ride home?" Hope began walking around the side of the house, toward the drive-way, with Jane beside her.

"No, thank you. Sally dropped me off and will pick me up when she's done with her errands for the Inn."

"You're still going inside?"

"Of course, dear. I came to check on Audrey and I intend to." Jane turned and strolled along the grass to the front door.

Hope pulled open her car door and slid onto the driver's seat. She fished her keys out of her purse and started the ignition. Before she shifted the car into gear, she lowered the window and stared at the beautiful Federal-period house for a moment. Hope had spent so much time there over the years. So how come she really didn't know the two people who lived there?

Chapter Sixteen

"Rice pilaf? That sounds so fancy to make. It's really easy to make?" Elaine snapped the thin spaghetti into thirds. Her pile of bracelets jingled on her wrist as she sprinkled the broken spaghetti into the pan. She'd donned a pink cupcake-print apron over her body-skimming red sheath dress and provided one for Hope, too.

"It's very easy and it's one of those recipes that will become your go-to." Hope cracked several eggs into a deep dish in preparation for the Parmesan chicken recipe.

Elaine paused. "I never thought I'd have a go-to recipe. I mean, I have my go-to shoes." She glanced at her four-inch-plus platform nude pumps. She elongated one leg, pointing her foot. "These are perfect for every occasion."

Hope eyed her student's ridiculously high-heeled shoes. "Good to know."

"Okay, what's next? The rice pilaf is all set. What are you doing?"

"We're going to prepare the Parmesan chicken. This is a way to kick up a regular chicken cutlet. Take the wedge of Parmesan cheese and grate it. Use the box grater."

Hope saw the confusion on Elaine's face, so she pointed to the stainless four-sided grater. "Just run the wedge of cheese up and down on the side."

Elaine flashed a grateful smile as she reached forward to grab the grater, unwrapped the wedge of cheese, and proceeded to grate a pile of cheese.

"You're doing a good job." Hope whisked the eggs with salt, black pepper, and a dash of red pepper flakes.

"This really isn't hard. Where did you learn to cook?"

"My mom, mostly. Then I experimented a lot. I was either in the kitchen or at the library."

"It's nice your mom took time to teach you how to cook. I bet she did a lot with you and your sister."

Hope nodded. Her mom loved cooking and had a recipe box stuffed with cards. Most were creased, stained, or marked up. One day Hope planned to create a cookbook from those beloved recipes. That was, if she could ever pry the recipe box from her mom's hands. "She did. Your mom didn't cook?"

Elaine shrugged as she set the box grater to the side. She had a billowy pile of cheese in front of her. "She cooked. But there were a lot of frozen meals and boxed mac and cheese. She worked so many jobs. She really didn't have time to cook."

Hope looked at Elaine. Sadness clouded her bright eyes. Hope knew very little about Elaine. She sensed Elaine didn't have a happy childhood. Given what she'd seen since moving back to Jefferson, she guessed Elaine didn't have a lot of girlfriends. And she doubted Elaine ever adhered to the number one rule of the girlfriend code—never go after another friend's man.

"Listen to me, rambling on." Elaine dipped her head, breaking eye contact while she wiped her hand on a towel. "What's next?"

"We have a salad to make, plus dressing." Hope grabbed a large bowl from the counter behind them. She was in awe of the space Elaine had in her kitchen. Dark walnut cabinets were topped with slabs of gold-flecked white marble, while three square pendants hung over the massive island topped with soapstone. Luxuries such as a dedicated beverage center, dual dishwashers, and a huge glass-front refrigerator indicated money was no object when the kitchen was designed. Too bad the room wasn't used to its fullest potential. For the next twenty minutes, Hope guided Elaine through the recipes and, to her surprise, Elaine adapted quickly to cooking. While Hope tried to concentrate on the food, her mind was busy thinking about the murders and the plan she and Jane had cooked up. The big question was, how on earth was she going to do it? She couldn't possibly search Elaine's house. First, the place was gigantic, and it would take hours to go from room to room. Second, her search of Harrison's office ended up with an unfriendly encounter with him. Third, much to her surprise, she was having a good time with Elaine, and the last thing she wanted to do was to ruin that.

No, she wasn't going to snoop through Elaine's home.

"It seems like we're doing well. Is there a restroom close by?" Hope asked.

"Down the hall." Elaine pointed in the direction of the swinging kitchen door. "You passed it on the way in here. Want me to show you?"

"No, I think I can manage." Hope didn't recall a bathroom but then there were a lot of doors in the mini-mansion. She walked out of the kitchen and stood for a moment in the hallway. The highly polished cherrywood floor laid out in front of her led down a hall with numerous doors, some open, some closed. She proceeded down the hall in hopes of coming across the bathroom.

She grasped the knob of one door and gently opened it, then peered inside. A sitting room.

She closed the door and continued down the hall.

She grasped another knob and pushed open the door. She peered in. A den. She closed the door and continued down the hall.

Gosh, the place needed one of those mall maps, the one that points to a location and says, "You're here," with other areas color-coded.

She heard a deep voice ahead and followed until she came across a partially opened door.

"No, there's nothing for anyone to find out." The voice belonged to Lionel.

She was surprised to find him home in the middle of the day. Elaine hadn't mentioned he was there.

But then again, the place was so big he could have easily entered without Elaine knowing. Just like he could have done at Audrey's house the day of the garden tour.

"Look, she's got nothing. We're good."

Hope edged closer to the opening. Who was Lionel talking to? What was he talking about and who was the "she" he was referring to?

"Look, Peaches got herself killed. She was up to something," Lionel said.

Cyndi Lauper's "Girls Just Want to Have Fun" blared.

Claire's ringtone.

Shoot.

"What the hell is that noise?" Lionel asked.

Hope pulled the phone out of the back pocket of her pants to shut it off, but she fumbled and it slipped out of her hands and landed on the floor.

Double shoot.

She quickly bent down to grab her phone. The study door swung open. She glanced up, with the phone in her hand.

Lionel was glaring down on her. "What are you doing here?"

"I'm sorry. I dropped my phone. I, I was on my way to the bathroom."

"It's at the other side of the house," he snapped.

"I guess I got lost. I'm sorry I disturbed you." She turned and dashed away.

But Lionel's heavy footsteps left no doubt he was right behind her and beyond angry at her eavesdropping. She pushed open the swinging door, hoping to find refuge with her cooking student. Never in a million years did she ever believe she'd be happy to see Elaine.

"There you are. I thought you got lost. This house is so huge." Elaine flipped over the chicken cutlets with a tong. "Look how golden brown they are." She beamed with pride.

"Uh, yeah, I guess I did." Hope darted around the island and joined Elaine.

The kitchen door swung open with force and Lionel burst into the room. "What the hell is she doing here?" He pointed a stubby finger at Hope. His breath was labored from chasing Hope. The fifty-something man had a receding hairline and a deep scowl on his tanned face. His shirttails were pulled out of his waistband, while his large belly pulled at the buttons of his shirt, and rolled-up sleeves revealed thick hairy forearms and an ostentatious watch. He looked more like a used-car salesman than a successful businessman.

"She's giving me a cooking lesson. Look, I made Parmesan chicken and—"

"What the hell do you need a cooking lesson for? I pay Muriel to cook and clean." His gaze darted around the kitchen. "Where the hell is Muriel?"

"She's running errands," Elaine answered.

"When she gets back, have her clean up this mess. And get her the hell out of here." Lionel waved his hand at Hope.

Elaine stepped away from Hope, putting a wide distance between them. "Why? What's wrong, honey-poo?"

Lionel took a step forward. "She's not here to

teach you to cook. She's here to snoop. She was over at the Blooms' house, where she was snooping around. She's trying to clear her sister, and she'll obviously do anything to do that."

Elaine's head swung around to Hope. Her eyes were wide with confusion. "You were?"

"I was there, but I wasn't snooping."

"Going through the rooms of people's homes you have no business in is snooping. And I found her skulking outside my office just now."

"You said you had to go to the bathroom. You lied to me? You used me?" Elaine asked.

"I told you, the women of this town don't want to be your friends. I warned you. Now you see I'm right. Now get her out of here!" Lionel turned to leave the kitchen.

"Who were you talking to? Was it Harrison?" Hope prayed that the show of Lionel's temper was about as far as he'd take it.

Lionel stopped and turned to face her. His cheeks puffed out, and his glare hit her hard. Maybe she hadn't seen the full extent of his temper. But since she'd already gone that far, there was no turning back.

"You said, 'There's nothing for anyone to find out.' What were you talking about?" Hope asked.

Lionel's jaw clenched and blotchy redness spread from his neck to his face. Was he going to have a heart attack? Stroke? Would she need to call 911?

"Get her out of here!" Lionel shouted.

No heart attack. No stroke. Just an order.

"Now!" Lionel turned again and stormed out of the kitchen.

Elaine walked over to the table and snatched up

Hope's jacket and purse. "I'll take back my apron," Elaine said in a cool tone.

Hope's head lowered. This wasn't the way she wanted their cooking lesson to end. She untied the apron and then took it off. She handed the apron to Elaine in exchange for her jacket and purse.

"I wasn't snooping, I swear. This is all a big mistake. But, I did overhear a part of his conversation. Why is he so worried about someone finding out something?" Hope's mind raced with the possibilities. Murder, of course, or maybe there were some shady dealings with his development. If there were shady dealings, maybe that got Peaches killed. Either by Lionel or someone else. "How much do you know about your husband's business?"

Elaine shook her head. "I thought you were different. I thought I'd finally found a friend." Elaine's lips quivered and tears welled in her eyes.

"You did. I mean, I'd like to be your friend. And as a friend, I want to help you."

"By suspecting my husband of murder? Friends don't suspect friends of murder. You can leave out the back door." Elaine spun around and stomped out of the kitchen.

Hope exited the house and headed to her vehicle as fast as she could. Settled behind the steering wheel, she inhaled a deep breath. Then she slammed her palms down on the steering wheel.

She wasn't solving the murders, she was alienating people. That wasn't what she envisioned when she made the decision to return home. She glanced over at the passenger seat, where her trusty composition notebook sat. Maybe it was time to toss the notebook and her amateur sleuthing. She had a blog that needed her attention, sponsors she needed to write posts for, and chocolate chip cookie recipes still to be tested. Her time was better spent working rather than sleuthing.

As she backed her vehicle out of the Whitcombs' driveway, her cell phone rang. She commanded her SUV's communication system to answer the call from Claire.

"You won't believe this. Logan got suspended from school today. He got into a fight with another kid who said something about the murders."

Hope's heart sank. Her nephew was a good kid, who didn't get into trouble. He was just defending his mother.

"There's nothing that can be worked out?"

"No. The school has a zero-tolerance policy. I have to call Andy and tell him. He's going to flip. This is now affecting my children." Her voice was strained with worry.

"Where are you?"

"I just arrived at a new listing on Sugar Tree Road. I'm doing a walk-through. Why don't you meet me at my house in an hour?"

"Sounds good. See you then." Hope disconnected the call and arrived at a stop sign. She had every intention of going straight, to head home, a few minutes ago. Now, she needed to follow up on what Meg had shared about seeing Peaches with a man the day before her murder. The blog post she had to write could wait. Her sister needed her.

Hope parked her vehicle in a space of the Village Square shopping center. The stretch of retail space and professional offices was a hub of activity midday and on Saturdays for errands and appointments. The Village Square housed small retailers such as a dry cleaner, a deli, and a shoe repair shop, along with accounting and law offices. As she exited her SUV, she noticed a pickup truck angled beside one of the dividers and saw Wallace Green, the owner of Green Landscaping, mulching the divider. Everywhere she looked in town, people were getting ready for spring flowers. Within a few weeks, bright, cheerful flowers would be blooming all along the parking-lot divider, which reminded her she needed to start spending more time outside. Otherwise, her garden beds would be overtaken by weeds.

She slung her purse over her shoulder, closed the car door, and walked toward Wallace. "Hi, Wallace." She waved.

Wallace looked up from the mulch pile he was spreading evenly over the garden bed.

"Hi, Hope. I'm trying to get this down before we get another downpour." He grinned. Deep lines creased around his brown eyes. He was dressed for a day of yard work in dirt-stained khakis, a polo shirt, and a baseball cap with his company's name.

"Good luck. I just heard on the radio it's supposed to be another bad storm coming through."

"We do need the rain, just not all at once. What brings you here? Getting some lunch?" He glanced toward the deli.

"No, I'm looking for information." Hope's plan was to speak to a shop owner and get the telephone number of the management company of the shopping center. "Maybe you can help me."

"Sure, what do you need?"

"The name and telephone number of the management company of this property."

"Thinking about opening a store? There are a few vacancies." Wallace tossed down another shovelful of mulch from the back of his truck.

"No. I wanted to find out if there is video of the parking lot. You know, like surveillance video."

"Cameras are everywhere. Look, on all of those posts are cameras." He pointed upward.

Hope's gaze followed and she saw them. Some good news, finally. "Perfect."

"Why are you interested in them?"

"I want to see if I can look at the footage from a few days ago."

"Hope, I don't know what you're up to, but does it have to do with the murders? I've been hearing things about Claire."

Of course he had been. "She didn't do anything." Hope heard her defensive tone and immediately regretted it. She'd already alienated enough people for one day and she didn't want to add Wallace to that list.

Wallace gave her a sympathetic look. "I believe you. But I doubt the management company will hand over any video to you. It's a police matter. You should tell them about whatever theory you have."

"You're right. Thanks." Hope couldn't argue with Wallace. He had a point. The police should be tracking down the lead. Well, she thought it was a lead. Would Detective Reid agree with her? She doubted he would. Glancing over Wallace's shoulder, she saw her opportunity to find out. Detective

Reid was exiting the deli. "Have a good afternoon." She broke away to cross the parking lot.

"Oh, those cookies you baked for the library's sale were awesome. I told Beth to get the recipes from your blog," Wallace called out as she stepped up on to the sidewalk and approached Detective Reid.

"Ms. Early, I suppose you're not here to get lunch," Detective Reid said.

"No, I'm not. I have come across some information that may be helpful in finding the person who killed Peaches and most likely killed Vanessa."

"What would that be?"

"Peaches was seen the day before her murder having what appeared to be a serious conversation with a man here."

He arched a brow, but he didn't look the least bit curious about her new lead. "That's it?"

"Yes. I know it's not a smoking gun, but it's something. Right?"

"Not really. Ms. McCoy was a real estate agent, and I'm sure during the course of her workday she had many serious conversations. It doesn't mean the man she spoke with killed her."

"So you won't follow up?"

"Do you know who the man was?"

Hope shook her head. She didn't.

"How did you come across this information?"

"Someone mentioned it to me."

"Does that person know who he is?"

"No. But surely you can watch the video from the cameras," she said pointed to the posts.

"Ms. Early, I believe I cautioned you against investigating on your own."

"You told me to bring any information I had to you directly. And that's what I'm doing." *So there.*

"Don't play games with me."

"I'm not. I'm telling you what I learned, and I expect you to do your job and investigate any and all leads that could expose the killer of Peaches and Vanessa."

"I don't work for you."

"You work for this town, Detective Reid." Hope spun around and walked briskly to her vehicle. The man was infuriating. He held Claire's future in his hands. She had to find a way to get him to look beyond Claire as a suspect. Since he wouldn't listen to her suggestions, she had no choice but to find evidence. Which meant she needed to find the man Peaches was talking to the day before her murder.

As Hope turned her vehicle onto Sterling Road, raindrops began falling. The cloudy then sunny day had turned cloudy again, and another round of heavy rain was due to start at any moment. By the time Hope reached High Ridge Road, the gentle rain had turned fierce, leaving the blacktop slippery and her windshield wipers working overtime.

Born and raised in Connecticut, she was no stranger to bad weather—snow, sleet, and rain—but High Ridge Road rattled the most experienced, confident driver. The barely two-lane-wide road was hugged tightly on one side by a towering wall of rock, while the other side was edged by a guardrail and a forest of maples, spruces, and balsam firs.

As if the worsening conditions weren't bad enough, her cell phone rang and the caller was identified. Corey Lucas.

"What is it, Corey?"

"I've left *how many* messages for you?"

"I didn't count them. Look, I'm busy here, so if you can get to the point, I would greatly appreciate it."

"There's a new reality . . . it starts taping . . . casting . . ." His voice faded in and out. "Audition tapes are being viewed now so . . . yeah, yeah. I want two of those shirts . . ." His voice faded again. "Sorry, I'm at Barney's."

Barney's? Hope rolled her eyes, which wasn't a smart thing to do while driving in a storm. She needed to get off the phone before she either drove off the road or said something to Corey she'd regret.

"I'm not interested in doing another reality show." She negotiated a curve in the road.

"The show is focused around . . ." The line went silent.

"Corey?"

Dead silence. She'd hit the spot on the road where there was no signal.

She commanded her car's syncing system to turn off and noticed that somewhere between her phone ringing and losing the connection, the rain had turned blinding.

She eased off the accelerator. She hated that road. She hated storms.

Her wipers slashed at the rain at top speed. She considered pulling over to wait out the storm as it passed, but the road was so narrow there wasn't a safe spot to do that. Just a few more feet until she reached the turn for Holly Lane. Surely she could make it there.

A flicker in the rearview mirror caught her attention. A white van. Another poor driver caught in the torrential storm.

Rain assaulted her windshield as the wind picked up, whipping through the tall trees. A boom of thunder shattered the silence.

"Idiot." She approached the narrowest, steepest part of High Ridge Road. She shifted to second gear to assist her vehicle in slowing down, without the risk of hydroplaning.

The van behind her didn't appear to slow down. Did the driver have a death wish?

The road descended and she applied pressure to her brakes.

The van narrowed the small gap between them.

The stupid driver seemed to have a death wish—hers. The last thing anyone wanted to do on that road was speed.

"Idiot," she shouted into the rearview mirror. Who was the driver? She couldn't get a good look at him or her because she needed to keep her eyes on the road.

Her palms were clammy as they gripped the steering wheel tighter as she came to a tight curve. God, she would have given anything to be back on the very straight streets of Manhattan, cabbies and all.

Her heart slammed against her chest as her vehicle hugged the road around the curve. She concentrated on keeping both her breathing and the car steady. The road descended again and her eyes widened in terror as the van closed in on her vehicle.

The hit came hard.

Her vehicle jolted forward.

She screamed as her body lunged forward. Her fingers tightened around the steering wheel. She struggled to maintain control of her vehicle, but her hands weren't strong enough to pull the wheel back straight.

Tears streamed down her face. Why was he doing this to her? Who was he?

Another hard hit came.

She lost all control.

Her car swerved to the right.

Desperate, she slammed on the brakes and pulled with all her strength to regain control of the wheel. But it was no use.

Her car crashed into the guardrail, taking out a chunk of the metal, her vehicle plunging down the embankment.

Her scream faded and everything went black.

Chapter Seventeen

Hope shifted as light penetrated her sleepy eyelids. She started to roll over until every muscle in her body screamed. Flashes of heavy rain, slippery blacktop, and a van whizzed through her mind. The pieces of her drive to meet Claire across town came together. She was intentionally driven off the road by a van. But why?

"Things a little fuzzy, dear? Completely understandable."

Hope struggled to lift herself upright. What was Jane doing in her bedroom?

"It's good to see you wake. I made you a cup of tea and cinnamon toast." Jane set a tray on the bureau.

"Breakfast?"

"Yes, dear. You've been sleeping most of the time since we got you home two days ago. Your body needed the rest."

Hope's forehead crinkled. Her mind was blurred with vague images of strobe lights, white coats, and cold stethoscopes. "I was in the hospital?'

"For a little bit. I think they should have kept you but you know what it's like with insurance companies today. In and out and good luck." Jane plumped up the pillows behind Hope and eased her charge back into them. She went for the tray and then set it over Hope's lap.

"Why didn't somebody wake me?"

"As I said, you needed to rest. You woke up a few times, which was good since it allowed you to take the pain pills prescribed to you. Then you fell back to sleep every time. Don't you remember, dear?"

"No, not really. You've been here all this time? I can't believe I've lost two days."

Jane smiled. "Yes. Along with Sally, and Claire has been here, too. But she has a family to take care of, so we told her we'd look after you. Now drink your tea."

"No coffee?"

"No, dear. You're recuperating and you need tea for that."

Hope took a sip. It was bad enough she felt as if she belonged in a body cast, but to begin the day without coffee was beyond cruel. "How long am I supposed to recuperate for?"

"Don't be impatient."

"Who, me?" Hope nibbled on the toast. Her teeth even hurt. "I'm sorry I worried you."

"The accident wasn't your fault."

"I guess it wasn't." Hope recalled how fast the van came out of nowhere. "The van was speeding."

Hope finished one slice of toast and immediately reached for a second slice. When Jane set the tray on her lap, she didn't think she was hungry enough to eat anything. She was wrong. She was starving, and it was a good thing there were four slices of toast on the plate. But maybe six would have been better.

"That's right. The driver intended to run you off the road and kill you."

Hope choked on the toast. "What?"

"There, there. Are you okay? You've survived a murder attempt, so don't go choking on my cinnamon toast."

"Murder attempt?" Hope wiped her mouth with a napkin. "You really think so?"

"Peaches was murdered for a specific reason. Vanessa was killed most likely because she knew something—"

"And I was almost killed because I'm making the killer nervous."

"Exactly." Jane nodded her head. "The murderer in my mystery series always became sloppy and made mistakes, which ultimately led to the arrest. Think, Hope. Think."

"About what?"

"The past few days. You've talked to the murderer at least once."

A shiver shot down Hope's spine. Had she really spoken to the killer? Was she that close to the person responsible for two deaths?

"I need a notepad." Jane looked around the room.

"In my nightstand." Hope pointed.

"My sleuth, Barbara Neill, always used a stenography pad." Jane pulled opened the nightstand drawer and retrieved a pad and pen.

"I've talked to several people. Including you."

Jane laughed. "I can assure you I didn't kill anyone other than on paper."

"Shut up! Jane is a suspect now?" Drew exclaimed from the doorway. He scooted into the room and discarded a vase of flowers onto the bureau.

"I most certainly am not," Jane said firmly.

"I smell cinnamon toast." Drew followed the scent to Hope's bed and snatched a slice. "I didn't have breakfast. You won't believe the morning I had."

"Really?" Hope glared at Drew. For once her drama would trump his. "I was run off a road, so I win."

Drew shrugged. "I guess."

"Now, who have you spoken to since the first murder?" Jane settled on a chair, ready to take notes.

The bedroom was sparsely furnished with just the basics—triple dresser, wingback chair, and a bed—and Hope expected it to stay that way until the first floor was fully remodeled. While she waited to upgrade her bedroom, she had indulged in a queen-sized bed and luxurious bedding. Beneath her six-hundred-thread-count sheets was a down featherbed that welcomed her tired body every night. Her European down pillows were like laying her head on a cloud. She'd created the perfect spot to collapse in.

"I'm not sure my mind is clear enough to make any list."

"Do your best," Jane encouraged.

Hope took another drink of tea. "Maretta, Alfred, Audrey, Elaine, Harrison, Claire, Sally, Meg, Amy at Alfred's office, Kent, and Wallace."

"Wallace Green, the owner of Green Landscaping?" Drew snatched the last slice of toast.

"I made that for Hope's breakfast, not yours," Jane scolded.

When Drew finished chewing, he flashed a sheepish grin. "Sorry."

Jane returned her attention to Hope "Why did you speak with him?"

"Meg said she saw Peaches in a serious conversation the day before her murder at Village Square. So I went over there after I left Elaine's to see if they had any video footage so I could see who he was. I ran into Wallace because he was working there and he said there is video at the shopping center, but he doubted I would get to see any of it."

"The police would be able to get access to the video." Drew stretched out along the foot of the bed and propped his head up with one bent arm.

"That's what Detective Reid said when I ran into him at Village Square, and he doesn't think it's significant."

"How absurd. Everything is significant." Jane jotted down some notes.

"My head is throbbing." Hope shifted again, trying to get comfortable, but she suspected it would be days before she'd be comfortable again. Her gaze drifted to the vase of flowers on the dresser. Creamy roses, pink daisies, and peach alstroemeria, with white larkspur and assorted greens, completed the breathtaking arrangement. She smiled.

"Those flowers are beautiful. Who are they from?" she asked.

"Let's find out." Drew dashed over to the vase and plucked out the gift card. He came back to the bed and handed the envelope to Hope. "I'm dying to know."

Hope opened the envelope and pulled out the gift card. "Get Well Soon, Your Friend Always, Audrey." She held the small card to her chest and fought back the tears that threatened to burst like a dam. She wasn't sure how much damage she'd done to their friendship when she visited the other day. The fact the card wasn't also signed by Harrison didn't escape Hope's notice. She doubted he would be as forgiving or understanding as Audrey.

"That was very thoughtful of her," Jane said.

"Especially after what happened the other day." Hope slipped the card back into the envelope.

"What happened the other day?" Ethan asked from the doorway.

Jane and Drew's heads swung around to the door, while Hope wanted to slide under the covers, but her body wouldn't cooperate. It wouldn't move an inch.

"Is there something you need to tell me?" Ethan moved into the room, filling the space in a way Hope hadn't expected. A healthy dose of masculine energy radiated from him, putting all her senses on alert. Too exhausted and sore to act on her awareness, she tugged her coverlet up closer to her shoulders. The signal she needed to rest should be clear. Right?

"I have to tidy up the kitchen." Jane scooted out of the room.

"I'll help." Drew left, right on Jane's heels.

Ethan stepped forward and hesitated for a moment before he sat on the edge of Hope's bed. Once he'd settled, her head spun. Maybe it was his closeness to her; maybe it was the intimacy of him being on her bed. Or maybe it was just the pain medication. That seemed to be the reasonable explanation.

"I believe your accident is related to the murders. I think you're making someone very nervous," Ethan said.

"That's what Jane thinks, too."

Ethan's dark eyes lightened a touch, and his façade of control and toughness vanished. He reached out and caressed her cheek. "I didn't mean what I said the other day to come off as an order. I just don't want you to be my next murder investigation."

Tears welled up in Hope's eyes again, and feelings that hadn't been stirred since falling head over heels in love years ago with Tim choked her, leaving her unable to speak.

He leaned into her. "So, what happened at Audrey's house?"

"I, I'll tell you. I promise. But right now, I need to sleep some more. I'm sorry." Her heart raced, and she could barely catch her breath because his lips were just a taste away. For the first time, she wondered what it would be like to kiss him. Would he be gentle or would he be hungry? Before she could decide, his cell phone buzzed, interrupting their moment. She fell back into her pillows, wondering if she kissed him, would he kiss her back?

"Chief Cahill." He stood and walked toward the window.

Hope's head throbbed. Apparently her muscles and bones wanted a little more company in hurting. It must be time for another pill. She reached over to the nightstand to grab the bottle. Before she'd swallowed the pill in the palm of her hand, she weighed the consequences of becoming more under the influence.

She had been just about to kiss Ethan. What would be next? Stripping?

Oh, God, she hoped not as she downed the pill.

"I have to go." Ethan replaced his cell phone in its holder on his belt. "I trust you'll stay out of trouble. Get some rest." He kissed her gently on the forehead before walking out of the room.

Crisis averted. There'd be no locking lips with Ethan. As she heard the bedroom door close, she snuggled under the covers and let the pain medication do its thing. Her heavy eyelids closed, and she drifted off to sleep. Her sleep was busy with the sounds of tires screeching on the road, flashes of bright lights, and the bodies of Peaches and Vanessa. Eventually her exhaustion triumphed over her nightmares, and when her eyes opened again, she squinted at the clock on her nightstand. It was dinnertime. She had to stop sleeping so much. With her covers loosened, Hope pulled her body upright. She leaned over and switched on the lamp, which cast a soft light. She glanced out the windows. The sun was setting. Where had the day gone? A change in venue was in order. She pulled the covers off completely and swung her legs over the side of the bed. *So far, so good.* She slid into her slippers and reached for her robe. Standing up, she realized taking a walk might not be such a good idea. Her legs wobbled. They felt like wet noodles. She couldn't help wondering if she'd ever feel good again. A piece of paper on the nightstand caught her attention. Jane had left her a note. She and Sally had gone out to run an errand and would be back to prepare supper. She set the note back down and headed for the door. By the time she reached the hallway, she felt like she was a year older. Heck, she'd be celebrating the big five-O by the time she made it down to the kitchen if her pace didn't pick up.

Forget the big five-O. By the time she reached the kitchen, she'd come to the conclusion her body felt like it was the big seven-O. At the bottom of the stairs, she had to pause for a moment. How could she be exhausted after sleeping the day away?

Evening had fallen with a heavy dose of wind. Spring storms were unpredictable, and any moment she could lose power. The windows were rattled by strong gusts, and the eerie high-pitched whistling sound swift winds made filled the night air. If she was an easily scared person, she'd check for dial tones and carry around her chef's knife just in case.

Even though she'd dismissed Jane's earlier suggestion that the car accident was really a murder attempt, she had second thoughts now.

Had she really spoken to the killer since the day of the garden tour? Did the murderer know she was trying to uncover him or her? If only she could tell the murderer how little she knew, it would save so much time and energy for everyone.

She found an ounce of energy and got to the kitchen island. Not sure when the Merrifields left, she didn't know when they'd return, so brewing a pot of coffee crossed her mind. She weighed those consequences. The worst would have Jane chiding her for drinking coffee while she recuperated. Heck, she'd been run off the road by a murderer, so what was a lecture or two?

With freshly ground hazelnut coffee brewing, she retrieved her cell phone from her purse and checked her messages. Her friends and out-of-state family members were checking in on her. And, of course, there was Corey. He sent his well wishes with instructions to call him. She scrolled past his message to scan a few more before she set the phone down. At some point she'd reply to everyone, but now she just wanted coffee. She glanced over at the coffeepot. She had a few more minutes before the coffee would be ready, so she moved over to the table. She needed to rest. The *Gazette* newspaper was unfolded and sprawled out on the table. An article recounting her accident graced the front page. "Way to go, Hope." She skimmed the article, looking to fill in the gaps of her fuzzy memory. There were statements from the police and a "no comment" from the hospital on her condition at the time she was brought by ambulance to the emergency room. There was also information on the van that forced her off the road. The white van was found abandoned a few miles away from the accident scene, and it belonged to Wallace Green. She looked up from the newspaper. Could it have been just a coincidence that right after she spoke to Wallace about looking for video footage of Peaches the day before her murder that she was run off the road by a van owned by Wallace? She grabbed her cell phone and scrolled through her voice mails, she'd seen one from Wallace.

Hey, Hope, I just heard about the accident. Hope you're doing okay. Can't believe one of my vans was stolen. Take care. Talk soon.

After listening to the message and hearing the genuine concern in his voice, she doubted he drove her off the road. And according to the article, the van was stolen from his home, where he ran his business from. There were no leads on who stole the van or how it was taken from the driveway.

Hope set her phone down and gathered and folded the newspaper.

Why would someone steal one of Wallace's vans? Why risk being seen at his home, where his wife took care of the administrative work and his guys were coming and going all day? Maybe it was his wife? Hope shook her head. Now she was being silly. The Greens weren't murderers.

A creak in the wood floor behind her startled Hope. She began to turn, to look over her shoulder, but before she could move, a gloved hand clapped over her mouth. She struggled against the grip, her eyes watering with pain and fear. A tiny gap in the glove let in some air and she screamed but knew no one could hear her as she was yanked off the chair.

Chapter Eighteen

Hope's chair crashed onto the floor as her body, too sluggish from medication to fight back, was dragged across the kitchen. Panic welled. She couldn't breathe.

Struggling, she freed her right elbow and jammed it into the intruder's stomach. The hold on her was momentarily loosened. Hope took the opportunity to break free.

She lunged forward. The intruder grabbed her by her hair so hard Hope thought she'd been scalped. Again, the heavy hand pulled her back.

Pain raged. No matter how much she hurt, she had to fight to escape.

She tamped down her fear. She needed to think. To come up with a getaway plan. She wouldn't end up like Peaches or Vanessa.

In a split second, from somewhere buried in her mind, she remembered a self-defense expert's advice. Drop down. The intruder wouldn't expect her to fall. On the floor, she'd have more leverage, even if only for a split second.

It had to work.

She inhaled a deep breath and braced her body for an onslaught of agony. She softened her knees and dropped to the floor.

Her body hit the pumpkin pine floor. Hard.

She heard voices.

Sally and Jane were back.

Oh, God, would they be hurt?

Her attacker froze. He. She. Whoever. Must have heard them also. Hope tried to lift her body up, but she didn't have the strength. Black boots stepped over her and a heel skimmed the side of her head.

In a flash, the intruder was out the back door.

Hope struggled to rise and heard Jane and Sally's simultaneous gasps as they entered the kitchen from the hall.

"What happened? Did you fall?" Sally rushed to Hope's side to assist her up.

"You should have stayed in bed," Jane scolded as she dropped her purse on the table.

"And why is the back door open?" Sally asked.

"Why did you come downstairs?" Jane asked.

The rapid fire of questions dizzied Hope even more. She needed to catch her breath before she could answer them.

"I didn't fall."

"Well, then, how did you end up on the floor?" Sally settled Hope on a chair at the table.

"Someone . . . someone was here. I don't know who it was. I was grabbed and dragged." Hope wrapped her arms around her torso to steady her shaking body.

"What?" both Merrifield women blurted out in unison.

"I was sitting right there," Hope pointed to the toppled-over chair.

Sally walked around to the other side of the table and lifted the chair up and pushed it in under the table. "Maybe now you'll keep your doors locked."

"The murderer was here," Jane said.

"What makes you think it was the murderer? It could have been a crazy fan. Situations like that happen when you're on television and write about your life every single day." Sally walked over to the counter to retrieve the cordless phone.

"Do you have a stalker?" Jane asked.

Hope tried to shrug, but it hurt too much.

"This is Sally Merrifield," she said into the phone. "There's been a break-in at Hope Early's house."

Stalker. Intruder. Murderer. It didn't matter which label applied to the person who'd just broken into Hope's home. She looked at her hands. They trembled. The wave of shock and surprise from being grabbed still spun in her head. She still felt the forceful grip the person had on her. The attack happened so fast. Just like the car accident. Drowsy with medication, she couldn't tell if the person was male or female. The description she would give to the police would be sketchy, at best. She wasn't concerned with the person's height or girth. She just wanted to get away. Now she wanted to rest her aching body, but her nerves wouldn't allow her.

Sally moved to the window and looked out while she continued to talk to the 911 operator.

"I don't think it was a stalker. I think it was the murderer. He didn't accomplish what he set out to do on the road so he or she came here to finish it." Jane spoke calmly, as if she were discussing a plot for a novel.

"You're not making me feel very good right now," Hope said.

Jane patted Hope's hand. "I'm sorry, dear. I get carried away, but this is so intriguing. Believe that I never, ever want to see you hurt. This is getting far too dangerous. The murderer has been in your house. God only knows what might have happened if we hadn't arrived when we did."

"Still not making me feel better."

Jane shook her head in frustration. "Sally is much better at this stuff than I am."

Hope raised a questioning eyebrow. Even that hurt.

The back door swung open and Drew entered.

Jane's head lifted. "No! Fingerprints!"

Drew looked at the doorknob in confusion and then back to Jane. "What are you talking about?"

"He wore gloves," Hope told Jane.

"The police are on their way." Sally joined Hope and Jane at the table and set the phone down.

"Police?" Drew's pale green eyes bulged. "Someone tell me what happened."

Jane let go of Hope's hand. "The murderer broke in and attacked Hope."

"We don't know it was the murderer," Sally corrected. "It could have been a stalker or just a burglar."

"Oh. My. God. Are you okay?" Drew rushed to Hope's side.

"I think so. Hard to tell. I'm so sore from the car accident."

"Hazelnut? I smell hazelnut. You made coffee, Hope?" Jane frowned. She stood and walked over to the coffeemaker. "What did I tell you about drinking tea while you recuperate?"

Sally stood and walked over to her sister-in-law. "Jane, someone just tried to kill her. If she wants to drink coffee, let her have coffee."

"I can't believe this. I'm so glad you weren't hurt or worse." Drew rubbed Hope's arm absently and a slight smile curled. "You know what this means?"

"She's in danger," Jane replied.

Drew hesitated for a moment. "Yes. She is."

Hope narrowed her gaze on him. "You're thinking about a story."

Drew hung his head in shame. "I was."

Sirens wailed outside.

"The police are here," Sally said.

"I shouldn't put a story before you." Drew lifted his head and took Jane's abandoned seat. "But this is just too irresistible."

"Of course it is." Hope wanted to be angry, but she couldn't. She was the one who put herself in the situation by sticking her nose into something she had no business with. But she didn't know any other way to help Claire.

The sirens grew louder.

"Ethan is going to freak when he finds out." Hope didn't want to imagine what he was going to say.

Sally approached Hope with a full cup of coffee. "Here you go."

The gentle fragrance of hazelnut wafted up Hope's nose. Her hands, still shaky, reached for the cup.

"He's going to want to put me in a bubble."

"Maybe he should. If we'd arrived later, you could be dead," Sally said.

"That person was in my house, and I'll be damned if he or she is going to get away with that."

"You're not going to stop?" Drew asked.

Hope shook her head. "No. Now it's personal."

Sally escorted the responding police officers into the house and one took Hope's statement while the other officer searched the house. Hope was confident the intruder had left but maybe the officer was looking for some evidence. After recounting what happened after she got out of bed, Hope retreated to her bedroom to take a shower. The hot water felt good on her sore body, and the few moments alone allowed her to compose herself. She dressed in a pair of yoga pants and a hoodie then headed back downstairs. She retrieved her composition notebook from her office and settled at the table to jot down some notes. Jane had prepared her a cup of tea while she wrote in the notebook.

The intruder was as tall as or taller than Hope, based on where she was grabbed around her torso. There were no indicators of whether it was a man or woman. If she hadn't taken those pain pills, maybe she would have been more alert. The gloves were black.

Her hand paused over the page. What else?

The sleeves were black.

Why couldn't she remember any more?

It happened so fast, and she was fighting for her life. Noticing details wasn't a priority.

Why hadn't she gotten a look at her intruder's face?

All she had to do was look up when she dropped to the floor.

"Are you sure you don't want to go to the hospital?"

Startled, Hope looked up and found Detective Reid approaching her from the hall. She quickly closed the notebook.

"I'm sure. I wasn't hurt. Just scared to death." The truth was she couldn't tell which soreness came from which incident—car accident or being manhandled by some lunatic.

"Are you working?" Reid eyed the notebook.

"Just making some notes." That wasn't entirely a lie. She doubted he would approve of what she was making notes of.

"You didn't get a good look at the person who grabbed you?" Reid sat across the table from Hope.

"No, I didn't."

Reid nodded. "Do you have any idea how the intruder got in?"

"The back door was closed when I came downstairs. But I didn't check the front door. I usually don't lock my doors. Nobody does in Jefferson." A definite difference from her years in New York City. Her apartment door had had three locks on it. Her ritual every night after coming home was to make sure all three locks were locked. And sometimes in the middle of the night she got out of bed to double-check. When she made the move back to Jefferson and spent her first night in her new home, she didn't get up in the middle of the night to check the one lock on her front door. She'd had a peaceful night's sleep that night. Now she wasn't sure if she would ever sleep soundly again.

"It's always a good idea to lock your doors. Have you received any type of threats? Perhaps from a fan?"

Hope shook her head. "I'm not that big of a celebrity to have obsessive fans."

"We need to look at all possibilities," Detective Reid said.

"It was the murderer." Jane ambled over to Detective Reid with a cup of tea.

Reid accepted the mug and took a sip. "Mrs. Merrifield, while I am not ruling out a connection to the recent murders—"

"Don't forget about Hope's car accident," Jane said.

"I'm not. I cannot jump to the conclusion the murderer caused the car accident or assaulted Ms. Early today."

"May I quote you?" Drew said from the doorway of the hall.

"No, you may not." He set the cup on the table, flipped his notepad closed, and stood.

"You have my assurance I will do my best to find the person responsible for your accident and for entering your house tonight."

Hope didn't have much choice but to accept Reid at his word. Ethan had told her Reid was a good detective. She'd have to trust Reid to do his job. "I appreciate that."

"Do you know where your sister was tonight?"

Hope was caught off guard. Why was he asking about Claire? "Are you suggesting my sister did this to me?"

"It's just a question."

"No, it's not."

"You probably should get some rest." Reid exited the kitchen through the mudroom.

"I can't believe that man." Hope grabbed hold of the mug and took a long drink, then grimaced because the tea had gotten cold.

Drew came to the table in a split second with a cup of coffee. He slid it in front of Hope.

"Bless you," she whispered, before taking a grateful drink of coffee. She caught Jane's disapproving look from the island.

"Are you sure you want to pursue this?" He pulled a chair closer to Hope and sat.

"I don't have a choice. Reid is determined to pin the murders on Claire, and the killer thinks I know something. I have to see this through."

Chapter Nineteen

After Hope's alarm blared, jolting her out of her first good night's sleep in days, she dragged her weary bones out of bed and into the shower. She didn't expect to sleep so well, given what had happened the day before. Maybe it was because she was exhausted, physically and mentally, that her body just gave in to sleep. Regardless of the reason, she was glad to finally have had a good night's rest.

In the shower, she stood under the spray of hot water longer than usual, an indulgence she rarely afforded herself because of her schedule. Since she had moved back to Jefferson, pampering had taken a backseat to barn chores, home restoration, and work. Remodeling her home and building her business had all fallen onto her shoulders. She didn't have a partner or a backup plan. She threw her list of things to do out the window and lathered up with her favorite vanilla goat milk soap.

The soap was crafted by Edie Barlow, a fellow contestant on *The Sweet Taste of Success*. After Edie's fifteen minutes of fame, she packed it in and headed to Vermont to raise goats and make bath products from their milk. Hope's city friends thought she was crazy for wanting to move back to Connecticut to blog and raise chickens, but at least Hope had her roots in the country, unlike the city-born Edie. Edie's friends and colleagues thought she needed to be committed because she was trading in her Jimmy Choos for barn boots to milk goats.

There were a lot of negative things that came from being on reality television, but they were balanced out by the friendships Hope made along the way.

Dried off and her hair blown dry, she dressed in a pair of jeans and a Henley top then pulled on a pair of socks before walking out of her bedroom. Downstairs she made a quick breakfast of a smoothie with a banana, a few frozen strawberries, and a heaping scoop of protein powder. She'd discarded the pain pills. She needed to be alert and coherent. Not only for her safety, but she had some work to do and she'd figure out a way to cope with the pain.

With her smoothie gone, she headed out to the barn to collect eggs and do her morning chores. In the mudroom, she slipped on her work boots. There was a chill in the morning air and the breeze wasn't as soft as a spring breeze should feel. There were still hints of winter as the wind whipped through the air.

She crossed the yard to the barn, where she'd converted one of the stalls into the chicken coop. Making a home for her chickens in the unused stall saved her a little money, plus the barn provided an extra layer of protection against predators and was well-ventilated and out of the harsh weather. She'd made a few modifications to the stall and in time, she'd moved her chicks in and added an outdoor pen so her chickens could get fresh air. While she didn't have any concrete proof, she believed happy chickens produced more eggs. She planned on filling the barn with other animals, but that was way down on her list of things to do once her home was finished. So, for the meantime, the chickens had the place all to themselves.

Slower than usual, Hope fed the chickens, filled up their water containers, and did a spot check of her girls for any scratches, coughs, or anything out of the ordinary. Some hens were more cooperative than others. Helga didn't appreciate Hope's concern and didn't hide her feelings when Hope attempted to pick her up. Hope couldn't imagine how Helga would respond if she needed medical attention. Dealing with an angry hen made fending off an intruder feel like a piece of cake.

On the way back to the house, she heard a car engine. She made a detour to the front of the house. Audrey's luxury car pulled into her driveway. As she approached, Audrey stepped out of the car and then retrieved a fruit basket from the backseat. A moment later, Bigelow jumped out of the car and took off investigating, paying particular attention to a maple tree.

"Hey!" Hope called out.

Audrey looked up at the greeting and smiled. With her hands full, she closed the car door with her hip. She was dressed in a bright floral dress

that accentuated her blue eyes. Her aviator sunglasses were pushed up onto her head, pulling back
her dark hair and revealing clear, unswollen eyes.
She looked relaxed and tranquil, a stark contrast to
the last time Hope saw her.

"You're doing an amazing job on this house,"
Audrey said. "I apologize for just dropping by. But
I was worried if I called you'd tell me not to come
over."

"Why would I?"

"Harrison wasn't very hospitable to you. He's
been under a lot of pressure at work and with the
murder . . . well, let's just say it didn't help."

Bigelow raced past his owner to Hope. She
leaned forward and cupped his face in her hands
and the dog stood still for a nanosecond, just long
enough for Hope to say, "Good morning, Bigelow.
How are you doing?" The dog wagged his tail
feverishly as his eyes widened with excitement. His
energy was contagious, and instantly Hope began
to feel a bit more uplifted.

"Please, come in." Hope led Audrey around to
the mudroom, where she kicked off her boots and
slipped on a pair of suede mules. They continued
through to the kitchen.

"What a beautiful kitchen." Audrey set the basket on the island. "When are you going to have a
housewarming party?"

"I really haven't thought of having one." Hope
inspected the basket of apples, oranges, and pears
Audrey had given her. She found a bar of dark
chocolate tucked among the fruit. Audrey knew
her well.

"Why not?"

Hope shrugged. "I guess I've been so focused on renovating this place. I have no idea of when I'll be done."

"You shouldn't wait. If nothing else comes out of these tragedies, the one thing we should realize is life is short. Too short sometimes."

Hope paused. Audrey had a point. She didn't need to have every room perfectly renovated and decorated to celebrate her new home with her friends and family. It could be years before she was done with the interior and exterior, and what a shame it would be not to take the moment to celebrate.

"I think you're right. I'm going to have a housewarming party. I'll get right on it."

Bigelow nudged Hope's leg, and she glanced down. He looked at her with his warm brown eyes. She loved that dog, and seeing him reminded her how much she wanted one of her own. The building she lived in back in New York had a strict no-pets policy, and one of the things she'd looked forward to by moving back to Jefferson was getting a dog. While she loved her chickens, they weren't cuddly, and she questioned their loyalty. As the projects wound down around her house, she promised herself she'd get a dog. Until then she would get her dose of puppy love from Bigelow.

"Good. If you need anything, just let me know."

"I will." Hope pulled out a canister of dog biscuits she always kept on hand for canine visitors and offered Bigelow a snack. He gobbled it up eagerly and gave her a sad-eyes look only a dog could pull off, and she melted and he got another biscuit. She closed the canister, signaling to the pup snack time was over, so he trotted away and found a corner in the family room where the morning sun streamed in to curl up and take a snooze.

"I wanted to come over and check on you, to make sure you're okay. When I heard about the accident, I felt so horrible it happened just hours after you left our home. Then I heard last night someone broke in here and grabbed you. Are you okay?"

Hope reached out and covered Audrey's hand with hers. "I'm okay. A little sore from the accident. But I'm okay."

"Are you sure? I can't imagine being attacked in my own home."

Hope squeezed Audrey's hand before letting go. "I'm sure."

"I also wanted to tell you that you were right."

"About what?"

"About hiding in my house. After you left, I headed out for a run. A long run to clear my mind."

"Did it?"

"Yes. By the time I came home, I knew I wasn't going to stay inside my house like a prisoner. Peaches' death was unfortunate, and I am confident the police will find the person responsible. And that person will have to deal with the shame of having done something so horrific."

"Good for you. How many miles did it take?"

Audrey laughed. "About six."

"Six? I'm lucky I can do three these days."

"I think you and I need to run together. I'll make a marathoner out of you."

Hope shook her head. Every year when she

lived in New York City, she found a spot to watch the annual marathon and looked on in awe of athletes who ran by her. She'd never run a marathon or a half-marathon. Unlike Audrey, she had no desire to put herself through twenty-six grueling miles.

"I'd be happy with running up to six miles." With all the recipes she tested for her blog, Hope needed to exercise regularly. She found running not only burned a bunch of calories, but the time spent zoned out gave her the chance to clear her mind. She needed to run soon. Though she doubted she would get very far since every muscle still ached. Maybe a long walk would suffice.

"We'll see." Audrey smiled.

Hope admired Audrey's confidence. Audrey always knew what she wanted and went for it and got it. Unlike Hope, who thought she'd always be a magazine editor. Then one spontaneous decision turned her life upside down and she landed as a divorced blogger living back in her hometown. There was one thing she wouldn't end up being and that was a marathon runner. No matter how much Audrey believed she could convert Hope.

"I'm going to try and salvage my book launch. You know that old saying about any publicity is good publicity? Well, it's not true. Calista told me my career is now officially on life support."

Hope grimaced. "Ouch."

"All this negative press is swirling around, and if I do an interview, I'll be asked about the murder."

"I'm sorry." Hope poured two cups of coffee and pulled out a container of plain Greek yogurt with a basket of blueberries, a canister of homemade granola, and a jar of locally sourced honey. With a couple of glass canning jars, she whipped up a healthy breakfast for the both of them. She served the breakfast parfait with a couple of her oatmeal-cherry-chocolate bars.

Audrey drew in a deep breath. "While I may not be able to save my writing career, I can do something else."

Hope's interest was piqued. "What are you planning on doing?"

"I've decided to run for mayor. Scandal is supposed to be good for politicians, right?"

Hope shrugged. She had no idea of the inner workings of a political career but thought it had a lot of similarities to reality television. Both were docudramas based on one part reality, one part fiction, and one part morbid curiosity, with a fleeting acquaintance to the truth.

"I just don't want things to get weird between us."

"Why would they?" Hope scooped a spoonful of parfait. The tartness of the yogurt mixed with the sweetness of the honey and the crunchiness of the granola made for a refreshing breakfast.

"I heard Claire is thinking of running for mayor. That may put you in the middle."

Oh. Hope hadn't given that much thought. Her sister and her good friend both going after the same thing. High school all over again, just this time around it wasn't a boy, it was a political office. No good was going to come out of that. Especially for Hope.

"We're all adults. It'll be fine." Now it was Hope's turn to be confident. She plunged her spoon into the parfait, seeking a blueberry.

Seemingly satisfied with Hope's assurance, Audrey dove into the parfait. "This is so yummy."

"And easy." Hope took a spoonful herself. She embraced simplicity as often as she could. That was one of the catalysts for starting her blog when she was at the magazine.

Audrey took a bite of the oatmeal-cherry-chocolate bar, and her eyes lit up as she chewed. "I love your bars."

"Thank you." Hope had decided a few weeks earlier to challenge herself to revamp a basic oatmeal-raisin bar recipe she'd been making for years. Tired of the same old thing, on a whim she'd replaced the raisins with dried cherries and dumped in some left-over mini-chocolate chips. Within twenty-four minutes, she had a new favorite bar recipe that could rival any brand of healthy bars.

"Speaking of your cooking, how did your lesson go with Elaine?"

Hope shrugged. "Good. She did surprisingly well." She was surprised by how well Elaine had settled into the lesson and followed directions. Hope wasn't sure what to expect when Elaine begged for the cooking lesson, but it had turned out better than she thought it would. Until Hope messed things up by snooping. Hope inwardly cringed. Between Lionel shouting at her and humiliating Elaine in front of her, Hope wanted to crawl under a rock. But the worst part was the look of hurt and betrayal on Elaine's face caused by Hope. Somehow, some way, she needed to make things right with Elaine.

"Really? She doesn't strike me as a Suzy Home-maker type."

"Guess we all have sides of ourselves others rarely see." Hope scraped the jar with her spoon to get the very last of the yogurt-granola mix.

"I really hate to bring this up, but are you going to Peaches' funeral?" Audrey wiped her hands on a napkin.

Hope nodded. "I feel like I should pay my respects. How about you?"

"I'm going, but I'm not going to Maretta's for the reception. It's so sad that Peaches didn't have any family. Thank goodness the Kingstons stepped forward to take care of the arrangements." Audrey glanced at her watch. "I should get going. We both have to get ready for the service. I'm glad you're feeling better. I was so worried."

"I appreciate that you stopped by to check on me." Hope walked Audrey and Bigelow to the front door.

"That's what friends do." Audrey hugged Hope. "Please be careful," she whispered.

Hope nodded, then let go of her friend. She stepped back into her house and closed and locked the door after Audrey and Bigelow had descended the porch steps.

She would be careful as she continued searching for the killer.

There were only three things that got Claire to church—weddings, funerals, and Christmas service and only because they were fashion events. By the end, she'd have a list of the top-ten best-dressed and a list of the top-ten "should go out and buy a mirror." That was the reason Hope did all she could to avoid going to church with her sister.

But for Peaches' funeral, Hope needed the ride.

She also needed her sister to zip up her black sheath dress. While Hope struggled to look decent enough to appear in public, Claire looked mourning perfect in a black trench coat, her blond hair swept back into a sleek bun and a stylish clutch in her hand. But Hope had had the foresight to wear a pair of wedge pumps, which made navigating the terrain at the cemetery effortless, while Claire found her stiletto heels sinking into the moist soil as she walked to Peaches' grave.

The burial was somber and chilly. Only a handful of mourners drove out to the cemetery to say their final farewells. As Peaches had no family, Alfred and Maretta had taken on the responsibility of burying the thirty-five-year-old. Hope knew Alfred felt it was the least he could do while Maretta strove to do the least she could for a woman she disliked. She'd chosen the no-frills coffin and the simplest floral arrangements.

The cool March air nipped through Hope's trench coat. She craved a hot cup of something. Even a cup of tea would have been welcomed. When the priest finished the service, she walked back to Claire's luxury sedan, along with Jane and Sally, mostly because they moved at her speed—slow.

"You need to speak with Rusty Collins," Jane said as the three of them walked across the lawn.

"Why?"

"He owns the house Peaches rented. I'm sure he'd let you look around," Jane said.

Hope doubted Rusty would let her inside the house. For that to happen, he'd actually have to do a favor. He was a curmudgeon of a man, short on patience and long on grudges. As far as she knew, Rusty didn't do favors. For anyone.

"The police have removed their crime scene tape," Sally added.

"How do you know that?" Hope approached a few bumpy patches. Luckily, she didn't lose her balance and managed to stay upright.

"We drove by there this morning, on the way back from the market," Sally said.

Hope winced. She'd definitely overdone it. She should have passed on the burial. She never thought she'd see the day she couldn't keep up with the Merrifields. Her struggle didn't go unnoticed by Jane, who slowed down a bit, no doubt to give a lecture.

"You really should be home. You're not fully recovered," Jane said.

Sally waved a dismissive hand. "Stop mothering her. She's a grown woman, and if she wants to be out hunting down a murderer, then we can't stop her."

"I'm not exactly hunting. I'm barely walking." Hope muttered. She made it to her sister's car, and the Merrifields continued to their car. She slid into the passenger seat, and Claire started the ignition. Hope reached into her purse for her cell phone. She looked up Rusty's phone number. If everything went well, she'd have access to Peaches' home by the end of the day.

"What are you doing?" Claire asked.

"Looking for a number. Rusty Collins." Hope typed in the search field.

"Why?"

"He owns the house Peaches lived in. I want to see if I can look around."

"Why?"

"To look for clues."

"You're now a target. Don't you think you should stop this sleuthing thing?"

Hope glanced at her sister. "No. If anything, I need to do more."

"That doesn't make sense."

"It does to me." Hope looked at her phone. "He's not listed. I guess we'll drive over to the gas station."

"No," Claire said sharply and a little too quickly.

Hope's head swung around and was surprised with Claire's look. "You got banned, didn't you?" Rusty was a legend in Jefferson for his banning customers at his gas station for minor infractions, such as pulling into a bay in the wrong direction. He was a stickler for traffic control. And he chased off banned customers who dared to buy gas. Hope wondered how he'd managed to stay in business for as long as he had.

Claire shook her head. "Never mind about the gas station. I have his number because he lists his house through our agency."

A tapping at the car window startled Hope. She dropped the phone into her purse and glanced over to the window.

Detective Reid.

She lowered the window. "Is there something I can help you with?"

"I just wanted to see how you're feeling." His face was closed. He had that unexpressive cop look going so it was hard to tell if he was truly concerned about her.

"That's very considerate of you. Do you still think my sister tried to kill me?"

"I cannot comment on an ongoing investigation."

"Of course." With her index finger, Hope pressed the window control button and the window rapidly rose, putting a barrier between her and the detective. If only that button worked on everything in her life. Now that would be a really good thing.

Chapter Twenty

"Are you sure you want to go in there? I can take you home," Claire said as she pulled into a space outside Maretta's home for the funeral reception.

"I'm sure. It's the right thing to do. Right?" A sliver of doubt wriggled its way into Hope's head. The last time she was in the Kingston house, it wasn't pleasant. Maretta had accused Hope of skulking around as if she were a criminal.

When they entered the house, Hope looked around for Maretta. Her quick scan turned up a small cluster of mourners in the living room, while a few others milled around what she expected to be an uninspired buffet set up in the dining room.

Drew strode out of the dining room with a cup of coffee. "Slim pickings."

"What did you expect?" Hope slung her purse over her shoulder.

Claire caught up with Hope. "I'm going to call

Rusty and see if we can stop over at Peaches' house on the way home."

"Have you seen Maretta?" Hope asked Drew.

"There she is." Drew pointed to the staircase. "I'd hate to be in her shoes."

"Some people like sensible shoes, Drew."

The older woman stepped off the staircase and disappeared into the living room.

"I'm talking about having to host a wake for a woman you despise."

"Oh. I don't think she despised Peaches." Hope glanced back to the dining room and spotted Meg Griffin at the buffet table. Should she or shouldn't she approach Meg? The last few times hadn't turned out so well. But they lived in the same small town now and they needed to find a way to coexist peacefully. It probably would have helped if Hope didn't suspect her of murder, but then again no friendship was without its ups and downs, right?

"Be right back." Hope broke away from Drew to walk into the dining room. She approached the dining table that had been set up as a makeshift buffet. "Navigating a buffet can be challenging," she said in a light, casual tone and hoped for the best.

"Tell me about it." Meg scooped up some baked ziti. "Everything is so calorie laden. Look at this ziti."

Hope tried not to. Processed mozzarella clumped over bland, watery sauce and soggy penne.

"The salad looks pretty safe. I mean, not too high in calories."

"I heard about the accident and what happened at your house yesterday. But since you're sticking your nose into matters that don't concern you, you can't be surprised by the turn of events, can you?" Meg dropped the serving spoon back onto the tray and set her plate on the table. She turned and marched away.

That didn't go well. Lots of ups and downs.

Somber guests begun to stir around the buffet, and Hope decided it was time to make herself scarce. She grabbed Meg's discarded plate and weaved through the small group to reach the kitchen, where she tossed the heavy-duty paper plate into the trash. She moved over to the sink, turned on the faucet, and washed her hands.

Out of the corner of her eye she saw Maretta approach. Even if she hadn't spotted the woman, she would have sensed an extra gloomy cloud hovering nearby.

"You certainly have been a busy bee these days," Maretta said.

"Hello, Maretta." Hope wiped her hand on a paper towel.

"A blog, radio interviews, remodeling a house, and investigating a murder. How do you find the time?"

"I did write a post a couple weeks ago on time management."

"Don't be flippant with me, Hope Elizabeth Early."

Ouch. Hope's full name. Maretta was unquestionably angry.

"I'm just asking a few questions."

"You're asking a lot of questions."

"There's no law against that."

"There should be. Just like there's a law against trespassing."

Maretta wasn't going to let it go. Ten years from now, Maretta would still be bringing up the night Hope found Vanessa's dead body, but the crime she would emphasize would be trespassing and not the murder. "Vanessa invited me the other night. And I was invited here today, just like everybody else."

Maretta moved closer to Hope. "Trying to get justice is an admirable thing."

A compliment? Had Hope heard right?

"However, snooping is not. I have guests to attend to, and I'm sure you can show yourself out." Maretta swung around and walked out of her kitchen.

How was it possible Hope was welcomed into thousands of homes every day, thanks to her blog, but she was quickly becoming persona non grata to the people she'd known for years? She shouldn't wait to be asked a second time to leave. She tossed the paper towel into the trash when movement out the window over the sink caught her attention.

She moved closer to the window and peered out. There was a woman stacking boxes on the small front porch of the carriage house. Was she Vanessa's sister? She also recalled someone saying her sister would be arriving to take care of the funeral arrangements. A pang of sorrow cut through Hope's heart. How awful for the woman to have to bury her sister. Chills skittered up Hope's body at

the brief thought of having to make such arrangements for Claire.

Hope only caught a glimpse of the woman,
dressed in a pair of dark leggings and a beige cro-
chet tunic, before she turned and walked back
into the house. Hope closed her eyes to try to recall her name. *Vera.*

She considered whether or not to go out to the
carriage house and decided to go. Vera shouldn't
be alone during the process of packing up her sister's life. Pulling open the back door, she stepped
outside. Apprehension stopped her. What if the
woman wasn't Vera? She shook off the silly thought
because the killer wouldn't be packing Vanessa's
belongings, nor would she be there during the day
with a main house full of people.

Hope walked along the bluestone path to the
cottage, which was built for Alfred's mother with
an emphasis on large windows to let the sunshine
in and to have a view of the beautiful garden
Maretta tended to. The late Mrs. Kingston loved
gardening and that was, other than Alfred himself,
the only thing Maretta and her mother-in-law had
in common. Hope glanced around and saw that,
like every other garden in town, it was waking
slowly from its dormant winter state. Daffodils dotted the garden beds, and Hope noticed there was
one large clump in the perfect viewing location
from the front porch. No doubt Mrs. Kingston had
enjoyed a morning cup of tea in the kitchen nook,
which was bumped out onto the porch, staring at
the perky, yellow flowers.

Hope climbed the two steps of the porch and, at

the threshold of the front door, she pushed the door open and leaned in. Her breath caught.

Vanessa?

Hope did a quick mental regrouping. The resemblance was remarkable. The woman wasn't Vanessa. She was her sister.

"May I help you?"

"I . . . I'm sorry. You must be Vera," Hope said.

The woman nodded. "Yes. And you are Hope Early. I recognize you from *The Sweet Taste of Success.* You should have won," Vera approached and extended a hand.

Hope shook Vera's hand.

Vera was a couple of inches taller than her sister but had the same heart-shaped face with big brown eyes.

"I'm sorry for your loss."

"I was told you were the person who found her." Vera moved back to a large box she was packing with pillows and throws. Vanessa did love accessories and cozy throws to curl up with at night on the sofa.

Hope cast her eyes downward for a moment. She wasn't prepared to relive that night over again, and she didn't think Vera wanted to hear the details.

"I also heard you found the other woman. How awful. Vanessa said Jefferson was a nice place to live." She placed a heavy emphasis on the word "was."

Hope lifted her gaze to Vera. "It is. What's happened is very out of character for our town. Are you packing up Vanessa's belongings by yourself?"

Vera nodded. "Luckily, Van wasn't a pack rat."

"She was very organized." Hope glanced around the living space, which consisted of the living room and eat-in kitchen. Prior to the moving boxes scattered around, the space had been tidy. As a renter, Vanessa couldn't add too many personal touches, but everything had a place and she had kept a spotless home.

"We got that from our mother. She was an accountant."

"That explains Vanessa's love of spreadsheets."

"And mine, too. Though, it's not helping me much finding a new job. But right now I can't think about that. I told Mrs. Kingston I would have everything cleared out by the end of the week."

"That's not a lot of time. I'm happy to help. You shouldn't be doing this by yourself. I have a sister. I can't imagine having to do this."

Vera's lip quivered. She appeared to have it all together but Hope expected that inside she was on the verge of falling apart.

"Thank you. I rented a storage unit to store Vanessa's things because I really can't go through the stuff. Not yet." Vera's strong façade broke. Tears streamed down her cheeks, and she tried to wipe them away with her hands. But there were too many tears.

Hope dashed over to the fireplace and snatched a box of tissues off the mantel. She extended the box to Vera, who pulled out a couple of tissues.

Vera wiped her face dry and drew in a shaky breath to steady herself. She appeared embarrassed by her show of emotion. She stepped over to the desk, which was set against the bedroom wall, and deposited the used tissues in the small trash basket. A large box sat on top of the desk, and there was a spread of files next to it.

"Did Vanessa leave her laptop at your house?"

"No. Why do you ask?" Hope peeked inside of the box of pillows and throws. The throws were scrunched up and just tossed in on top of the pillows. Vera was grieving and not thinking clearly about small things. She had far more important things to focus on than pillows and throws.

Vera looked over her shoulder. "Because I can't find hers. I've looked everywhere. It's strange."

Hope glanced up. Somehow she'd resist repacking the box. She stepped away, putting distance between herself and the temptation. She joined Vera at the desk.

What could have happened to Vanessa's bright pink laptop? She always carried it with her when she came to work at Hope's house. She had a sleek leather bag she toted the laptop around in.

"Did you find the laptop bag?"

"Yes." Vera pointed to the floor by the desk.

Hope picked up the bag and unzipped it. Inside were the mouse and a packet of computer wipes. Where on earth was the laptop? Did the murderer take the computer? If so, why? How were Vanessa and her computer connected to Peaches' murder?

"Did Vanessa ever mention Peaches McCoy to you?"

"Not really. She may have said something because the name is familiar to me, but I don't remember what Vanessa said. She mostly talked about you and

Audrey Bloom." Vera dropped the files into the box and then reached for the round pen holder of markers, pens, and pencils.

"Wait, you don't want any ink leaks." Hope scooted over to the small but efficient kitchen and searched for sealable plastic bags. With the box in hand, she returned to Vera and dumped the contents of the pen holder into a Baggie and sealed it.

Vera smiled. She looked relieved someone else was taking control. "Thank you."

"Let's get some work done."

Together, they continued to pack up the desk and corner bookshelf. Even with her love of technology, Vanessa had preferred print books and indulged in hardcover editions because she loved how they felt in her hands when she settled down to read. Three more boxes were filled, and Vera decided to call it a day. She wanted to take the boxes to the storage unit and head back to her room at the Merrifield Inn.

"The bedroom is cleared out and now this area. I just have the kitchen to pack up and a few things in the living room. Then I'll have a moving company come and move the furniture out."

"Let me know when you want to pack up the kitchen. I'll be here."

"Thank you. I really appreciate your help."

"If you need anything, don't hesitate to call me." Hope pulled out her planner from her purse and wrote her information on a sheet of paper and handed it to Vera. "Anytime. I mean it."

Vera took the sheet of paper and nodded.

Hope left the carriage house and headed to the

street, where she found Claire exiting Maretta's house.

"I'm ready to go," Hope told her sister.

"What were you doing out there?" Claire tied the belt around her trench coat.

"Helping Vanessa's sister pack up things."

"She's here? That's so sad." Claire tucked her clutch under her arm and started walking.

"It was." Hope followed her sister.

"Where is she staying?"

"At the Inn. Maybe I should invite her to dinner. She probably hasn't had a home-cooked meal in days."

"You're probably right. That would be a nice gesture. It must be hard for her being here all alone," Claire's voice was low and serious with a hint of sympathy.

"You know, Vera couldn't find Vanessa's laptop. She always had it with her."

"Perhaps the killer took it."

"That's what I was thinking. But why? What could have been on the laptop worth killing for? And how is this all connected to Peaches' murder?" The more Hope investigated, the more questions kept popping up. She'd love at least one solid answer. Just one.

"Hey, you!" a loud voice bellowed.

Hope glanced over her shoulder and saw Lionel Whitcomb coming at them, pointing a stubby finger in their direction.

"What's his problem?" Claire asked.

"My guess is his problem is me," Hope said.

"Listen, lady, I have something to tell you." Lionel came to a stop. He was dressed in a bad-fitting jacket that pulled at the shoulder seams. His prominent belly stuck out, straining his shirt buttons. His thinning brown hair was combed over in an attempt to cover his balding scalp. His dark eyes, covered by a thick, bushy unibrow, were fixed on her. The man needed a good waxing. And a lesson in manners.

"My sister has a name, Lionel." Claire rested a hand on her hip.

Lionel shot a warning look to Claire. "I'm not talking to you."

"And we're not talking to you." Hope moved to step away. He might treat his wife and colleagues rudely, but she wasn't going to stand for it.

"Hey, I'm not done with you," he shouted.

"Lionel, there's no reason to raise your voice when speaking with us," Claire said. Her sister had used the even-toned, professional voice she'd honed in her years of real estate. More than once Claire had to talk a buyer or seller down off a ledge.

Lionel barely looked at Claire, but he clearly ignored her advice. "You came into my house under false pretenses, looking for dirt to soil my good reputation."

"I'm just looking for the truth," Hope said.

Lionel's sagging cheeks puffed out, and Hope was certain that if she looked close enough, she could see steam coming out of his hairy ears.

"You can't handle the truth," he said.

"What would that be?" Hope stepped forward, staring at the schoolyard bully.

"Your sister killed Peaches and then offed Vanessa because she knew about the murder." Lionel seemed to have solved the murder all nice and tidy.

"I did no such thing," Claire protested.

"Why would Claire kill Peaches?" Hope asked.

"To get the listing. She's been begging me for months for the listing. But she didn't have the chops to handle a deal as big as my development."

"I do so have the chops. And to be honest, I wouldn't take your listing now even if you begged me," Claire said.

"If you two don't stay out of my business, you'll be begging me when I'm done with you," Lionel warned.

"Where were you when Peaches was murdered?" Hope asked.

Lionel's face scrunched up, and his eyes bulged with fury. "What did I just say to you?"

"Where was your wife on the nights of the murders? And who were you talking with on the telephone when I was at your house? Who were you referring to when you said, 'She's got nothing. We're good.' Who were you talking to?"

"You've got a lot of nerve, lady."

Claire tugged on Hope's coat sleeve. "Stop poking the bear."

Hope shrugged off her sister's hold. Lionel was becoming unhinged. Causing a scene on the street in the middle of the day. What didn't he want Hope to find out? Was he covering for Elaine? No, he didn't seem the type of man who would stand by his wife. He was more the type who would cut his losses and dump any liabilities as fast as he could. Maybe Peaches became a liability for him and he killed her.

"No alibis for either of you? Or, are you each other's alibis?" Hope asked.

"I'm warning you!"

Hope spun around, pulling Claire with her, and walked away. She raised a waving hand to signal she was done with him. He had a bad temper, and it was possible Peaches had crossed him in their business dealings or she could have pushed for more money. Hope had to find out where he was when both murders occurred.

Chapter Twenty-one

"You're quiet. What's wrong?" Hope eased deeper into the heated passenger seat of Claire's car. Her rental SUV came with the bare minimums and while she never considered herself a materialistic person, she did miss the few added luxuries her damaged vehicle had, like heated seats.

Claire made a noncommittal sound. She looked pensive when Hope expected her to look outraged at the scene Lionel Whitcomb just caused. Claire wasn't a pushover and, like Hope, she didn't suffer fools. So, what was up?

"Don't make me pull out my cell and call Mother," Hope warned.

Claire flicked a glance at Hope and then turned her attention back to the road. "I was just thinking about Vera. How is she doing?" Claire flicked on the turn signal and made a left onto Dorchester Road, where Peaches' rental home was located.

The quiet road was lined with Cape Cods and ranch-style homes built in the 1950s. The front yards were neat and manicured, while the homes were well-maintained. That was the Jefferson Vanessa had told her sister about and the Jefferson that Hope grew up in. Not the Jefferson of the past few days filled with murder.

"She seems okay, but she's probably in shock. Her sister is dead." Hope looked at the mailboxes for the house numbers.

Peaches' home should be coming up soon.

"Do you want me to be like Vera?" Claire's sharpness laced through her voice.

Hope looked at her sister. The question was unexpected, and she didn't have an answer for it.

"Planning a funeral for my sister? Packing away all of your belongings? And, what the heck would I do with those chickens?"

Hope sighed. "Nothing is going to happen to me." An image of Claire with Hope's feisty hen, Helga, flashed in her mind. Egg collection would become a blood sport because Helga had been known to attack with very little provocation.

"Like you weren't run off the road or grabbed by some psycho in your kitchen?" Claire slowed as they approached the house Peaches had called home before her untimely death.

Hope opened her mouth to say something but immediately closed it. She couldn't argue with Claire. By digging into the murders, she had put a target on herself.

"And I couldn't forgive myself if you're the next victim. This is getting too dangerous. I want you to stop. I'll hire a lawyer and a private investigator so you can go back to just being my sister. My very much alive sister."

Her sister's plea hit Hope hard, leaving her a mixed bundle of emotions. She had to gather herself or else she'd sound like a blubbering fool.

"Even if I stop right this minute, I'm still a threat to the killer. He or she thinks I know something. I might as well see this through. I promise I'll be careful."

"Promise?"

"Promise. Now, let's go inside." Hope stepped out of the parked car and followed Claire along the weathered brick path to the front door of the simple ranch house painted white with beige trim. Nondescript bushes served as landscape.

"Two bedrooms, one bath." Claire unlocked the lockbox attached to the doorknob and entered.

Hope shook her head. She wasn't renting the house, she was searching it. "What's going to happen to all of her stuff?" Hope continued to follow her sister.

Claire shrugged. "Maybe Maretta and Alfred will take care of it like they did the funeral. What exactly are we looking for?"

Hope looked around the spacious combination living and dining room. Beige and boring. Nothing indicated a successful thirtysomething real estate agent lived there up until a few days ago. There weren't any photographs or personal touches, nothing but beige.

"I haven't a clue. I guess something out of the ordinary." Hope sifted through a pile of magazines on the pale wood coffee table. The neat piles consisted of mostly interior-decorating magazines filled with tips and techniques Peaches didn't bother to apply to her home.

"Huh. She had an interest in decorating. Though, you wouldn't know it by looking around this place." Claire walked into the dining area, which was a small square shape just off the kitchen.

"I'm going to check her bedroom." Hope walked down the short hall, past the bathroom and an un-furnished spare bedroom. She found the master bedroom minimally furnished with a queen-size bed, dresser, and a full-length mirror. Peaches did-n't indulge on possessions. So what did she do with the money she earned?

"More boring." Claire came into the room be-hind Hope. "Oooh, let's look through her closet." She dashed over to the plain wood door and opened it to reveal a stash of clothes.

"So this is where her money went?"

Claire picked through the clothes and the handbags on the top shelf in lightning speed. "Im-pressive."

"What?"

"These bags are all real. There's a small fortune tucked up on that shelf." She pulled one open. "Since there's no next of kin, who gets them?" She petted the luxurious hobo bag.

"They could be donated to the Village Donation Center," Hope suggested.

Claire gasped. "Donated?"

Hope took the bag from her sister's hold and tossed it back onto the shelf. Claire gasped again at the manhandling of the ridiculously priced handbag.

"We have work to do." Hope shut the closet door and walked over to the dresser.

"Again, what are we looking for?"

Hope opened a few drawers. "I found her unmentionables."

"Let's keep it that way."

"What's this?" Hope pulled out a lingerie bag and gingerly opened it.

"Hmm, isn't that interesting. Shouldn't it be in the nightstand?" Claire peered over Hope's shoulder.

Hope clumsily bundled the bag up and stuffed it back into the drawer.

"What? You never saw one before?"

"Yes, I've seen one before." At her bridal shower Hope received a few adult toys as gag gifts.

"You're beet red. I know what I'm getting you for Christmas," Claire teased.

"Stop."

"I'll have no choice if you don't start dating."

Hope rolled her eyes.

"Along with some cats."

"I'm not ready. Besides, I'm way too busy to date," Hope said.

"Liar."

"Nuh-uh."

"Ethan hangs around a lot at your house. You're telling me you aren't the least bit interested?"

Hope tilted her head. She didn't know how she felt about Ethan. They'd been friends since high school, they went to each other's weddings, and she'd gone to his children's christenings. She

needed friends at this point in her life, and she
worried if they moved beyond being friends, something could go wrong and she could lose him. So
far her choice in men hadn't been the best.

"We're just friends," Hope said firmly.

Claire shook her head. "If you don't use it, you
will lose it. Mark my words."

"Duly noted."

Claire pointed to the closed nightstand drawer.
"I wonder what's in the nightstand."

"A phone book? Bible?"

"Seriously? A Bible?" Claire went to the small
piece of furniture and pulled open the top drawer.
"A small address book." She thumbed through it.
"It's pretty empty. Must be her personal one." She
tossed it back into the drawer and a bunch of business cards fell out, landing on the beige carpet.

"I know it's a rental, but this house doesn't seem
like a home. Vanessa lived in a rental but it felt like
a home."

"This is interesting." Claire scooped up the
fallen cards.

"What?"

"Matthew Roydon, Criminal Defense Attorney,"
Claire read from a card.

Hope snatched the card out of her sister's hand.
"Matthew Roydon. Matt."

"So?"

"Peaches was texting someone named Matt just
before she was killed. Why was she texting a lawyer?"
And could he be the man Meg saw her with the day
before the murder?

"What text message? How do you know?"

Hope slipped the card into her pocket. Did she

finally have something that could lead her in the direction of the killer? Or at least in the direction of an answer? She glanced into the drawer. A layer of newspapers lined the drawer. She pulled them out and spread them out on the bed. They were all cut up. The newspapers looked like Swiss cheese.

"What on earth? Oh my goodness. I know what she was doing!" Claire grabbed hold of Hope's forearm and squeezed.

"Would you let go of me?" Hope shook her arm free of Claire's hold.

"It's obvious. These are all cut up. She was sending ransom notes."

"Really? Ransom notes? Who did she kidnap?"

"Well, why else would you cut newspapers up?"

"These are old newspapers." Hope sorted through them. They were all from the Hartford area from eleven years ago. It seemed Peaches had clipped out articles by the odd shapes left in the remaining pages.

"Okay, so if she didn't use the papers for ransom notes, maybe she used them for decoupage."

Hope shot her sister a sideways glance. "I wonder what the articles were about."

"Maybe they were real estate articles."

"Possibly." Hope gathered up all the newspapers and picked them up. Since the police had released the house and left the newspapers, they obviously didn't consider them pertinent to the murder.

"You're taking them?"

Hope nodded. "I think we found something."

"What exactly did you find?" a woman's voice said from the opposite side of the room.

Chapter Twenty-two

Hope nearly jumped out of her skin at the sound of the vaguely familiar voice. She swung around and breathed a sigh of relief when she saw Iva Johnson in the doorway with a plastic caddy filled with cleaning supplies in one hand and the other rested on her hip.

"We could ask you that same question," Claire said.

"Hmmpff." Iva lifted her chin and strode into the room. She reached the bed, dropped the caddy, and sorted through her spray bottles. "You ladies thinking about renting the place?"

"Rusty said we could have a look around. Why are you here?" Claire asked.

Iva glanced at her caddy then back up to Claire. "What does it look like? I cleaned for Ms. McCoy, and Mr. Collins asked me to keep this place neat until it gets rented again. So I do have a right to be here. I'm not snooping." She yanked out one of the spray bottles. "I'm just doing my job."

"There isn't much to clean when no one lives in the house."

"Regardless, I do have a few things I need to get done. I have other clients." With her spray bottle and a cleaning cloth, Iva headed into the adjoining bathroom.

"What's with the two of you?" Hope asked Claire.

"She does a really good job cleaning. Not only does she make spots disappear, she also works the same magic on jewelry. She's always been sneaky, you know that."

"Are you sure?"

"She cleaned for me a few years ago so I'm certain. Are we done here?"

"I want to ask her a couple of questions first. Give me a few minutes." Hope didn't know how much Iva could tell her. Or even if she would tell her anything. If Iva wasn't above stealing from clients, then she certainly wasn't above gossiping about them. She guessed it was worth a shot.

Claire shook her head. "Good luck. You know she hasn't changed one bit since high school." Her heels clicked on the hardwood floor as she exited the room.

Iva poked her head out of the bathroom. "You're still here?"

Hope swung around.

The once-beautiful girl she knew from high school had gotten older and bitter.

"Since you worked for Peaches, you may know something that could help the police solve her murder."

Iva stepped out of the bathroom, both hands on her hips now. "Let me get this straight. You're trying to solve murders now? Always the overachiever. Guess some things never change. Big-time New York City magazine editor. Television celebrity. And now you're playing detective. Guess you want to make sure the murders get pinned on someone other than your sister."

Alcohol and pills might have stolen whatever dreams Iva had back in school, but jealousy and bitterness took away any chance she ever had at being happy. Hope didn't want to travel down the road of defending her successes to Iva.

She turned away. She was done wasting her time. "My mistake."

"I, I don't think I know anything that would help. Except . . ."

Hope stopped and looked over her shoulder, unsure whether to trust Iva wasn't about to unleash more snarkiness.

"Except what?"

"Mr. Whitcomb spent a lot of time here."

"They were in business together. It's reasonable they had meetings."

Iva rolled her eyes. "In the bedroom?"

"What?" Hope turned completely around to face Iva.

"For a smart businessman, he was cheap and careless." Iva busied herself by smoothing down the bed comforter. "Do you see how he dresses? He looks like a slob. Anyway, one morning I found his wallet on the floor right over there." She gestured to the side of the bed.

"How do you know it was his?"

"I didn't look inside, if that's what you're asking. I just recognized it because I'd seen it at his house. I clean there, too."

"Did you clean for Vanessa Jordan?"

Iva shook her head. "Never."

Hope considered what Iva said as she made her way back to the living room. Peaches and Lionel were having an affair. Did Elaine know? She probably was used to being the "other woman," but how did she feel about being the betrayed wife? Would she have murdered Peaches? But what could her motive for killing Vanessa have been? Or did Lionel kill Peaches? Maybe Peaches was threatening to make trouble for him. But why kill Vanessa?

Hope needed to review Vanessa's résumé. Maybe there was something in her past that connected her to Peaches and explained how their murders were connected.

"Can we go now?" Claire had settled on the sofa with a magazine.

"Yes." Hope continued past her sister to the front door. She opened the door and found Ethan on the doorstep. At first she was startled by his unexpected presence, but once that passed, her heart fluttered for a moment. All six feet of him filled the doorway, and his gaze was fixed on Hope. Though, his visit probably wasn't social.

"What are you doing here?" he asked in a suspicious tone.

Hope bit her lower lip. Darn. She had two options. The first option was to tell him the truth, which guaranteed a lecture on how she should stay out of police business. Option number two was to tell him the tiniest white lie, almost microscopic, really. Not wanting a lecture, she went with the latter.

"I'm looking for a rental. My current residence isn't working for me anymore."

"This isn't funny," Ethan warned.

"I know. Trust me, I know." She had the bruises to prove how much she was aware that what she was doing wasn't a game. "We have to go." Hope gestured for Claire to follow her. They walked past Ethan to Claire's car.

"If Reid finds out you were here, he'll arrest you." Ethan followed them to Claire's car.

"Looking at houses isn't a crime," Hope replied.

"Interfering in an ongoing criminal investigation is."

Hope flashed a smile. "Then it's a good thing I was just looking at a house, right?" She dashed around the passenger side and slid onto the seat.

"Was that a lovers' spat?" Claire asked in a whisper when she opened the driver's side door.

"Get in." Hope just wanted to go home, soak in a hot tub of water because her body ached, and then dig into Vanessa's past. She was certain there was a connection between the two murder victims. She just had to find it.

Hope waved to Drew as he bustled into the kitchen with a large pizza box. He'd called earlier to say he would stop to pick up dinner and come over. Not having to cook sounded like heaven to Hope. Even though her blog revolved mostly around what she cooked, a night off every now and then was welcomed. After returning home earlier, she'd soaked her aching body in a hot tub to ease away the day she'd had. She went to a funeral, helped a woman pack up her dead sister's belongings, and searched through the drawers of another dead woman.

When she'd climbed out of the tub, she'd dried off and dressed to finish painting the rest of the dining room while she waited for Drew. Her clean-up was interrupted by a telephone call from Corey Lucas.

"You haven't returned any of my calls," Corey said in an exaggerated whiny voice.

Hope cradled her cordless phone as she washed her hands and Drew set the pizza box on the island. After drying her hands, she gestured to Drew to get the plates out of the cabinets. She was starving.

"Some things have been happening here."

"I heard about your car accident. Are you okay?"

Hope filled him in on her minor injuries and lingering soreness. For some odd reason, he seemed interested in the details. She paused and wondered what he was really up to. Corey didn't like details because of his short attention span, which was what made him a perfect fit for reality television.

"Good that you weren't seriously hurt. Now, for the reason why I've called you so many times. I just wanted to give you a heads-up."

Drew set the table and moved the pizza box over there. Next up was the beverages, and he pulled out two bottles of beer from her refrigerator.

"A heads-up about what?" Hope walked to the table. She needed to end the call soon because there was a slice of pizza, heavy on the vegetables, calling her name. Drew lifted up the top of the box, and the aroma of melted cheese, sauce, and vegetables wafted up to her. Time to say bye-bye to Corey.

"A reality show . . ."

Hope sighed. No wonder he listened to all the details about her accident. He had an agenda. "Corey, I told you I don't want to do another reality show."

"Yeah, yeah, I know. This isn't about you. There's a new show about to begin taping called *Life After the Big D*."

"*Life After the Big D*? What's it about?"

"Rebuilding your life after a divorce."

"Divorce? Gosh, is there nothing off limits for a reality show?"

"No, not really. Look, I thought you should know Tim signed on to do the show."

"What?"

Hope straightened up and for a moment she saw red as a wave of anger flashed through her. She was speechless, and perhaps that was for the best because the words that immediately came to mind weren't polite.

"Hope? Are you still there?" Corey asked.

"I'm here," Hope said eventually, when she was certain her voice wouldn't crack. Tears welled up in her eyes, but she didn't want to cry, and she didn't want Corey to know she was about to cry. She was done crying over Tim.

"The show is going to follow him around as he begins dating again, you know, finding love again . . ."

Hope dropped down onto the chair as Corey's words were muffled. Her mind raced with thoughts of betrayal, anger, and vengeance. How could Tim do such a thing? Appear on a national television show and air their dirty laundry. Her jaw clenched. Like he had to rebuild his life after their divorce. She was the one who lost the condo, she was the one who was unemployed when the divorce papers were served, and she was the one who was cheated on.

"Are you serious? He's really going to do that? Why would you sign him?" she asked when she snapped out of her thoughts.

"Whoa, it's not my production. The show belongs to Neptune. It's an Alan Snyder show. I've gotta run. Just thought you should know."

"Thanks." Hope disconnected the call. "I think."

"Ah, honey. Tim is cashing in on his fifteen minutes of fame. *Life After the Big D* follows seven New Yorkers as they reenter the dating world as newly divorced and search for their one true love," Drew said.

"What?" Hope looked up.

"I Googled it." He held up his phone so Hope could see his screen.

Of course he did. Ever the reporter. He could find out anything. All he needed was his cell phone and a search engine.

"Ugh," Hope pushed away the dish in front of her. Her appetite was gone.

"Hey, there," Drew pulled his chair closer to

Hope. He lifted a slice of pizza out of the box and plopped it on the plate and pushed it in front of her.

"No, I can't eat anything now."

"You have to eat. Or you'll leave me no choice but to call Jane and you'll be drinking chamomile tea in no time."

Hope eyed Drew carefully. He wasn't bluffing. He would call Jane. And Jane would make a pot of tea. She reached for the slice of pizza and took a bite.

"That's my girl." Drew gave a triumphant smile.

Hope chewed and swallowed. "Do you think Tim is going to talk about me? About us?"

"Absolutely. It's the only way he can stay relevant."

Hope believed the old saying of honesty was the best policy, but once in a while she would prefer Drew not be so honest. A little white lie would have gone a long way at that moment, because there was a sliver of hope Tim wouldn't overshare about their marriage on television. Sure, it was the teeniest, tiniest sliver of hope, but she needed to hold on to that, and it would have been nice to hear Drew say that.

"Enough about your lousy ex." Drew reached for a slice of pizza. He selected the largest slice with the thickest crust.

"You're right. There's nothing I can do about Tim and his decision to do a reality show."

"Claire called on my way over here and told me Ethan showed up at Peaches' house. When you and I talked earlier, you left that part out."

Hope shrugged. "It was no big deal. He was just there to lecture me. Again."

"He's worried about you."

"I'm a big girl. I can take care of myself."

"Why are you fighting this?" Drew took a bite of pizza.

"Because Detective Reid seems to be hyper-focused on pinning the murders on Claire."

Drew wiped his mouth with a napkin then took a drink of beer. "I'm not talking about the murders. I'm talking about you and Ethan."

Hope opened her mouth to protest. She didn't know how many times she needed to remind those close to her she wasn't ready to date or look for a new relationship. She also doubted Ethan was looking for a relationship, either. They were two divorcees with enough baggage to fill a minivan. He had his own divorce drama to recover from and two young children to focus on.

Maybe a little bit of honesty would help Drew understand she simply wasn't ready to date again. "My heart is broken."

The biggest smile Hope ever saw covered Drew's face. Not exactly what she expected after sharing her pain.

So much for honesty. "That makes you happy?"

Drew tilted his head sideways and sighed. "Don't you know yet?"

"Know what?"

"That you're on the mend. I can see it. We can all see it."

"I don't understand."

Drew thumped his palm against his forehead.

"Duh. The way you look at Ethan says it all. You're falling in love with him."

"You're crazy." Hope took another bite of pizza and chewed. Drew was wrong. She wasn't falling in love with Ethan. She was in love with Ethan, which scared her more than the murderer trying to kill her.

Chapter Twenty-three

The commercial break was over and Hope was back on the air with Morning Pete. His crew was especially lively. Maybe it was because spring was finally in the air or they were overcaffeinated. Whatever the reason, Hope had an uneasy feeling in her stomach each time she was back live with them. Something bad was going to happen. She just knew it. She'd been popping in between their weather and traffic reports and blocks of music. She glanced at her watch. Just a few minutes left before she was off the air and her apple pie was out of the oven.

The fragrance of a high pile of apples baking with cinnamon and nutmeg in a buttery crust wafted through the kitchen. Hope's mouth watered in anticipation of a heaping forkful of pie. But alas, the pie was not for her. It was for Ethan. A peace offering of sorts. A tasty way to say, "I'm sorry."

"So, how does it work with your recipes?" Morning Pete prompted Hope out of her apple pie daydream.

"I thoroughly test each recipe I share on my blog. My readers depend upon that. They expect to be able to prepare the recipes in their own kitchens."

"These days, recipe testing seems to be taking a backseat to your new hobby," Morning Pete said.

Hope paused for a moment. There it was. The something bad that was going to happen.

She wasn't sure where Morning Pete was going, but she had a good idea of what he was hinting at.

"Recipe testing never takes a backseat." She smiled. Even though she knew the radio host, his crew, and their listeners couldn't see her, they could hear her smile. It was a trick a friend of hers taught her years ago, a little piece of experience she'd picked up working her way through college as a customer-service representative. "Let them hear you smile," she often said. Maybe not reacting would deter Morning Pete from going any further with whatever he was planning on doing.

"You've found two dead bodies. What's going on in your quaint little town?" He chuckled loudly. In the background, Hope heard his crew join in the laughter.

Her plan to thwart his plan hadn't worked. He clearly didn't "see" her smile.

"Sources say you're an integral part of the murder investigations." Cindy Dee was Morning Pete's sidekick and provided the estrogen to the program.

Hope looked at her watch again. Why did it feel like time had stalled?

"How does a blogger shift gears to become an amateur sleuth?" Cindy Dee asked.

Hope was determined not to react to the questions. She was there to promote her blog, not discuss the murders in town. She glanced at her watch. The second hand barely moved.

"Is it true your sister is a murder suspect?" Morning Pete asked.

"It's *person of interest*," Uncle Gio corrected. He was the morning program's resident prankster and thorn in Morning Pete's side.

Hope shook her head. She was done with the circus freak show. The handful of new readers weren't worth suffering the fools of morning radio. "I'm not here to discuss the murders of two women, one of whom was my assistant and my friend. And, for the record, my sister had nothing to do with either murder. And to be clear, I am not an integral part of the investigation. Thank you for having me on. It's been a pleasure." Her final sign-off was far from pleasant. But it felt good.

She clicked off the phone and dropped it on the table. Never again would she be a guest on that show. She needed to be more choosy in the future when promotional opportunities presented themselves.

A few moments passed, allowing her to reflect on her final appearance on Morning Pete's show. It wasn't the sign-off she'd hoped for. She'd practically told him off and hung up on him and his audience. In hindsight, she could see how her spontaneous reaction wasn't a good one. Maybe nobody really noticed. People were busy in the morning, getting ready for work, making breakfast, getting the kids up, and they probably weren't really that wide awake. Yeah, they probably didn't even notice Hope lost her cool.

The back door opened and she looked over her shoulder. Ethan entered and relief flooded her. Her rock was there, but could she lean on him after how badly she treated him the day before?

"Hey, good morning." Ethan walked over to the counter and poured himself a cup of coffee. He didn't appear to be holding a grudge. "I heard you on the radio. Your segment ended rather abruptly."

Hope shrugged. There wasn't anything she could do about it at that point. She didn't want to talk about the radio show or how every person in the state and Rhode Island now knew her sister was a suspect in two murders. *Good going, Hope.*

"He was just doing his job. It's all about ratings for guys like him."

Hope nodded. "Yeah, ratings." She twirled the telephone handset, staring intently on the mindless task.

Ethan sat across from Hope, set his mug on the table and rested his arms on the table. "Talk to me."

Hope looked up. Ethan watched her with an intensity that made her heart beat a little faster. Could she get away with not admitting how she really felt about him? Would he be able to tell she was keeping a secret? It was a risk she had to take. Saying her feelings out loud would only complicate things. Keeping the secret was the best thing for both of their sakes.

"I found out last night Tim signed on to do a reality show about life after divorce and finding true love."

"Ouch."

"I guess I should lower my expectations of how low Tim will sink to hurt me. I kind of feel sorry for him."

"Why?"

"I went on *The Sweet Taste of Success* to pursue a passion, a dream, and he's doing his show to find love. The sad fact is the reality TV machine will chew him up and spit him out and he'll be alone at the end. The show has no intention of finding him a happily ever after."

"Have you found yours?" Ethan took a drink of his coffee.

As Hope opened her mouth to reply, the oven timer beeped and she had a reason not to answer. Thankfully. "I do owe you an apology for my behavior yesterday."

"Is there something that goes with the apology?" He made an exaggerated sniffing motion.

Hope laughed as she stood and walked over to the double ovens. "I was going to bring this by later." She opened the bottom oven door. She reached in and pulled out a hot, bubbling pie and swiftly set it on the cooling rack.

Ethan shifted in his seat, twisting around to look at her and the pie. "Thank you for the apology. The pie isn't necessary, but I'll take it anyway."

"I behaved poorly yesterday. I was rude. To be honest, I didn't want another lecture about investigating on my own."

"That's what you should be with me all the time—honest." He shifted his gaze to the coffee mug and took a drink.

The word stung Hope. Honesty was important

to Ethan. His ex-wife was far from honest. She lied to him, she cheated on him, and she broke his heart. Even though Hope had the best of intentions and she was doing the right thing for her family, she had been deceptive.

"There's nothing that you can do that the police can't."

Hope leaned against the counter and crossed her arms over her chest. He had a point, but Detective Reid seemed to be more interested in making sure Claire's new wardrobe consisted primarily of orange. It was Hope's job, as Claire's sister, to protect her and that was what she was going to do. She was going to keep Claire out of prison and out of orange jumpsuits.

"Where's Vanessa's laptop?"

"What?"

"Her computer. Where is it? She always had it with her and now it's missing."

"How do you know that?" Ethan stood and walked over to her. He rested both hands on his hips and stood firmly.

Hope wasn't sure if he knew about the missing computer and wanted to keep it quiet or if he didn't know about the computer, which meant his officers missed something. Either way, he didn't look happy with her. *Again.*

"I was helping her sister pack up her belongings yesterday." Hope set the potholders on the counter and walked past Ethan to enter her office. She heard his footsteps behind her as he followed her. She began making her housewarming party invitations after she assembled the pie and put it in the oven to bake, She could easily purchase invitations at the store, but she preferred to take the time to hand make the cards. She gathered her card stock, her rubber stamps, and her ink pads. The night before she wrote up the guest list and set it on her worktable, along with her trusty camera to photograph each step for a blog post. Now, she just needed to decide how she would decorate the cards. Staring down at the craft table, she was torn between two stamps, a bird trio or a flutter of butterflies for the card cover. Maybe she could do half and half.

"Of course you were just helping."

Hope ignored Ethan's sarcasm and grabbed the butterfly stamp. Butterflies it would be. A sign of spring and rebirth.

"What's with all the newspapers?"

Oh, no. Hope swung around. Her eyes widened. *Shoot.* Ethan stood at her desk, sifting through the clippings she took from Peaches's house the day before. How was she going to explain stealing them?

"Hope?"

Hearing her name snapped Hope out of her panic.

"Ah . . . for a craft project." She scooted over to the desk and gathered up the newspapers in lightning speed. When she sat down the night before to go through them, she noticed the pages appeared to be from the first few pages of the *Hartford Daily* newspaper, so whatever was cut out was considered news. What made the front part of a newspaper were crimes, like a hit-and-run. Or was it possible Peaches was involved in a crime eleven years ago? Hope could see her fibbing a little to close a real estate deal but not committing a crime worthy of the front page. Peaches could have been involved in real estate fraud. News like that made the front page. Hope didn't think about that last night. And Harrison was a mortgage broker. Could that have been the reason Peaches was in his home office? Was she looking for evidence? Maybe she was trying to make a deal with a prosecutor if she'd gotten caught up in something illegal. She had a card from a criminal defense attorney. He could have been negotiating the deal. So maybe her murder wasn't about the hit-and-run but her turning on a business associate. Harrison or Lionel. Or both men. She wouldn't put it past Lionel to cheat people. But how would Harrison be involved?

"I shouldn't have left all of this out. It's too messy." Hope hurriedly gathered all the papers, stacked them, and set them aside. Out of sight, out of trouble and no explaining necessary.

"It's a work in progress. A little messy is okay."

"Have you determined if Peaches and Lionel Whitcomb were having an affair?"

"What?"

"They had a close business relationship, and I found out from Iva Johnson that she found Lionel's wallet in Peaches' bedroom one day while she was cleaning. That's an odd place for a man to drop his wallet, don't you think?"

"Look, Hope, I need you to back off of the murder investigations."

Hope looked up from her desk and studied Ethan for a moment. He looked serious.

A lump caught in her throat. Something must have happened. She swallowed hard and braced herself before asking, "What aren't you telling me?"

"Detective Reid is building a compelling case

against Claire. What she's going to need is a good lawyer and a sister to lean on, not an amateur sleuth putting her life in danger."

Hope's knees nearly buckled. There couldn't be a compelling case against Claire. She wasn't guilty of murder.

"How, how can he be building a case against her? She didn't kill anyone."

"He's uncovered some more evidence."

"What kind of evidence?"

"I'm not at liberty to say. I've already said too much. But I thought you should hear it from me."

Hope shook her head. "You barely said anything." She couldn't believe that a seemingly intelligent man like Detective Reid could believe her sister was a murderer. "I need to know. You know Claire. Tell me honestly, do you think she's a killer?"

Ethan shook his head. "No, I don't."

Hope reached out for Ethan's hand and squeezed it. She needed his reassurance because she was terrified. "Good."

"What are you going to do?"

Hope didn't have an option but to continue with her own investigation. Her sister wasn't going to be prosecuted for crimes she didn't commit.

"Well, since Morning Pete has just announced to the whole state I was an integral part of the murder investigation, I'm not going to disappoint. I'm going to find the killer, prove my sister is innocent, and then I think I'll make a pan of brownies."

*   *   *

Hope checked her messages. Her cell phone was blowing up with texts and e-mails from the people she knew back in New York City. She wasn't the only person who'd found out about Tim's upcoming appearance on *Life After the Big D.* She shoved her phone back into her purse and continued through the entry hall of the Merrifield Inn. Perhaps Vera could shed some light on a connection between Vanessa and Peaches. She hadn't heard from Vera since the day of Peaches' funeral, so she didn't know what her plans were for the day. Hope decided to catch her first thing in the morning.

The Inn's reception area was quaint and opened to the front sitting room, which was furnished with antiques and quilts. Hope was certain they were all Merrifield family treasures. In addition to scattered area rugs, well-read books, and strategically placed flower arrangements, the Inn came with its own ghost. Or at least so legend had it. Legend was good for businesses in quaint New England towns.

"Good morning, Hope," Jane said from behind the reception desk. The older woman smiled warmly and looked genuinely pleased to see Hope, which was a nice change of pace considering it seemed few people in town were happy to see her. "Come to visit Vera?"

Hope wondered if Jane had already pumped the woman for information. A pot of chamomile tea, a couple slices of toast, and a piece of chocolate served along with a few well-thought-out questions about Vanessa's past. Vera wouldn't even have realized she'd been interrogated by the time Jane was done with her.

Hope approached Jane and rested her arms on the counter. "Yes, I am."

Jane leaned forward. "She's very sad. That's to be expected. I brought her a tray last night since she didn't come down for supper."

Hope's heart squeezed. She couldn't imagine being alone in a strange town dealing with her sister's death.

"When she returned yesterday afternoon, we chatted a bit." Jane's bright lips formed an innocent smile, as if they'd discussed the weather or which antique shop to visit.

"What did you two chat about?"

"Vanessa. The poor child bounced around here and there for years. Which means there is a chance she had crossed paths with Peaches at some point. Find where they connected and we'll find the killer," Jane advised.

"I'll do my best."

Jane patted Hope's hand. "Of course you will. Claire's name needs to be cleared in this awful matter. Now go see Vera. She's out on the patio having breakfast. I practically had to force her to eat something."

Hope made a beeline for the patio. Spring was a fickle season in New England. One day it could snow and the next day it could hit over eighty-five degrees, and somewhere in between there was bound to be a rainstorm. Hope likened the season to a box of chocolates. You never knew what you were going to get until you bit into one. The past few days had been rainy and gloomy and felt more like autumn than spring, but today was a beautiful spring day with lots of sunshine and warmth. Stepping onto the patio, she was greeted by the bright morning sun. She lifted her hand to shield her eyes and scanned the brick patio for Vera. The patio was compact but fit five tables comfortably. From any seat, you had a view of the deep, narrow lot of land that comprised the Inn. The landscaping was simple and uncluttered, with tall fencing for privacy from the neighboring homes. In a few weeks, the garden would be lush with color and texture, thanks to Sally's keen gardening eye. The spot was perfect for a relaxing meal or cup of tea late in the day. Hope soaked in some of the serenity of the simple garden as she approached Vera, who sat at a table by the edge of the patio.

As Hope reached the table, she noticed Vera looked deep in thought. She reconsidered her decision to question her. Could she really intrude on a grieving sister?

"Hope? What are you doing here?" Vera glanced up. She looked tired and sad and lost, and it broke Hope's heart. Her eyes were hooded, deep bags circled underneath, and her face was drawn and pale. Hope noticed Vera's breakfast had barely been touched. Jane wasn't going to be happy.

"I came to check on you. To see how you're holding up. May I join you?"

Vera blushed. "Where are my manners? Yes, yes, please do."

Hope seated herself across from Vera. "I hope you're comfortable here. Jane is a wonderful innkeeper."

Vera nodded. "She has been such a dear. She

kind of reminds me of our, I mean, my grand-mother. I have to remember it's just me now." She let out a nervous laugh.

"I'm so very sorry for your loss. I can't change anything that has happened, but I want to, no, I plan to make sure the person who is responsible for Vanessa's death is found and sent to prison."

"I've heard talk your sister is a suspect. Is that true?"

"Yes, it is. But Claire isn't a murderer. She had professional disagreements with Peaches McCoy, which makes her a person of interest in the murders. I assure you she is not the person responsible for your sister's death. Or Peaches McCoy's death. That's why I'm here. I want to ask you a few questions, if you're up to it."

Vera pushed her plate away and then rested her elbows on the table. "Maybe helping you will make me feel a little better. What do you want to know?"

Hope wasn't sure what the etiquette was in asking a woman if she knew why her sister was murdered. A handbook would have been helpful.

"Vanessa was the second victim, but she was present the day of Peaches' murder. So I wondered if Vanessa could have been the intended victim the day of the garden tour. After all, she was invited and several people knew she would be there. Unlike Peaches, who just showed up uninvited."

"I have no idea why anyone would want to kill Vanessa. She didn't have any enemies."

"Then perhaps she saw or heard something," Hope thought out loud.

"I guess that's always a possibility."

"Why did Vanessa move to Jefferson? What was she doing when she came here?"

"Oh, Van moved around a lot. She didn't plant roots, our grandmother always used to say. She held so many jobs. She liked variety."

"What kind of jobs did she have?"

"She worked as an administrative assistant for various companies over the years. She never stayed in one spot too long. I think she had a new place to live with each job. She truly had a nomad's soul."

"There's nothing you can think of that could explain why she was killed?"

Vera shook her head. "I'm sorry. Van had one of those personalities that everybody loved. That's why she did so well adjusting to new jobs. I wish I could be more help."

"No, no, you've helped. Now it's my turn to reciprocate. I have a few errands to run, but I can be at her house later to help finish the packing."

"I have appointments to make the arrangements for Vanessa, so I won't be doing any packing today." A wave of grief swept over Vera's face.

Hope nodded her understanding that the "arrangements" Vera would be setting up were the funeral. "Call me if you need anything." She stood and walked back into the Inn, and waved good-bye to Jane, who was on the telephone, as she passed through to the front door. She descended the front steps to the sidewalk and right into Elaine Whitcomb's path.

"Oh," Elaine said in a cool tone.

"Good morning, Elaine. I'm so glad I've run into

you." Hope wanted to make things right between them. She'd seen a side of Elaine's life no one else had, and she knew Elaine needed a friend.

"I really don't have time." Elaine stepped forward. She wore stilettos in a leopard pattern, leaving Hope to wonder how she got from point A to point B without falling over.

"Wait, please, Elaine. I want to apologize."

"For what, exactly? Coming to my house under false pretenses? Snooping around my home? Or insinuating I'm a murderer?"

Hope cringed. She was guilty on all counts. She couldn't explain because no one would understand. Heck, she had a hard time understanding her willingness to put herself in danger to find a killer.

"I'm trying to find the truth, the person who murdered two people. You have to understand I have to ask questions."

"I understand you used me and you suspect me of murder."

"Let me explain."

Elaine raised an index finger, signaling to Hope to stop talking. "Just so you know, I've unfriended you, unfollowed you, and unsubscribed from your newsletter."

Hope gasped. She had no idea Elaine was social-media savvy.

A sliver of a smile touched Elaine's lips. She looked proud of herself. Putting Hope in her place seemed to be an ego boost for the woman.

"When did Lionel first meet Peaches? Could they have been more than just business colleagues?"

"Seriously? Hmmppff." Elaine swung around and marched away.

Hope let out a sigh as Elaine disappeared into a shop. She'd deal with Elaine's hurt feelings later. After she found the murderer. A quick motion caught her attention from the direction of where Elaine had disappeared.

Drew was speed walking toward her, gesturing to her with one hand as he held his cell phone in the other. As he got closer, he swiped his phone screen, shoved it into his pants pocket, and linked his arm with Hope's.

"What's going on?" Hope asked.

The door of the Inn opened, and Jane descended the front steps. The skirt of her floral printed dress flowed in the breeze created by her fast pace. "It's good you're still here, Hope."

"Only because I ran into Elaine."

"How did that go?" Jane asked.

"Never mind about Elaine." Drew rolled his eyes. "You won't believe what I found out."

Chapter Twenty-four

Hope followed Drew and Jane into The Coffee Clique. The morning rush had come and gone, leaving them with their pick of tables. Jane claimed one by slapping down her black purse and sitting, then gave her order to Hope.

Hope joined Drew at the counter, where he was studying the overhead menu. She pushed her sunglasses up into her hair. The overpriced, oversized shades had become her favorite accessory because she still looked like hell. Restless nights did that to a girl. The past few days haunted her like a bad movie. A yawn escaped. Whatever she ordered needed to be an extra-large.

There was a woman ahead of them placing her order. "A short café, no sugar, whipped cream, dry with half-skim and half-milk. Don't use two percent. A pump of peppermint, mix it with the milk," the woman said to the teenage boy behind the counter.

"What are you getting?" Drew asked.

Hope shrugged. French vanilla, hazelnut, raspberry aromas mingled in the air, dizzying her with endless possibilities. All of the choices overwhelmed her.

The woman ahead of them took her hot beverage and walked out of the shop. Hope and Drew moved up.

Still not sure what she wanted, she chose to start with Jane's order first. "I'll take a tea with a spot of milk." Hope moved up to the counter.

"Spot?" the teenager asked with a puzzled look.

Hope stared at the young man. He had no problem with the dry, half-milk-pump of peppermint woman, but an order of tea confused him? And what exactly was a dry coffee?

"It means a little amount," Hope said.

"Oh, why didn't you say so?" He reached for a mug.

"I did. I'll also take a large coffee with milk."

"More than a spot?" He laughed.

Hope nodded. "Please."

"Plain coffee? So boring. I'll have a double, extra frothy latte with cream and an apple muffin," Drew said. "I hit the gym this morning so I can splurge."

Hope paid for her beverages, picked up the cups, and walked back to the table. She sat and took a long drink of her coffee. Heaven. All that was missing was a cinnamon bun, but since she'd already indulged in one this week, she resisted diving into another.

"You look tired, dear. That horrible Morning Pete must have worn you out. Sally and I listened this morning. All he wanted to do was spread gossip to please his listeners. You don't need him." Jane sipped her tea.

"Do you want to hear what they said after you hung up?" Drew joined them at the table.

"No, I want to hear what had you practically running down Main Street."

"Technically, I wasn't running. Anyhoo, the stories cut out of the newspapers were all about a fatal hit-and-run accident eleven years ago in New Haven." Drew blew on his coffee before taking a sip.

"Terrible thing. A fifty-eight-year-old woman was crossing Church Street and was struck by a dark sedan. There were only a couple of witnesses, but they couldn't provide much detail. The driver never stopped, and the woman died right there on the road," Jane said.

Hope drank her coffee and considered what Drew and Jane had just said. The dots were finally connecting. "That woman was Peaches' mother."

Drew nodded enthusiastically. "Mary Beth McCoy. The detective on the case was Matt Royson, who is now a criminal defense attorney." He broke off a piece of his muffin and popped it into his mouth.

Hope pulled out her composition notebook and pen from her purse. It barely fit, but she didn't want to be without it. She opened it and flipped to an empty page.

"So, what do we know so far? Peaches' mother was killed by a hit-and-run driver. The lead detective on the case is now a lawyer, and Peaches was apparently in contact with him because we found his card in her address book. She was also texting him the day she died. She cut out articles about the accident from the newspapers. Then she went to an event she wasn't invited to and was murdered there." Hope jotted down those notes as they came to her.

"Quite a puzzle." Jane snatched a piece of Drew's muffin.

"Hey," Drew exclaimed.

Jane smiled as she chewed.

Drew returned his attention to Hope. "We're missing something."

"Yes. We're missing something. It has to be . . . do you think it's possible the driver of that car eleven years ago was at the garden tour?" Hope asked.

Drew straightened up and his eyes widened. "I think you're on to something."

"Yet, nobody knew she was going to show up. Back to square one. This is so frustrating. We have information, but it doesn't seem to fit together." Hope let out a sigh and put her pen down. She sipped her coffee and thought. She was so close to an answer, but nothing made sense, nothing went together. All the pieces of the puzzle were right in front of her, yet a piece or two seemed to be missing. She just needed to find those pieces to complete the puzzle.

"Complete. Finish. That's it," Hope murmured.

"What did you say, dear?" Jane asked.

Hope looked up from her notebook. "Closure. Gilbert told me Peaches had finally found closure in her mother's death. How do you find closure in a cold case?"

"By finding the person responsible." Jane wiped

her hands with a napkin. She'd eaten the remaining half of Drew's muffin.

Hope's eyes widened and she pointed her index finger at Jane. "Exactly. Peaches found out who the driver of that car was."

"And the driver found out she knew," Drew surmised.

"So he or she killed Peaches to keep the secret," Jane said.

Hope nodded with excitement. They were right. "Now we just have to find out who that person is."

"This person seemed intent on keeping his or her identity a secret, hence murdering two people to do just that," Jane said.

"I'll do some more research on the hit-and-run," Drew said.

"We need to take a step back and look at everything we know. Let our subconscious do its job," Jane suggested.

"I wish Detective Reid would follow your advice. He seems determined to make sure Claire goes to prison for the murders. I mean, if none of this is clear to us, how could it possibly be clear to him? The man has tunnel vision." Hope raised her cup for another sip.

Drew cleared his throat and gestured for Hope to turn around. He was trying to tell her something.

"He's behind me, isn't he?" she whispered.

Drew and Jane nodded in unison.

Hope looked over her shoulder. The detective was standing there with a smirk and a large coffee cup. She quickly closed her notebook and slipped it back into her purse.

"Good morning. It's a beautiful day, isn't it?" He lifted his cup and took a sip.

"Yes, it is," Jane said.

"I hope the three of you aren't still investigating the murders. Our police station has small accommodations, and I'd hate to arrest all three of you for interfering in official police business. You might feel cramped."

"Thank you for your concern. However, we're just having a friendly conversation about what a beautiful day it is and what our plans are." Hope doubted Detective Reid wanted to hear the actual details of their discussion. Though he probably heard her last comments about the investigation. She cringed inwardly.

"That's correct, Detective. I have to get back to the Inn," Jane said.

"I have an interview lined up over at the middle school about the Spring Fling dance." Drew pulled back his empty plate from Jane and pouted.

Detective Reid nodded, seemingly pleased by their plans. "And what about you, Ms. Early? What will you be up to today?"

Hope locked onto his gaze. "I'll be meeting with a lawyer."

For the past two years Hope had had the task of meeting with various attorneys, due to her divorce, expanding her blog into a full-fledged business, and buying her new home. She'd signed her name on countless legal documents, written obscenely large checks, and gotten on a first-name basis with several legal secretaries. However, none of those secretaries were as friendly as the one in Matthew Roydon's office.

"You were cheated. You should have won *The Sweet Taste of Success.* That marble cheesecake you made had me drooling," Stacey, the energetic secretary, said from behind her desk.

"That's very kind of you to say." With any luck, engaging in pleasant small talk with her new friend would get her into Roydon's office just a few feet away.

"Tell me, just between us, was Olivia Dunn really such a diva?" Stacey's blue eyes were wide with curiosity. Everyone loved gossip and behind-the-scenes tidbits.

Hope considered for a moment before answering. She'd learned quickly during her time in the spotlight that a few ill-chosen words could become a viral sound bite in a heartbeat.

"Olivia had her moments. You know, it's a very stressful situation to be in. I'm sure someone else on the show believed I had diva moments." Luckily Hope's meltdowns weren't caught on camera, unlike the winner of *The Sweet Taste of Success.*

Lauren Temple had many meltdowns and the producers ate up her drama. She knew how to command attention just as well as she knew how to proof bread dough.

Stacey shook her head. "You were one of the best bakers on the show. Milton was awesome, too. But that Lauren chick sure knew how to work the camera and the judges. No one stood a chance against her. If she ever decided to change careers, she should be a trial lawyer."

Hope laughed. She could envision Lauren doing

battle with a prosecutor and charming the jury. "That sounds perfect for her."

"I'm sorry. Here I am talking your head off about your show, and you're here to see Mr. Roydon. Lucky for you, his trial got postponed so he's available. Let me tell him you're here." Stacey disappeared into the back office and returned a few moments later. She led Hope into the lawyer's office.

"Good afternoon, Ms. Early." Matthew Roydon came around from behind his desk. Over six feet tall, he had intense caramel eyes and broad shoulders that filled out his tailored suit nicely.

"Thank you for seeing me on such short notice." Hope took the seat Mr. Roydon gestured to in front of his impressive desk. Could she get the ex-cop turned lawyer to cooperate with her? Seated, she inhaled a deep breath to calm the butterflies flittering around in her stomach. The worst he could do was ask her to leave. Right?

"What can I do for you?" Mr. Roydon returned to his tall leather chair and rested his forearms on the desk.

"I'm here about Peaches McCoy," Hope said.

Mr. Roydon leaned back. "I'm not sure how I can assist you."

"You are aware she was murdered."

"I am." Mr. Roydon's facial expression didn't change. There was no sign of grief or sadness. He had a good poker face, which Hope guessed came in handy at trial.

"Were you representing her in a criminal matter?"

"I'm unable to answer that question."

Hope nodded. Darn attorney-client privilege. It was time to move on to her second theory.

"You were the detective on her mother's case eleven years ago."

"Where are you going with this, Ms. Early?"

Hope shifted in her seat. Those butterflies that fluttered earlier were swirling around violently in her stomach like a tornado. She wasn't in an acquaintance's home asking questions, she was sitting in a lawyer's office asking about a cold case he couldn't close. She'd definitely upped the ante in her amateur sleuthing.

"I think there's a chance her mother's death had something to do with her murder. Peaches was texting you the day she died."

His brows arched as he leaned forward. "How do you know that?"

"That's not important. Do you know why she would cut out articles about her mother's fatal accident from newspapers?"

"I have no idea."

"Do you know Lionel Whitcomb?"

"What exactly is it you do, Ms. Early?" he asked pointedly.

"I'm a blogger."

"Crime blogger?"

Hope shook her head. "No, lifestyle and food blogger. I mostly blog about food. Recipes, entertaining tips, things like that." Whatever credibility she had when she walked into the office was now gone. Most people didn't understand blogging and thought it only a hobby for people who were tech geeks, anti-social, or bored.

Mr. Roydon pushed back his chair and stood, which confirmed Hope's fear. "I'm sorry. I really am busy. I don't have time for your fishing expedition."

Hope shimmied to the edge of her seat. She wasn't going to be thrown out of his office, not when she knew he had some information that could ultimately help Claire. She just needed to convince him to share that information.

"I really think there's a connection. Is there anything you can tell me about Mrs. McCoy's murder eleven years ago?"

"It is officially a cold case with no active leads."

"How does a woman get run down on a busy street and nobody sees the driver?"

Mr. Roydon shrugged. "Good question." He moved back to his chair and sat down. Hope sensed his reluctance to talk, but it appeared he would. "It was very late. Mrs. McCoy was on her way home from her cleaning job at a medical practice. There weren't cameras everywhere like now. How does any of this concern you?" His voice softened, and his gaze on her was no longer suspicious. He looked genuinely concerned.

Hope took a deep breath. It felt like a heavy weight was lifted from her shoulders. She wasn't being tossed out and maybe she could get some answers.

"My sister is suspected in Peaches' murder and possibly in a second murder."

Mr. Roydon nodded. "I heard about another woman being murdered."

"Did Peaches ever mention Vanessa Jordan's name to you?"

"No, not that I recall."

"Vanessa was my assistant, and she was present the day Peaches was murdered. It doesn't take a rocket scientist to see that those murders are connected, and the police are focused on my sister."

Mr. Roydon leaned forward again and clasped his hands on his desk. "It sounds like your sister needs an attorney more than she needs a sister investigating on her own."

"Point taken," Hope agreed.

"But I have a feeling you're not the type of person who can sit around and do nothing. You have to do something. Am I right?" His gaze fixed on her with precision.

Hope cleared her throat to buy time so the tingly, warm feeling shooting through her body had time to settle down. She blinked to break their eye contact. "Yes . . . yes, you're right."

Mr. Roydon tipped his head before he plucked a business card out of the holder, then stood and walked around his desk. "Peaches and I kept in contact over the years. There are some cases a cop can't let go of, and her mother's case was that one for me. Mrs. McCoy was a nice lady who worked hard to keep a roof over her daughter's head. She deserves justice."

"Did you meet with Peaches in Jefferson the day before her murder?"

"Ms. Early, you shouldn't be investigating real crimes."

Hope ignored his warning. He wasn't the first to caution her, and she doubted he would be the last.

"I think Peaches was looking for justice for her mother."

"In Jefferson?"

Hope nodded. "It's possible."

"But unlikely. If the police couldn't track down the driver of the car, I doubt Peaches could have." He handed Hope his business card. "Just in case your sister needs to hire an attorney. Or if you find yourself in trouble for interfering in a police investigation." He grinned before pushing away from his desk. "It was a pleasure meeting you. Have a nice day, Ms. Early." He flashed a smile, no doubt the same smile he used on jurors to win a lot of cases.

Hope stood, a little dazed by the abrupt ending of their conversation, but he must have a lot of work to do and she did show up without an appointment. She walked to the opened door and exited with a soft, "Thank you for your time."

As the door close behind her, she remembered Mr. Roydon wasn't the only person with a lot of work to do. With Vanessa gone, Hope was behind on everything, and chasing leads that were dead ends weren't helping with her to-do list.

"Did Mr. Roydon speak with you about the retainer?" Stacey asked as Hope walked out into the reception area.

"Huh? Oh, no, I'm not retaining Mr. Roydon. Actually, I don't need a lawyer. I wanted to ask him about Peaches McCoy." Hope hitched her purse over her shoulder. If her luck turned around, she wouldn't hit traffic on the drive back to Jefferson.

"You knew Peaches?" Stacey stood and walked around her desk.

"Yes. Actually, I found her . . ."

Stacey's shocked look told Hope nothing more needed to be said. Stacey appeared to be a sharp gal, so she was able to fill in the blanks.

"How horrible. I can't imagine." Stacey moved over to the small waiting area that consisted of a sofa and coffee table. She straightened the stacks of magazines sprawled out on the table.

"Did you ever meet Peaches?"

Stacey nodded. "Sure. She came in here a lot. She had a connection with Mr. Roydon. You know he was a detective who worked her mother's case. It's cold. No leads. No nothing."

"There were no suspects?"

"I don't think so. Mr. Roydon hates unanswered questions. I can tell you Mrs. McCoy's death eats at him. For a while, Peaches seemed to be doing better. You know, she'd moved on with her life and built a successful career. Then out of the blue she packed up and moved to Jefferson. She left the real estate team she'd built from the ground up to start all over. It didn't make sense."

"She never said why she made such a big change in her life?" Hope asked.

"No, guess it will remain a mystery. At least for us. She was really close to one other agent. Betsy . . . Betsy Callahan. That's her name. She was the first agent to join Peaches on her team. I hope the police find her killer. It would be a shame to have both murders unsolved." The telephone rang, and Stacey excused herself.

Hope agreed. And if she had anything to do with it, the murders wouldn't remain a mystery. She'd see to that.

Chapter Twenty-five

After an online search for real estate agent Betsy Callahan, Hope entered a spacious two-bedroom penthouse overlooking Long Island Sound and spied Peaches McCoy's protégée. Hope recognized her from the photograph on the sign in the lobby, announcing the open house. A handsome woman, Betsy worked the room like the pro she was. She exuded the same confidence Peaches had and made small talk easily with strangers. Betsy glanced over and spotted Hope.

Like a predator zeroing on its prey, she disengaged from the small group of people that surrounded her. They dispersed into various areas of the apartment, while Betsy made her way to Hope with stealth precision.

The impeccably polished woman extended her hand to Hope and dove right into her opening pitch. "Welcome to the Bayview and its crown jewel. I'm Betsy Callahan, and this is fourteen hundred square feet of luxe living with magnificent views and a private terrace. Full amenities included."

"It certainly is breathtaking." Hope removed her hand from Betsy's firm grip. "Actually, I'm not in the market. I've just purchased a new home."

"Oh," Betsy's hopeful expression soured as she took back her hand. "Well, then how can I help you?" She glanced over her shoulder, no doubt checking to see if any of the potential buyers needed her assistance to write up an offer.

"I'm here to speak to you about Peaches McCoy," Hope said. "She was murdered a few days ago."

"Yes, I know. I was shocked when I heard."

"I'm hoping you can help me."

"Who are you?" Betsy's voice tightened with irritation.

"Hope Early. I knew Peaches." It wasn't exactly a lie. She did have a nodding acquaintance with the late real estate agent. "I have reason to believe her death is connected to her mother's fatal hit-and-run eleven years ago."

"Seriously? Look, I'm a little busy here. So, if you don't mind—"

"Oh. My. Goodness. Hope Early!" a high-pitched voice called out from across the well-staged living room.

Hope lifted her head and saw a tall woman clad in animal print from head to toe and blinged out from her earlobes to her slender fingers. She rushed over to Hope and grabbed her hand and pumped it sharply.

"It's really you. I can't believe it. You were my favorite on that show. I can't believe I'm meeting a celebrity. Do you live in this building? Oh. My. Goodness. If I buy this apartment, could I be living next to a celebrity?"

"Celebrity?" Betsy's interest in Hope piqued again.

The woman cast a confused look at Betsy. "You don't know who Hope Early is? Do you live under a rock?"

"Of course I know." Betsy gave a nervous laugh.

"Betsy was just helping me with something, weren't you?" Hope grinned widely because the bordering-on-rude real estate agent had to help her now.

"Right. I'm happy to help in any way I can. And if you don't mind, Mrs. White, I just need a few moments to speak with Hope privately."

"Sure. No problem. I'm going to finish looking around. I do love this place. Before I forget," the woman dug into her quilted leather purse and pulled out a business card. "My husband is a dentist, and I'm sure you'll love him. He does a lot of famous teeth." She handed the card to Hope and then walked away.

"Thank you." Hope shoved the card into her purse as her fan walked away.

"Now, what can I do for you, Ms. Early?" Betsy asked all sweet and nice now that she believed Hope was somebody important.

Hope hated to admit it, but the little bit of celebrity status that appearing on *The Sweet Taste of Success* gave her did help every now and then. And it helped with Betsy Callahan. The woman didn't want to be bothered by Hope Early, one of Peaches' friends, but when she realized she was talking to Hope Early, the celebrity, the woman was practically falling over herself to be helpful.

Hope shook off her irritation. "Do you know why Peaches left her successful business and moved to Jefferson to take a job at a small real estate office?"

Betsy shrugged. "No. She called me into her office one morning and told me she was closing her business. Just like that."

"You had no idea?"

"I wish I had. That would have put me in a better position. I hate being blindsided. But I guess she decided there was more to life than making a deal."

"Why do you say that?"

"About six months prior to her closing up shop and moving out to the country, she joined a gym and started going every day. I guess she got on some health kick that ballooned into a complete life change."

"Going to the gym was out of the ordinary for her?"

"Yes. Peaches hated working out. I have no idea how she stayed so slim." Betsy's voice held a hint of envy. "You know, what was really strange was the gym she joined was so far from her condo and from her office. That didn't make sense to me since there was a fitness center down the street from her building."

Could Peaches' move to Jefferson have been just what Betsy thought it was, a life change? Could it have been that simple and it had nothing to do with her mother's fatal accident? Could the clo-

sure Peaches had experienced have been accept-
ing that the driver of the car would never be identified?

"Is there anything else you can remember?"
Hope asked.

Betsy shook her head. "I'm sorry. I can't." She
leaned forward and in a low voice asked, "What
show are you on?"

"Oh, she mistook me for someone else. Have a
nice day." Hope fought back a smile at the woman's
obvious disappointment. She spun around and swiftly
exited the pricey apartment.

Flowers weren't the only things springing up as
the season changed. Signs for tag sales popped up
all over the place. Hope loved tag sales and had a
hard time passing one up. They were perfect for
finding treasures that could be lovingly restored or
used for props for photographs on her blog. She
rarely left a tag sale empty-handed. Taking the
back roads home to Jefferson, Hope could stop at
any tag sale that looked like she could get a few
good deals. Twenty minutes into her drive home,
she spotted a series of handmade signs that led her
to a raised-ranch house. She parked and got out.
There was decent activity at the tag sale, especially
over in the area where toys were grouped. Little
ones tried out the toys, while their moms calcu-
lated how much they would offer. Negotiating at
tag sales was an art.

Hope picked up a blue-and-white pitcher to
check the price sticker on the bottom. Ten dollars.
The pitcher wasn't a traditional Blue Willow pat-

tern and wasn't necessarily old, but it would make
a nice addition to her ever-growing collection of
blue-and-white accessories. But ten dollars was too
much for one item. She scanned the table, which
was set lengthwise up the driveway, and she spotted some other pieces she was confident she could
bundle together for a reasonable offer.

With her decision made to purchase the blue-
and-white pitcher, four crystal candlestick holders,
and a large tarnished copper pot, Hope made an
offer to the home owner that was accepted without a
counteroffer. While she loved finding diamonds in
the rough, she really didn't like haggling. The home
owner was kind enough to wrap the candlestick
holders, and Hope then packed up all the items in a
collapsible crate she kept in the back of the car.

She opened the cargo area door and slid in the
crate. She nestled it close to the two other filled
crates from a few earlier stops. She scored some
good deals.

Sifting through bins of kitchenware, searching
through home accessories, and browsing through
old books was a welcome distraction from her
meetings with Matt Roydon and Betsy Callahan.

She couldn't call either meeting a success. They
were more like a waste of time. Though, she did
have Roydon's card in case she or Claire needed
his services. He might not have been far off base
with his offer, at least for her representation. Because if Detective Reid found out about her visits
to Roydon and Callahan, he might very well consider her interfering with his investigation. Yes, it
would be a good idea to keep the charming attorney's number handy.

At a four-way-stop intersection, another tag sale sign was tacked to a utility pole. She glanced at the clock on her dashboard. She smiled. There was time for one more stop. Flicking on her blinker, she made a turn and followed the signs to another nearby sale. As she drove by the house, there was still quite a bit of inventory out so she found a spot on the side of the road to pull over. Parked, she grabbed her purse and got out of her rental car.

Hope browsed, but at the first few tables nothing caught her eye. Unlike Matt Roydon. That realization brought Hope to a halt, and another realization hit her. Those butterflies in her stomach had nothing to do with the investigation but more to do with the fact Matt Roydon was a very good-looking man. *Whoa.*

"Are you looking for anything particular?"

The female voice jogged Hope out of her thoughts. She looked over in the direction of the voice and found a young redhead holding a baby and with a toddler clutched to her leg.

"No, I'm just browsing."

"Take your time. Let me know if you have any questions." The mom walked away with her children.

Hope had a lot of questions and none of them could be answered at the tag sale. The question that nagged at her now was what was going on with her? She had feelings for Ethan, feelings she believed was love, but she also found Matt very attractive. So attractive she had butterflies in her stomach like a silly teenage girl when she met him.

Just as she was about to turn around and head back to the car, something caught her eye. She made a beeline to a back table. A collection of rolling pins.

One was a thick, mahogany rolling pin. She lifted it and felt the heft of its weight. Perfect. The others were of various shapes and condition. The mahogany rolling pin was the one she wanted. She decided to make an offer for all of them. Together they'd make a good photograph.

"You found something?" The young mom approached without her children in tow.

"How much for all of them?" Hope set the large rolling pin down.

"They were my grandma's. She loved to bake. I just don't have the time, you know? How does ten dollars sound for all of them?

Hope looked up and noticed dark circles around the young woman's eyes. Hosting a tag sale wasn't an easy task. There was a lot of prep work and then there was the cleanup. Add two kids under the age of three and it was a recipe for exhaustion. She wasn't going to haggle with the woman. In fact, she was getting a bargain.

"Ten dollars sounds good." Hope paid and then gathered up her new rolling pins. She placed them in the cargo area of her SUV. As she closed the cargo door, her cell phone rang. She pulled it out of her purse and saw her brother-in-law's name. She swiped the phone on. "Hey, what's up?"

"Claire's been arrested," Andy said.

Her stomach plummeted. Her breath caught in her throat, as if she'd been punched right in the gut. "How . . . how can that be? She's innocent."

"I don't know where you are, but you need to get back here now. I'm at the courthouse. We're making bail now. And then I'm taking her home."

"I'm on my way. I'll be there soon." Hope

swiped her phone off, got into her car and started the ignition. What the hell was Ethan thinking? How could he let Detective Reid do something so clearly wrong? The time they wasted arresting Claire meant they weren't looking for the real killer. She'd go straight to Claire's house and do her best to avoid Ethan because she didn't want another murder in Jefferson.

Hope dropped her purse on her kitchen island, rested her hands on the countertop, and inhaled several deep breaths. How could Claire have been arrested? It was insane that people believed Claire murdered two women she barely knew, in cold blood. Insane that a judge set bail rather than toss the outrageous charges. Insane. Just insane.

Another deep breath.

Just as Hope had crossed the Jefferson town line, Andy had called her to let her know Claire had taken a sleeping pill and gone to bed. Disappointed she wouldn't see her sister, Hope decided to continue to their house so she could see Andy and the kids. She wanted to hold them, let them know everything was going to be okay, despite the terrible mistake the police had made.

She made sure they had a good dinner before leaving. It wasn't a surprise when the meal she prepared was barely eaten. Everyone was too worried to have an appetite. She pushed herself away from the island and filled the teakettle. She wanted something warm, comforting, but she didn't need any caffeine. She figured it would be difficult enough to sleep without any added stimulation.

With the kettle filled, Hope set it on a stove burner and turned on the flame. While pulling out a mug from an upper cabinet, there was a knock on the back door, followed by the door opening. Ethan appeared.

The sight of him infuriated her, yet she had an urge to run into his arms. Rather than react, she pulled out another mug and set them both on the island.

"May I come in?" he asked with hesitation.

"Guess so." She hoped her tone didn't reveal either of her warring emotions.

"I'm probably the last person you want to see tonight, considering what happened today." He closed the door behind him and cautiously approached the island.

What did he expect her to do to him? After all, he was the one wearing the gun. A quick glance to her left reminded her she had a fully stocked knife block at her disposal. Maybe he was worried about that.

"Detective Reid would be a close second," Hope snapped.

"For what it's worth, Claire has a very good attorney."

She glared at him. "She wouldn't need a good attorney if she hadn't been arrested. I don't understand why she was arrested. You said you believe she's innocent."

"I do. But my job isn't about what I believe. It's about where the evidence takes us during an investigation. And it's taken us to Claire."

The kettle whistled and Hope poured hot water

into the mugs, then dropped a tea bag into each. "What evidence?"

"She and Ms. McCoy had a competitive relationship, Claire sent her threatening text messages, and Vanessa's laptop was found in the trunk of Claire's car."

"What?" She set the kettle down on a trivet with a thump. "That's not possible."

"We found it there. Though the hard drive was missing."

"Missing? So somebody stole the computer the night Vanessa was murdered and removed the hard drive, then planted it in Claire's car?"

"Our working theory is Claire did that."

"Please, Claire isn't a computer geek. She couldn't possibly remove a hard drive. She barely knows how to operate her refrigerator." The remodel of Claire's kitchen a year ago included a fancy refrigerator complete with a command center that allowed for home owners to create a shopping list, send photos, and listen to music. Claire barely knew how to work the ice machine in the freezer door. She'd never figure out how to remove a hard drive from a computer.

Ethan walked around the island to Hope. He reached out to her, but she pulled back. "I understand how you feel."

Hope placed her hands on her hips. Since Andy's call earlier, she'd felt helpless and out of sorts. Her sister was arrested, fingerprinted, and arraigned. It was surreal, like an out-of-body experience. A wave of emotion threated to undo her. But she wouldn't surrender to the fear that penetrated every fiber of her body. That was what the killer wanted and she had no intention of accommodating him or her.

"You have no idea how I feel. My only sister was arrested for crimes she didn't commit after you told me you believe she's innocent."

"Hope, you have to understand. I said that as your friend. But as the police chief, I have to—"

"Follow the evidence, I know." On any other day, she would have found comfort in Ethan's presence, but he now represented the cause of the pain that touched every part of her body. He couldn't be her rock. Not that day.

"I think I should go." Worry creased his forehead and regret flashed in his eyes.

"You should" was the only thing she could say in response.

He lowered his gaze and shook his head. He turned and walked out of her kitchen. An instant reflex to chase after him was tamped down by the heaviness of fear. More fear than she'd felt when she was forced off the road or when she was grabbed right there in her kitchen a few days earlier by an intruder. When she left New York to move back home, she believed she'd lost everything. She hadn't. She still had her sister, who was an anchor for Hope. A fun-loving, shoe-buying, loyal, and loving anchor in the middle of Hope's stormy love life and shattered career. If she couldn't prove Claire was innocent, then she would lose everything that truly mattered in her life.

Chapter Twenty-six

"You do know I heard you need to register them. Something about protecting everyone from bird flu." Gilbert Madison stood in the open doorway of the barn. He'd been out for his morning walk with Buddy when they stopped by for a visit.

"Yes, I heard." Hope wiped her hands on a towel. She appreciated Gilbert's diligence of keeping up with the legal aspects of owning chickens, but she wasn't in the mood for the chitchat. Up at the crack of dawn, she wanted to finish her chores and get over to Claire's house as soon as possible.

Helga and her peeps, yes—Hope knew it was a bad joke, but she couldn't resist—were fed and watered. It was the fastest feeding she'd ever done. An urge to spend as much time with Claire as possible drove her to breaking all previous time records. She gave herself a mental shake because she needed to stop thinking like that. Claire wasn't going anywhere.

Just like Gilbert, apparently. "Never thought we'd have to worry about bird flu."

Buddy slid down into a relaxed position on the barn floor. Great, he wasn't going anywhere, either.

"I'm sorry, Gilbert. I have to get going. I need to get over to Claire's." Hope started walking toward the barn door.

Gilbert shook his head. "I heard what happened yesterday. I'm sorry."

"Thank you." Hope closed the chicken-coop door and pulled off her work gloves.

"If there's anything we can do, please don't hesitate to let us know. Give Claire our best." Gilbert whistled and Buddy stood, and they both turned and headed to the road.

Hope followed them out of the barn, pulling closed the barn door behind her. Back in her house, she'd changed into a floral skirt and cardigan and slipped into a pair of ballet flats. She grabbed her purse and a canvas bag filled with ingredients for an egg casserole and a loaf of rustic white bread she had made the night before. Kneading the dough allowed her to get her frustrations out. She had a feeling she'd be baking a lot of bread in the coming days.

When Hope arrived at Claire's, she entered through the back door and found Evelyn, the housekeeper, unloading the dishwasher. On the surface, it looked like any other morning she arrived at her sister's home. She would exchange small talk with Evelyn as she passed through the kitchen to find Claire. But it wasn't like any other morning. Yesterday her sister was arrested for murder and had to post bail. She shook her head in disbelief. She still couldn't understand how that had happened.

Perhaps it was because Detective Reid was looking to close his case quickly. Arrest Claire, slap two murder cases closed, and head home for dinner. He probably had a good night's sleep believing the murderer had been caught. She doubted he considered for one minute he was wrong.

"Good to see you, Hope." Evelyn closed the dishwasher.

Hope dropped her purse and the canvas tote bag on the counter. "How is everyone?"

Evelyn shrugged. "The kids are really quiet. Your sister and Mr. Dixon are with the attorney."

An attorney that made house calls? His retainer must cost a fortune. "I'm going to start breakfast." Hope began unpacking the groceries and Evelyn made a quick exit to do laundry, allowing Hope to settle into the kitchen.

Cooking was Hope's center. It was where she went when life got out of balance. The mixing, the stirring, the measuring, it all calmed her. A dash here, a pinch there kept her focused on the task at hand so her mind couldn't replay over and over the problem she was trying to work through. Sometimes she veered off a recipe, sometimes she followed it exactly. Either way, what mattered was that when she was in the kitchen, she was in control and nothing could defeat her. By the time she was cleaning up, whatever her problem was usually seemed so much smaller and conquerable. Hope's mind was clearer, she had a plan of action to attack the problem, and she had something to eat. Win, win.

After cracking a dozen eggs, Hope whisked them vigorously, adding pinches of salt and a couple cracks of pepper from Claire's ginormous pepper mill. She then added a handful of chopped herbs. Once the eggs were beaten, she tore apart the loaf of bread.

"Ms. Early, what are you doing here?" a familiar deep voice said.

Hope looked over her shoulder. Her eyes bulged. What was Matt Roydon doing in Claire's kitchen? After the shock faded, she realized he was Claire's lawyer.

She set the loaf of bread down and grabbed a towel to wipe her hands. "I'm Claire's sister. I came over to make breakfast for my family. Are you her lawyer?"

He nodded. "I was retained by your brother-in-law. Thank you for giving him my card."

"I didn't." She studied Mr. Roydon. He looked competent. Hope recalled the diplomas on his office wall, but she didn't look close enough to see where he graduated from. At the time, she was a little distracted by his charming smile.

"Is my sister aware you were acquainted with Peaches?" She wasn't sure if there was some kind of conflict of interest since he knew one of the murder victims.

He grinned. Now he looked a little sexy. She needed him to look competent. Competent wasn't distracting.

"I disclosed my history with Peaches. I don't expect there to be any complications."

"Good." Satisfied he was transparent with her sister, Hope returned to putting together the egg casserole. She spread the large chunks of bread in the baking dish.

He moved farther into the room, closer to Hope. "I'm glad I have your approval. And you can call me Matt."

She glanced up. His grin had expanded into a charming smile, and his caramel eyes were a touch warmer than they had been the day before when they first met.

"I'm curious about how you plan on getting the charges dismissed." Hope lifted the mixing bowl and poured the egg mixture over the bread. She scraped the bowl until it was clean and then she set it in the sink. She sprinkled more herbs on top, lifted the dish, and scooted over to the oven.

"Let me." Matt opened the oven door.

"Thanks." Hope slid the dish onto the rack. She closed the door, set the timer, and returned to the counter to clean up. "So when you do you think you'll get those charges dismissed?"

"It's not that simple."

"She's innocent. She didn't murder anyone."

"I have a private investigator that works for me. I'm bringing him in on this."

Hope wiped down the counter with a sponge. "I have a theory."

He cocked his head sideways. "You do?"

"Yes, I do. There's no statute of limitations on murder, is there?"

Matt shook his head. His sandy blond hair was thick and neatly trimmed. His tailored gray blazer fit him perfectly, accentuating his masculine curves—broad shoulders, lean mid-section, and muscled arms. Why couldn't her brother-in-law have hired a paunchy, middle-aged lawyer? "No, there isn't."

"Just what I thought. I believe the person who killed Mary Beth McCoy was present at the garden tour and killed Peaches because he or she was worried what Peaches knew and would tell the police."

"I seem to recall you're a lifestyle and food blogger. Mostly food, though."

Hope tossed the sponge in the sink. "Yes, I am."

"Then perhaps you should focus on that and leave your sister's case to me and my professional investigator."

"Well, so far this murder investigation has been left to presumably the ultimate in investigators, the police, and somehow my sister was arrested. I know I'm not a professional, but I believe my theory is plausible, and the police should look into it." Hope opened a deep drawer and pulled out a handful of coffee pods. She dropped them into a basket and set it on the island.

"You're correct. You're not a professional investigator."

Hope ignored Matt's reaffirmation of what she wasn't as she set four coffee mugs next to the basket. She knew her capabilities and limitations and how far she was willing to go to prove her sister innocent. "There is also another theory."

"Do tell."

Hope glanced up and saw the look of amusement on Matt's face. She stifled her irritation because she needed his cooperation. "It's possible Peaches was caught up in some kind of illegal real estate dealings."

"Please, Hope, stop."

"Stop? No! My sister's future is on the line. There are other theories beside professional jealousy."

"Let me do my job."

"Can you at least confirm you weren't representing Peaches in a criminal case?"

"If it will get you to stop playing detective, I will confirm I was not representing Peaches in a criminal matter."

Hope smiled. "Thank you. Now we can focus on my first theory, that the hit-and-run driver eleven years ago may have killed Peaches."

"The police have completed their investigation. As far as they're concerned, they've found their murderer."

Hope gasped. Hearing those words spoken about Claire stung. "Ethan doesn't believe Claire is the killer."

Matt arched his brows. "Chief Ethan Cahill told you that? When?"

"Last night."

"Are you and Chief Cahill involved?"

"No. No . . . Not like you're suggesting."

"But he was at your house last night and confided in you."

"I'm not involved with anyone. We're friends. That's all." A heat surge shot through her body, and she had no doubt her cheeks were red from embarrassment. Matt was a trained detective and criminal defense attorney. Surely he could tell when someone wasn't being completely honest. While she and Ethan weren't romantically involved, they were close. At the moment, she didn't know how to label their relationship. Could there even be hope for a romance if Claire was prosecuted and found guilty of the murders?

"Hope? Did I lose you?"

"What? I'm sorry. What were you saying?"

"I understand you want to help Claire, but for her sake, I strongly suggest you stay out of this. There's a chance you could do more harm than good. She needs your support. She needs her sister and her family around her. Let me do my job."

Hope was speechless. Sure, she and Claire were different as night and day in some ways, but they always had each other's back. So sitting on the sidelines and doing nothing wasn't possible.

"I don't think I can do what you're asking, Matt."

"Please do," Claire said.

Hope looked past Matt. Claire was standing in the doorway. She was dressed impeccably in a coral dress and nude pumps. Her makeup was applied flawlessly, and her hair was pulled back in a neat bun. Being arrested, fingerprinted, and arraigned hadn't dampened her fashion sense.

"What?" Hope was completely confused by the shift in strategy.

Claire walked to Hope and took her hands. "Matt's right. There's a chance any further snooping could be damaging to my defense."

"You want me to do nothing to help you?"

"Please don't twist my words around. I'm the big sister, and I'm telling you to stop investigating. Do you understand?"

Hope hated when Claire pulled the big sister

routine. All her life Claire used that line when she wanted to get her way.

"If that's what you want." Given the serious looks on both their faces, Hope didn't feel she had a choice. She'd do her best to follow their instructions.

"Thank you." Claire hugged Hope. "You know, he's single," she whispered in Hope's ear.

"Glad we're all on the same page," Matt said with a hint of satisfaction.

Claire let go of Hope and focused her attention on Matt. "Please stay for breakfast. We have plenty of food."

"I appreciate the invitation. I'd love to stay." Matt unbuttoned his blazer and loosened his tie.

"Hope is an excellent cook," Claire said to Matt.

Hope caught the glint in Claire's eyes. Even though she was facing murder charges, she was playing matchmaker for her little sister.

"Come on, get in," Drew shouted, waving to Hope as she dashed down the front steps of her porch.

She hurried to the waiting car and slid into the passenger seat.

"Are you sure about this?" Hope had returned home from Claire's an hour earlier when Drew called to let her know he'd tracked down one of the witnesses of Mary Beth McCoy's hit-and-run. Drew spent the night before poring through articles about the accident and got a name and an address. It was a long shot, but maybe the woman recalled something from the night of the accident.

"Yes. Cora Mason saw the accident. Are you sure you want to do this? Remember what you were told?"

Hope thought for a moment. Earlier she was told to stay out of the investigation by her sister and her lawyer. She should do that, especially since there was a risk of hurting Claire's case. But what if Cora Mason knew something that could shed light on the person responsible for Mary Beth's death and there really was a connection between the hit-and-run and the two murders Claire was accused of? Hope had to take that chance. She just had to be careful.

"I'm sure."

"Okay. I've programmed the address in my GPS, so let's get going." Drew pulled out of Hope's driveway and, within minutes, they were on the highway leading to Norwalk, a city along the Long Island Sound. Traffic was heavy in some spots, but they arrived at Cora Mason's home in good time.

The two-story brick colonial had a small fenced yard and a straight row of daffodils just about to bloom. Hope exited the car, and, with Drew behind her, they approached the front gate and unlatched it.

"Let me do all the talking. I have years of experience getting information out of people." Drew dashed around Hope on the short concrete path to the porch and jogged up the four steps.

"Okay."

"Miss Mason may be reluctant at first, but I'll get what we need." Drew pressed the doorbell.

"Okay." Hope joined Drew on the porch.

Heavy footsteps approached the other side of the door before it swung open and a large, older woman appeared in a bright orange velour jogging set. Her dark red hair was set in a messy updo and her lips were a deep shade of burgundy.

"What can I do you for?" the woman asked in a husky voice.

"My name is Drew Adams. I'm a reporter for *North Country Gazette.* I'm here to ask you about the hit-and-run accident you witnessed eleven years ago. Mary Beth McCoy was killed in that accident."

"Reporter? What the hell does a reporter want to know about that for? It happened so long ago." The woman's gaze drifted to Hope. "Wait a second, you're that baking woman from television. A Sweet . . . Sweet taste . . . Wait, it'll come to me." She snapped her fingers.

Hope stepped forward and extended her hand. "I am Hope Early. I was on *The Sweet Taste of Success.*"

Cora Mason's face lit up. "That's right, honey. That's who you are. I loved your scones. I printed the recipe and made them. Delish. Come, come inside." She grabbed Hope's arm and led her inside. "You can come too, reporter. Shut the door."

Hope tossed a glance over her shoulder to Drew. She did her best to suppress the smile that tugged on her lips. Drew might have had years of experience in interviewing people, but she had been on reality television. It was about time it actually paid off.

Cora led them to the living room, which was brightly furnished and had a large picture window with a view of the main road. A well-worn recliner was angled in front of the television and a fern hung from the ceiling.

"Sit, sit. Make yourself comfortable." Cora gestured for them to sit on the sofa while she settled into the recliner. "Awful thing that happened back then. The woman was just crossing the street and then bam! Just like that." She slapped her hands together. "She was roadkill."

Hope cleared her throat at Cora Mason's bad choice of words. "Can you tell us if you saw the driver?"

"Nah. It was too dark. All I saw were the headlights. Why are you asking? You knew that woman?" Cora asked.

"No, I didn't. I knew her daughter. She was killed a few days ago." Hope tried not to be disappointed, but it was understandable the incident was a blur to Cora. "Her daughter's name was Peaches McCoy. Did she ever contact you?"

Cora shook her head. "No, you two are the only ones who have asked about that night since it happened." Her attention drifted to Drew. "Those are some nice kicks." Cora gestured to his sneakers.

Drew beamed. "Thanks. Just got them." He stared at his platinum and light gray running shoes.

"Not worried they'll get dirty?"

"By the time they get dirty, it'll be time to replace them."

"Wait a minute." Cora straightened. "Wait one darn minute. Running shoes. That's right. I forgot all about them. Yeah, that's what I saw."

"What did you see?" Hope asked.

"White sneakers. I was far away and it was dark,

so I couldn't tell you who got out of the car, but the person was wearing white sneakers," Cora said.

"The driver got out of the car?" Drew asked.

"Sure did. Got out, walked to the lady on the road, bent down to check on her, then ran back to the car and drove off. It happened so fast. But the person wore white sneakers. Gosh, I can't believe I forgot that." Cora smiled proudly.

Hope looked at Drew and sensed the look on his face was a reflection of hers. Neither was pleased or disappointed. What Cora told them was something. It just wasn't enough to find the person responsible for Mary Beth's death.

They said their good-byes to Cora, who insisted on a photograph with Hope for her Facebook page before they left.

"Want to head back home?" Drew asked as they approached his car.

"Sounds good." Hope's phone buzzed and she pulled it out of her purse. She saw Corey's name and sighed. "What is it?"

"Heard what happened with your sister. I'm sorry for your troubles." He almost sounded sincere.

"Thank you," Hope said cautiously.

"I was thinking we could do a mini-series focused around you and your sister getting ready for trial."

"What? I'm not going to be a part of that. Don't you have any boundaries?"

"I work in reality television, what do you think?" Corey snorted.

"Ugh. Not interested. Good-bye." Hope returned her phone to her purse.

"What did he want?" Drew asked after sliding into the car on the driver's side.

"A reality show revolving around prepping for Claire's trial."

"May not be a bad idea. You could gain some sympathy."

"You, too? I'm surrounded by crazy. Look, Claire isn't going to trial because she's not the killer."

"That's right. Claire would never wear white sneakers."

Hope laughed. Her sister had a very detailed list of fashion-don'ts and she adhered to that list. White sneakers weren't her thing. Shoes. In a flash, she saw the black boot that skimmed her head after she'd fallen to the floor in her kitchen and her assailant walked by her. The boot was familiar. But why?

Chapter Twenty-seven

Two aspirins and a cold compress didn't help Hope's headache, which she realized was a result of not eating since breakfast. With little appetite, she grabbed a granola bar, then settled at the table with her composition notebook to record her notes.

On a blank sheet of paper, she wrote *white sneakers on driver* on one line.

Cora Mason had recalled the driver of the car, gender unknown, wore those sneakers. The hit-and-run occurred late at night, so wearing a pair of sneakers seemed odd. Maybe the person wasn't only a bad driver with no conscience but also had bad fashion sense.

Hope took a bite of the granola bar and chewed. She studied the note, and her mind wandered to her conversation with Betsy Callahan. She recalled what Betsy said about Peaches suddenly joining a gym.

On the next line, Hope wrote "unexpected gym membership."

She stared at the two lines, hoping the driver's name would suddenly appear, like it was some magical word game. No such luck. She finished her granola bar and got up to get a glass of water. When she returned to her seat, she looked at the two lines again. They were connected somehow.

She drew a curved arrow from the first line to the second line and then a curved line from the second line to the first. "Who wears sneakers?" Ah-ha!

"Someone who works out at the gym." Hope was willing to bet her fancy stand mixer that the gym Peaches joined was located near the location of the hit-and-run. Peaches was looking for the driver. Hope grabbed her phone and texted Drew. His research skills were far beyond hers, and he could find out if there was a gym in the area of the hit-and-run eleven years ago a lot faster than if she tried. He replied with a simple "NP."

While she waited for Drew to get back to her, she finished making the invitations to her house-warming party. She still had to work on the menu and the decorations. As she addressed the envelopes, a pang of guilt hit her. With two murders and her sister arrested and out on bail, should she really be planning a party? It seemed so frivolous, but, on the other hand, they all needed a distraction. Decision made. She would go forward with her party.

She heard the notification ring on her phone and found a new text message, but it wasn't from Drew. It was from Audrey. While Drew kept his

texts short and sweet, Audrey wrote epic text messages. Audrey had decided to step down as president of the Society to Protect Jefferson and was
pulling together a last-minute meeting of the
group, and she wanted Hope there as moral support. Surprised by her friend's sudden decision,
Hope didn't hesitate to reply she'd be right over.

When Hope arrived at Audrey's house, the driveway was packed with cars. It appeared most of the
membership of TSPJ had showed up for the announcement. Sally's car was there, which meant
Jane was there and she could fill her in on the visit
to Cora Mason. As Hope approached the front
door, she was joined by Drew.

"It took a little while, but I found at the time of
the hit-and-run there was a gym three blocks away.
It was called The Fit Center." He twisted the doorknob and entered the house.

"So, it's possible the driver of the car was coming from the gym when the accident happened
and that's why Peaches joined the gym." Hope followed Drew through the foyer into the living room,
where the members had gathered.

She spotted Sally and Jane on the sofa, while
Maretta sat on a chair with her purse on her lap.
Audrey was seated on another chair in front of the
fireplace so she would be in view of everyone. Meg
stood beside her while the rest of the members
were scattered throughout the room.

"We'll never be able to get a membership list
from so long ago," Drew whispered.

"I know. But I still think the driver was present
the day of the garden tour."

"We just need to find out who belonged to the

Fit Center way back then. I guess we can rule out the Merrifields." Drew cast a glance to the elderly sisters-in-law.

"I think that's a safe assumption."

"Then that leaves us with the rest of the guest list."

Hope nodded. "And we can't rule out Harrison since Cora Mason couldn't make out the gender of the driver."

"Or anybody else who could have slipped in through the door in the study," Drew said.

Hope sighed. Just when she thought they were narrowing down the list of suspects, it kept growing.

"Thank you for coming on such short notice." Audrey looked out to the small group of people gathered in her living room. TSPJ wasn't a large group, but they were committed and determined to preserve their town from overdevelopment.

"I feel now is the time to step down as president for personal reasons. Meg will become our new president, and we will hold an election for a new vice president in the coming weeks. I have no doubt each of you will support Meg in her new position just like you've supported me. Thank you for coming today."

There had been speculation Audrey would step down if she decided to run for mayor. By the knowing nods and murmurs of understanding, Hope didn't find anyone surprised by the announcement. So Hope wasn't sure why Audrey wanted her there for moral support.

Drew snapped a few photographs and broke

away from Hope to interview Audrey and Meg for his article. The crowd dispersed into the sunroom, where Audrey had set out refreshments. South facing, the room was bright with the afternoon sun streaming in and simply furnished as a space to enjoy the view of Audrey's garden. A long teak-wood table was set with a punch bowl, several beverage pitchers, and platters of crudité and small appetizers. Hope poured a glass of iced tea and took a sip. Audrey had pulled together a nice spread on such short notice.

"This is reminiscent of the garden tour, isn't it?" Jane helped herself to a stuffed mushroom.

"I hope not. That day ended with a murder. I'd prefer that not happen today." Hope glanced around the room and everyone seemed relaxed and chatty. From the snippets of conversation she heard, the topic of discussion was preservation business, not murder. No doubt everyone knew Claire had been arrested the day before, but none of them were going to be disrespectful and discuss it in her presence, at least.

"How are you holding up?" Sally filled up a plate of fresh fruit, heavy on the cantaloupe slices.

Hope shrugged. "I've been better. Claire has a lawyer and he seems to know what he's doing."

"That's good. Hang in there, kiddo." Sally squeezed Hope's arm and then walked away to join another group of members.

"Drew tracked down one of the witnesses to Mary Beth McCoy's hit-and-run," Hope told Jane.

Jane's eyes brightened. "And what did you learn?"

Hope filled Jane in on the visit and the only new

piece of information they had uncovered. Though the white sneakers weren't exactly the clue that would lead them to the driver of the car. She also recapped her visit to Betsy Callahan.

"I do agree with your theory that the driver of the car was here the day of the garden tour. We should go through the guest list," Jane said.

"Yeah, we're on that." Drew joined Hope and Jane. "Well, we can rule out you and me." Drew gestured to Hope. "We were both away at college."

"Thanks for clearing me," Hope said dryly.

"And you don't drive, Jane. But what about Sally?" Drew asked with a teasing grin.

"Drew!" Hope exclaimed and heads turned in her direction. She felt her cheeks heat; no doubt they were flaming red. She quickly faked a smile and waved a motion for everyone to continue as they were.

Drew chuckled. "What? I'm just ruling people out."

"Why don't we do this later?" Jane suggested.

Hope thought that was a good idea, and they agreed to discuss the guest list later in private. Drew drifted over to another group to interview while Jane joined Sally back in the living room. Hope marveled at Jane's confidence that everything would come together to reveal the true killer. But she had doubts. She didn't see how the pieces would come together when none of them seemed to fit.

"I know Audrey appreciates that you came." Meg joined Hope.

"She put her heart and soul into TSPJ. I'm sure

it's difficult for her to step down," Hope said cautiously.

"I'm going to take good care of TSPJ. I don't want Audrey to worry about a thing. She needs to focus on salvaging her book career and running for mayor. Now that Claire will be out of the race, Audrey is a shoo-in."

Meg's callous comment caught Hope off guard. Even for Meg it was a low blow. It sounded as if Meg had already convicted Claire. Hope glanced around the room. Was that why they were so quiet on the topic? They'd already convicted Claire, too?

"Don't count my sister out yet."

"Right, she wouldn't be the first criminal to run for office," Meg said.

"How dare you!"

But the smirk on Meg's face didn't disappear. "Face it, the luster of the Early girls has been tarnished." Meg chuckled and strutted away.

Hope stood there frozen, struggling to get her rapid breathing under control while her whole body trembled. She didn't want to cause a scene. So she chose not to follow Meg and tell her off.

"Alfred and I will do whatever we can to help Claire," a voice said from behind.

Hope turned around and found Maretta standing there with her arms crossed over her chest and her purse dangled from her wrist. Even her usual sour look appeared to have softened a touch. Hope was shocked Maretta chose not to pounce on Claire's situation but instead offered support. Hope didn't know what to say.

"Cat got your tongue?" Maretta asked.

"No, I . . . thank you for your support," Hope stammered. "I'll let Claire know."

"Be sure you do. And we would appreciate knowing if Claire plans on returning to work. We have a business to run." Maretta released her arms and marched away, disappearing down the hallway.

Now that was the Maretta Kingston Hope knew. The other warm and almost fuzzy one freaked Hope out.

"Hey, I'm heading out." Drew returned to Hope. "Are you okay?" He reached out and touched her arm.

The small gesture nearly dissolved Hope into a crying hot mess. "I . . . I'm okay. Just a little tired. I'm going to be leaving soon. Do you want to come over for dinner?" She didn't want to be alone because she knew the events of the past few days would replay over and over in her mind. Hanging out with Drew for dinner and maybe a chick flick would give her a few hours of peace.

"Sure. Call you later." Drew waved good-bye.

Twenty minutes later the other guests had left and Hope was cleaning up the sunroom. The simple task of filling the dishwasher was a relief from chasing down leads from an eleven-year-old cold case.

The kitchen door swung open and Audrey entered. "Thanks so much for coming over. I really appreciate it. You didn't have to clean up."

"Are you sure you want to step down from TSPJ?" Hope closed the dishwasher's door and set the wash cycle.

Audrey was the type of person who when she made a commitment stuck to it. Walking away from a cause she was passionate about wasn't like Audrey.

"I am. I won't have time for the group when I'm mayor. It'll be a struggle to balance the work as mayor and write my next book."

"Your next book? So everything worked out with your publisher?" Hope ripped a paper towel off its roll and wiped the countertop.

"Somehow, despite the disastrous book launch that ended with a murder, my publisher is on-board for another book. I think it's going to be about entertaining in the garden." Audrey's voice was serene, and happiness radiated from her. She truly appeared to be in her glory.

"That's great." Hope crumpled the paper towel. Just a few days ago Audrey's career was in limbo and now it was soaring. She always managed to land on top somehow. Her life was perfect, wasn't it?

"Calista is thrilled with the sales so far. In fact, the book is heading back for a second printing." Audrey clasped her hands together, and her smile was from ear to ear. She looked as if she was going to burst with happiness.

"Really?" Hope tossed the paper towel into the trash bin. She wanted to be happy for Audrey, join in her moment of joy, but she couldn't. Not with murder charges hanging over her sister's head. All Claire did was show up at a garden tour and her life was turned upside down, while Audrey seemed to be profiting from the tragedy.

"Looks like I didn't need your help after all." Audrey propped a hand on her hip, and her big smile was gone.

"What are you talking about?"

"Calista told me she asked you to do some stuff for me on social media and that you politely declined. But no hard feelings. We both have a brand to protect. I know I'd do anything to protect my brand. So I completely understand, and I forgive you."

Audrey's so-called forgiveness pricked at Hope. There was nothing to forgive. Hope wasn't responsible for Audrey's image. Audrey's publisher had a publicity department responsible for that. But, for some reason, Hope didn't think Audrey would agree with her, so it was time to leave.

"I'm glad everything worked out for you. I better get going." Hope began to walk toward the door. Her plan was to go home, soak in a warm bath, and drink a glass or two of wine. She'd definitely earned a little pampering after the week she'd had.

"Wait. I have a bag full of clothes for the church collection. It's in the study."

Hope stopped. Her shoulders slumped. She'd forgotten about the clothing. Twice a year the church had a clothing drive, and Hope volunteered to collect the unused clothing from her friends.

"I'll wait here while you go get it." Hope had no desire to go into the study again. In fact, she never wanted to walk around another person's house ever again.

Audrey laughed. "Don't be silly. You can go and get it. Harrison is over that whole incident. In fact, I think you should come over to dinner next week."

"I'd like that, but right now I can't make any plans." Hope wanted to be available for Claire, so she didn't want to make any commitments. "Can I let you know later?"

"Sure, no problem. Go get the bag so I can let Bigelow out of the garage."

Hope turned and breathed deeply. She could go into the room. It was only a room. There wouldn't be another body in there. And since Harrison was gone, there wouldn't be an angry, scowling man in there, either. She made her way down the hall to the study with a plan. The plan was to pop into the room, grab the bag, and get out. No lingering or snooping. Just in and out. Simple. Right?

She pushed open the door and entered the room and saw the large shopping bag stuffed full.

Work the plan. Grab the bag and leave. Fast.

She walked directly to the bag, no detours, no side glances, and lifted it. She was surprised by how heavy the bag was. What did Audrey donate? She was always very generous when going through her closet. Hope lifted the bag and she turned to leave the room; one of the handles of the shopping bag broke, and the bag fell to the floor, landing on its side, and a bunch of stuff spilled out.

Hope squatted to gather up the clothing. She was going to need another bag. There were several sweaters and blouses and a loafer had fallen out. As she refolded the clothing, stopping a couple of times to admire Audrey's good taste, she realized none of that stuff was heavy. So, what was in the bottom of the bag? She dug into the bag and pulled out the other match to the loafer and some more tops and at the very bottom there was a pair of Moto ankle boots. She pulled one out and studied the boot.

Just like the one she saw when the person who broke into her house attacked her.

Chapter Twenty-eight

Hope straightened, the black boot still in her hand. It had to be a coincidence. Audrey's boot just looked similar. Yes, that was what it was. Similar. Chasing suspects and leads had her imagination working overtime. Audrey wasn't a killer.

Audrey was a good friend. She was a good neighbor and a good citizen who contributed endless amounts of hours to their community. And she was present when Peaches was murdered. And she was the one who was getting rid of boots that looked like the pair worn by the person who attacked Hope in her home. And that person was probably the same person who tried to drive her off the road. That person had stolen a van from Wallace's and followed Hope from Elaine's house.

"How did Elaine's cooking lesson go?"

Hope's hand trembled. Audrey had asked about the cooking lesson the other morning. How did she know about it? Hope hadn't told her, and she

doubted Elaine mentioned it to Audrey. They
weren't exactly friends.

"I ran six miles after you left."

Could she have run to Wallace's and stolen the
van? It was only a couple of miles from Audrey's
house. For a serious runner like Audrey, that was
an easy run. Hope's heartbeat increased to a scary
rate as the craziest idea she'd ever thought of
could actually be true.

Hope dropped the boot onto the pile of clothes.
She wasn't thinking clearly. What Meg said to her
earlier and her own guilt for dragging Claire into
this mess was clouding her thoughts. There had to
be a logical explanation for how Audrey knew
about the cooking lesson and why she was donat-
ing a pair of boots that looked exactly like the pair
Hope saw when she was lying on the floor after
being attacked. And she was going to ask Audrey.

Before she stepped forward to go and find Audrey, she caught a glimpse of the storage box tucked
in the corner. The last time she had been in the office, there were newspapers on top of the box.
They were gone now. She went to the box, removed
the cover and saw the papers inside. She pulled
out the clippings. They looked like the shapes of
the missing sections of the newspapers Hope
found in Peaches' bedroom.

She read through the clippings. They were all
about the hit-and-run accident that killed Mary
Beth McCoy. A wave of nausea rolled through her.
She was going to be sick. Audrey was the driver
that fateful night. There wasn't any other explanation. She killed Mrs. McCoy then Peaches and
then Vanessa. Hope's breathing became shallow,

and her head spun with the realization that her friend was a cold-blooded killer.

Friends don't suspect friends of murder.

Elaine's words echoed in Hope's mind. She was right, and that was why Hope never suspected Audrey. They were friends. At least she thought they were.

"Ethan," she whispered. She needed to call him, to tell him what she'd discovered. But her cell phone was in her purse, which was in the living room. *Shoot.* She looked around and saw a telephone on the desk. She dashed over to the desk, reached for the receiver, and dialed 911.

"You were just supposed to pick up the bag and leave," Audrey said coldly.

Hope twirled around. Audrey was standing there holding a gun pointed at her.

"Put the phone down," Audrey gestured with the gun. "Now!"

Hope replaced the receiver on the telephone. Her stomach plummeted as everything came together. Now there was no doubt. "You're the killer? How could you kill those women?" She hoped this was all a misunderstanding. There had to be a logical explanation why her good friend was pointing a gun at her.

"I didn't have a choice," Audrey said, her voice cool and calm.

"Of course you did. Mary Beth's death was an accident. The police will understand. You didn't mean to kill her when you left the gym that night."

"How do you know that?"

"It doesn't matter. What matters is you didn't set out to harm anyone that night."

"I didn't," she said.

"Good, good. We can tell the police that." Hope wanted to make Audrey believe she was still her friend and she was going to look out for her. She would keep that ruse long enough to get the gun away from Audrey and have the police arrest her.

"I was scared. She came out of nowhere. I panicked. I checked on her, but she was dead." Her words were flat, as if she was detached from the event. "The scandal would have ruined everything for me. I was getting married the following week." A smile grew. "My mother had everything planned, and I couldn't disappoint her."

"I understand." Even though Hope's stomach churned and panic filled her, she forced herself to remain calm. She had to. She was face-to-face with a killer and she needed to find a way to escape. Maybe if she kept talking, she could find an opening to make that escape. But the gun aimed at her made her doubt her plan.

"No, you don't. You don't understand what it's like to have to live up to unreasonable expectations. My mother had high standards, just like Harrison does. I've done everything I could to not disappoint them. They would have been so disappointed in me if they found out I hit that woman and killed her."

If Audrey hadn't been a murderer, Hope would have felt sorry for her. Perfection came at a high cost, and Audrey always seemed to strive to be the perfect daughter, wife, home keeper, and gardener. She definitely seemed to ace being the perfect killer. Three murders and she showed no remorse.

"Why did you kill Peaches?" Hope asked.

"Because she finally tracked me down. She spent years searching for the driver of the car, and she found me. But first, she decided to taunt me. She began sending those clippings anonymously. Then notes started to come, letting me know I was found out. That I had little time as a free woman. She was going to the police. But I wasn't going to prison. I wasn't going to have my picture on the front page of newspapers or be fodder on those ridiculous talk shows."

"That's why she came here the day of the tour?"

Audrey nodded. "I met her in here, and she told me she was going to call the cops so I would be arrested and led out in front of everybody. She had it all planned out. I let her believe I would turn myself in, then I returned from the outside and bashed her head with a rock."

Audrey's voice was callous and emotionless, and it sent chills down Hope's spine. She stepped back but stopped when Audrey waved the gun, signaling for Hope to stay still.

"What about Vanessa? Why did you kill her?"

"She was always curious, wasn't she? She found those clippings and asked about them. She did an Internet search and put it together. I had to stop her from going to the police. Just like I have to stop you."

"What? I . . . I'm not going to go to the police," Hope lied. She was willing to say anything to get away from Audrey.

"Of course you are. You're such a Goody Two-shoes."

"You're insane."

"Sticks and stones . . ."

"You're not going to get away with this." But yet, Hope had no plan to stop Audrey. Why couldn't she think of a way out? If she made a run for the patio doors, Audrey could shoot her. If she made a run for the door to the hallway, she'd have to take Audrey on physically, and Audrey had a gun. That damn gun.

"We're going to take a walk outside. There's a lovely spot that's perfect for you to die in. I hope you agree." Audrey gestured for Hope to turn around and walk toward the patio door. "I wasn't expecting to have to do this. So I'll need some time to figure out how to frame Claire for your murder. I guess I'll work out the details after my dinner date with Harrison."

Hope followed Audrey's instructions. What choice did she have? Audrey had the advantage over her. Where on earth did Audrey get the gun? Did it belong to Harrison? Was it loaded? Hope wasn't about to play Russian roulette to find out. Rather, she'd focus on figuring a way to escape. Her life depended upon it.

Audrey moved closer to Hope and shoved her forward to start walking. "Once we're outside go straight."

Anger and betrayal and hurt boiled inside of Hope, and she threw concocting a plan out the window. In one swooping motion, she stopped, leaned forward, and came back up with a sharp elbow into Audrey's midsection. A scream pierced Hope's ear. She dashed toward the patio door, but Audrey was right behind her.

Grabbed by her hair, Hope was yanked back, and the sound of gun cocking rattled her to her core. She stumbled backward, losing her balance, and her hand just missed the doorknob of the patio door.

Damn!

They both landed on the floor with a thump. The gun discharged. The loud bang rattled through Hope's body. But she wasn't shot. Her hands weren't on the gun. They still gripped Audrey's arms. Audrey didn't have the gun in her hands, either. Where did it go? No time to find out. She had one chance to escape. She was going to get out of the house—fast!

Before she could fully stand up, Audrey grabbed her leg and pulled her back to the floor. Hope landed on top of Audrey and, in a blur, Hope was tossed over. Audrey straddled her now and they struggled while Audrey stretched her arm to reach the gun that lay just inches from them on the floor.

Hope needed the gun. She tried to lift her arm, but Audrey had her pinned. She squeezed her eyes shut and, with every ounce of strength, she tried to unbalance Audrey by rocking her body.

Audrey cursed as she fought to remain steady as she extended her upper body to allow her finger-tips to reach the gun. Audrey leaned back and a triumphant smile curved on her lips. But it was quickly replaced by a look of shock.

"What the . . ." Audrey called out as she tumbled off Hope's body.

A blur of fur flew over Hope and a guttural growl filled the air.

"Get him off me!"

Hope struggled to sit up and saw Bigelow on top of Audrey. She didn't know where he came from, and she didn't care. She scrambled to her feet and dove for the gun.

"Bigelow!" she called.

The dog snapped to attention.

"Come, boy."

The brown dog trotted away from his conquest and over to Hope's side. Her shaky hands held the gun on Audrey, who lay on the floor bleeding from her head. Keeping the gun pointed on Audrey, Hope moved to the desk. Bigelow stood where he was, keeping an alert eye on Audrey.

Before she could dial 911 again, she heard sirens approaching and relief flooded through her. The first officer on the scene entered the study and directed Hope to put down the gun. She obeyed, happy to be rid of the weapon, and was escorted out of the room by a second officer. She was taken to the living room with Bigelow.

She sat on the edge of the sofa with Bigelow settled next to her. His pink tongue slobbered her tear-stained cheek. She smiled and hugged the dog.

"You saved my life, big guy. You're going to have a lifetime supply of homemade dog biscuits." She cupped his face with her hands and kissed him on the head.

A sound drew her attention from Bigelow to the doorway and she glanced over.

Ethan.

She'd never been so happy to see him before. A sudden urge to run to him hit her hard, but she couldn't move because she feared she'd just collapse. Her body still trembled, and she doubted her ability to control her movements. Her ears still rung from the gunshot, and her head pounded. All in all, staying seated was the best option for her.

"Are you okay?" He rushed to Hope's side, stretching one arm along the back of the sofa. He wore a pair of jeans and a fisherman's sweater, which he always looked relaxed and rested in. But not at that moment. He looked tense, and worry was etched all over his face.

"I'm sorry. I'm so sorry," she said, her voice barely a whisper.

"For what?"

She looked him and up down. "It's your day off and now you have . . ." Her words trailed off as tears flowed down her cheek.

"Hey, it's my casual Friday look." He grinned.

"It's not Friday," she replied.

"No, it's not." He lifted his hand and pushed back a lock of her hair and tucked it behind her ear and as his hand fell away. It caressed her check, gently wiping away the tears.

She smiled. Ethan was trying to lighten the moment, and she appreciated the effort.

"She killed them. She told me so, and she was going to kill me. She's crazy. If it weren't for Bigelow, I don't know if I would have gotten away from her." Her struggle with Audrey on the floor flashed in her mind. The weight of Audrey on top of her, the fight for the gun, and those agonizing moments of not knowing if she'd be killed overwhelmed her. Tears streamed down her face. She wiped them with a tissue an officer had handed her earlier. She couldn't even imagine how she looked. Her eyes must have been puffy and red, smeared with mascara and eye makeup, not to mention her hair, which had to look like a rat's nest, thanks to rolling around the floor with a psychotic killer. Thinking about how she looked seemed superficial since she had almost been murdered, but it was the safest thing to think about.

"Hey." Ethan gently tilted her chin up with his forefinger. "Look at me."

She met his dark eyes.

They held the gaze for a moment before he said, "Thank God you're safe. I don't know what I would have done if something happened to you." His voice was low and husky and comforting. He wrapped his arm around her and pulled her to him, and she went willingly.

She pressed against his chest, the steadiness of his heartbeat lulling her into a calmness she desperately needed. All of the bad things that had just happened faded away. She closed her eyes, shutting away the whole world and feeling safe for the first time in a long time.

"Excuse me, Chief."

Hope opened one eye, spied Detective Reid standing under the arched doorway, and frowned. She should have known he'd show up on the scene. She opened her other eye as she pulled herself out of Ethan's embrace. A chill wiggled through her body. And she disliked the detective a little bit more. Bigelow wasted no time in snuggling up to her. He laid his head on her lap. The sweetness of the dog nearly melted her heart.

"I have a few questions for Ms. Early, if you don't mind," Detective Reid said.

A flicker of irritation flashed on Ethan's face.

He stood and walked over to his detective, rested his hands on his hips, and glanced back over at Hope. "I think she should be examined by a doctor before any questioning."

"Ethan, I'm okay. Audrey didn't hurt me." Hope was eager to do whatever she needed to in order to get home and sink into a hot tub for an extended stay.

"I appreciate your willingness to cooperate, Ms. Early." The detective flipped open his notepad. "Before we begin, I want to read you your rights."

"What?" Hope leaned forward, jerking Bigelow up.

"It's only a formality, I assure you," the detective said.

"Formality? The woman tried to kill me. She had a gun and was pointing it at me. She told me she was going to kill me!" Hope exclaimed.

"Hope, I really think you should let the ambulance take you to the hospital before you make any further statements," Ethan said.

Detective Reid glanced at Ethan, his expression unreadable.

Hope inched to the edge of the sofa. "I'm telling you the truth."

"Unfortunately, Mrs. Bloom is unconscious and I'm unable to ask her any questions that would verify your story—"

"My story?" Hope asked.

"I will interview her as soon as I am able to. Until then, I need to follow the evidence."

Yeah, she'd heard that before, and her sister ended up arrested for murder. Hope was beyond confused. Detective Reid didn't believe Audrey confessed to the murders and had tried to kill Hope. In his law-and-order mind, he probably thought Hope concocted the whole story to frame Audrey for the murders Claire committed. Looking at him now, his expression was very readable.

"I'm telling you Audrey admitted everything. Hitting Mrs. McCoy with her car, killing Peaches because Peaches was going to turn her in, and killing Vanessa because she stumbled upon the truth. I can't believe this is happening. She had a gun!"

"From what we can ascertain at this time, the Blooms own that gun legally. Ms. Early, it is quite possible you were the assailant here and Mrs. Bloom was just protecting herself. After all, I understand you have been entering homes under false pretenses to search the premises," Detective Reid said.

"That's crazy!" Hope rubbed her face with her hands, pushing her hair off her face.

How did this get all twisted around?

Detective Reid stepped forward, heading for the chair opposite the sofa. "It's plausible, and I need to interview you and Mrs. Bloom."

"Ethan?" She looked at him. He had to stop Reid.

"We do need to know exactly what happened here, however, you are under no obligation to talk to the police as you can refuse or seek legal counsel first. I do think since you were involved in an altercation with Mrs. Bloom, you should be examined by a doctor before saying anything further." Ethan approached Hope and guided her up by her arm. "I will call Claire for you and have her meet you at the hospital."

"Maybe she should bring Matt with her and maybe I should stop talking." Hope let Ethan escort her out of the living room. Was this what Matt meant by there was a chance she could do more harm than good?

Chapter Twenty-nine

Hope's feet slapped the pavement. Her rhythm kept by a soundtrack she created for her moderate run. Five days after Audrey confessed to Hope about the murders, Harrison had packed his bags and Bigelow's, too. He decided to leave Jefferson while the divorce proceedings began, and he didn't want the dog. Hope offered to take him and give him a home.

For her first run with her new companion, she lowered the intensity so they both could get used to running together. She wasn't sure how it would work out, but Bigelow kept pace with her, his ears flapping and his eyes focused on the road. He'd been trained to run by Audrey, and Hope wondered, as they came to the end of their three miles, if he was disappointed by the shorter run. Glancing at her running buddy, he didn't look unhappy.

Hope checked her fitness tracker as they both waited at the intersection of Hartford Road and Main Street for a break in the mid-morning traffic to cross. Her heart rate was exactly where it needed to be, and she'd hit her calorie burn goal. Which meant she could hit The Coffee Clique for a latte. When the two-lane road was clear of traffic, she whistled to Bigelow and tugged on his leash, picked up her pace, and dashed across the road. Safely on the sidewalk, she returned to walking. She looked down at the dog again. She liked having him with her on the run. She felt as if she owed the dog a debt since he saved her life, and she loved him. She worried he wouldn't adjust easily to his new home, but from the moment Harrison dropped him off, with all of his toys, his bed, and a case of food, the dog seemed to settle in easily.

Hope and Bigelow reached the front door of The Coffee Clique, and then she realized she couldn't take a dog inside the coffee shop. Standing there, jonesing for a latte, she tried to figure out a solution.

"Why do you still have him?"

Hope swung her head. Claire was crossing Main Street from the real estate office.

Solution found. "Oh, hi. I'm glad to see you."

Bigelow lunged forward, and then jumped on Claire.

Hope pulled on the leash. The last thing she needed was Bigelow messing up Claire's tweed skirt or silk blouse. "No, Bigelow!"

Claire sighed and rolled her eyes as she pushed the dog down. When Bigelow was back on all fours,

Claire brushed away any dirt that might have transferred to her clothing. "If you must keep him, you really should get him trained."

"He likes you." Hope smiled as she patted his head.

"I know a trainer you can hire. I just sold him a house."

"He's just excitable. He'll calm down. Soon." Hope mustered as much confidence as she could in her new pet. But she wasn't sure. She'd never owned a dog before and wasn't sure if Bigelow would grow out of his extended puppyhood mentality. Maybe he would just take longer to mature. She definitely needed to get some books on dogs and that trainer's number.

"Do you want a latte?" Claire pulled open the front door of the shop.

Hope nodded. "And a cup of water for Bigelow?"

Claire threw a skeptical glance over her shoulder then nodded before stepping inside the shop. Hope squatted to meet Bigelow eye to eye. "Don't worry. She'll warm up to you. But you do need to have some manners around her."

Bigelow replied with a deep bark, followed by a low, steady growl.

He was so soft and warm and sweet, so when he growled and his body tensed, she was surprised. Hope stared at him and wondered what was wrong. His light brown eyes were fixated on something behind her. She looked over her shoulder. Detective Reid was approaching. *Great.* She stood, turned, and braced herself for more grief from the detective who followed the evidence. Though, she'd do as Matt told her to do—say nothing.

"Good morning, Ms. Early." He joined her and Bigelow. "I heard Mr. Bloom had given you his dog. Is he adjusting well?"

Bigelow let out another bark.

Hope pressed her lips together to keep the smile that tugged from spreading. For what he lacked in manners, he made up for in taste. Clearly, he didn't care for the detective.

"Yes, he's adjusting well. Don't let us keep you." Hope gestured to the front door of The Coffee Clique.

"You're not. But since I've run into you, I thought I might take this opportunity to give you an update on the investigation."

"My attorney told me not to speak to you." She stroked Bigelow's head, hoping it would calm him. The last thing she needed was for the dog to lunge and attack the detective. That would be wrong. Right?

Bigelow glanced upward as if to say, "No worries, I'm a lover not a fighter." He settled next to her, his compact but solid body resting against her leg.

The front door of the shop opened and Claire exited with a tray of two lattes and one cup of water. She came to a fast stop when she saw the detective.

"She's not supposed to be speaking with you. Neither of us are." Claire's words were clipped.

"It's okay. You don't have to speak to me. I'll do the talking."

Hope wasn't surprised by that statement. "What do you have to tell me?"

"I've concluded my investigation, and this morning Mrs. Bloom will be arraigned for the murders of Mary Beth McCoy, Peaches McCoy, and Vanessa Jordan."

"Excuse me?" Hope wasn't sure she'd heard the detective correctly.

"Audrey finally confessed?" Claire asked.

"Yes, she eventually did. There was mounting evidence against her, and the fact we found her fingerprint on the seat adjustment of the van she stole from Wallace Green seemed to leave her no choice but to confess. Criminals often overlook the smallest details." Detective Reid shoved his hands into his pants pockets and looked proud of himself for closing the case. The mounting evidence he was taking credit for was uncovered by Hope, but she wasn't holding her breath for a thank-you from him.

"One fingerprint somewhere it shouldn't have been. Wow." Hope took in the news. Relief, vindication, and joy whirled. She knew all along her sister was innocent and proving it almost got her killed before almost getting arrested. She was sure Reid wanted to slap handcuffs on her right there at the Bloom house the day Audrey attacked her and it was only because of Ethan he didn't. Having her examined by a doctor in the emergency room allowed enough time for Matt Roydon to arrive and intercept an official interview.

"Is that *all* you have to tell us, Detective Reid?" Claire asked.

Hope heard the tone in her sister's voice and knew Claire was looking for an apology for being accused and arrested for two murders.

Before he could answer, his cell phone buzzed and he pulled it out of its case on his belt. He looked at the phone. "I have to take this. Have a nice day, ladies." With the phone to his ear, he walked away.

"Can you believe him?" Claire asked.

Hope nodded. "Yes, I can." She took the cup of water from the tray Claire held and set it on the sidewalk for Bigelow. He eagerly lapped up the water. "He was thirsty." Maybe she was getting the hang of being a dog mom after all.

"So am I. Let's take these lattes back to your house," Claire suggested.

"Sounds good to me. Then I want to shower and get everything ready for the party tomorrow." Before Hope could remove the cup from Bigelow, someone shouted out her name.

She looked up. Vera Jordan was approaching them. Vera's resemblance to Vanessa made Hope's heart seize. She guessed it would take time for that to stop. Hope wasn't the only one who saw Vera. Bigelow noticed the woman walking toward them and got excited all over again. He pulled on his leash, and his dancing feet knocked over the cup, splashing Claire's red suede pumps.

"Oh! No!" Claire screeched as she jumped away from the puddle of spreading water, but it was too late. The tips of both shoes were soaked.

"Oh, boy." Hope grabbed the napkins tucked in the tray and feverishly patted the shoes to soak up

Debra Sennefelder

the water. "He didn't mean to do that. Right, Bigelow?" She grimaced as water stains set into the shoes. "I think I can fix this."

"He's a menace." Claire pointed at Bigelow.

Hope straightened. "Just let them dry. They'll need at least twenty-four hours. Then I'll rub them with a suede eraser and finish it off with a lint brush to restore the nap. You'll never know they got wet."

"What's going on?" Vera reached them and her forehead crinkled with confusion.

"That dog ruined my new shoes," Claire blurted out.

Hope let out an exasperated breath. "They're not ruined."

Claire pointed her manicured index finger at Hope. "You owe me a new pair of shoes. I'll send you a link later and I want two-day delivery." Claire lifted Hope's latte out of the tray and handed it to her. "I'm going back to the office." She crossed Main Street and disappeared inside the real estate office.

"Guess I interrupted at a bad time, huh?" Vera patted Bigelow on the head. "He's such a cutie."

"Don't worry about it. I'm glad you're coming tomorrow."

"Me too. Van would have wanted me to. And to be honest, I'd kind of like something to do other than crying."

"I understand. Then it's settled. I'll see you at my housewarming party. And remember, no presents. I have everything I need." Hope tugged at Bigelow's leash and began walking back home as Vera entered the Coffee Clique. She did have everything. She had a beautiful—well, it was going to be beautiful when she was done with the re-model—home, and a new career she loved, and her family. What more could a gal ask for?

"Oh, it's you." Elaine's voice sounded tight, as if she were surprised, but not in a good way. She let the door of the nail salon close behind her.

Hope stopped and flashed a big smile. "Good morning." She hadn't seen her since Elaine an-nounced she'd unfriended, unfollowed, and unsub-scribed from all of Hope's social-media platforms. Hope guessed from the unfriendly tone of Elaine's voice and the blank expression of her Botoxed face that Elaine was still upset with her.

"I guess we'll keep running into each other since we both live in town." Elaine placed both hands on her hips. Her hourglass figure was ac-centuated by the navy-blue wrap dress she wore and adorned by a lot of bling. Hope wondered if Lionel offered up a jewelry store as a way to apolo-gize for his indiscretion with Peaches.

"I think you're right," Hope answered.

"Well, I think you should move."

"What?"

Elaine nodded. "I lived here first. You're the one who moved to town a few months ago."

"Elaine, I was born and raised in this town," Hope reminded the woman.

Elaine shrugged. "But you left, then I came, and then you came back, so you should go."

The woman's logic perplexed Hope. And with about fifty people coming over tomorrow to cele-brate with her, she didn't really have the time to try and understand Elaine's logic. She wasn't really sure if she ever wanted to understand the woman's logic. "I'm not going anywhere. I've apologized for what I did and I hope someday you can forgive me and we can be friends. Until then, you'll just have to figure out a way to deal with seeing me out and about in my hometown." Hope tugged on Bigelow's leash and started walking again. "Oh," she said, glancing over her shoulder, "the invitation to my housewarming party still stands. I'd love for you to come." With a wave, Hope turned and continued along Main Street and waited for a break in traffic at the intersection to cross over to Hartford Road. She meant what she said to Elaine. She wanted them to be friends.

Bigelow walked leisurely while Hope sipped her latte. The spring morning air was filled with a sweetness from the blooming flowers, and a soft breeze swirled while birds chirped in the distance. Hope and Bigelow were going home. They had a party to prepare for.

As they walked, Hope's mind wondered to her first big event at her new home. Her heart swelled with pride. She was excited to show off her work-in-progress to all of her friends and family. The old farmhouse wasn't the first home she'd owned, that would be the condo on the Upper West Side in New York. While she did her best to make it a cozy home, the seventh-floor apartment was still a large rectangle divided into a few rooms. She'd hosted countless dinner parties there as well as brunches for friends on lazy Sundays. That was probably the thing she missed most about living in the city. Her box of a home didn't require so much work, so lazy Sundays were a way of life. Now her Sundays consisted of a lengthy to-do list, like every other day of the week.

A honk caught Hope's attention and she slowed down. Ethan's truck approached and pulled over to the curb. Bigelow's tail wagged feverishly and he pulled on the leash. For a little guy, he was strong. She definitely needed to hire a trainer.

With his window rolled town, Ethan leaned an arm on the door. "I was just at the deli and ran into Batts. He said your car is ready to be picked up. Come on. I'll give you two a ride over there."

Hope smiled. Syd Batts owned Batts & Sons Auto Repair, a fixture in Jefferson since Hope was a little girl.

"Great." She dashed around to the passenger side and pulled open the door then guided Bigelow up into the half-seat behind the driver and passenger seats. He sniffed the backseat before settling down.

"He sure is a happy fellow." Ethan pulled out onto the road. He was dressed in his civilian clothes, a pair of gray pants and a white shirt with a Windbreaker. As the chief of police, he didn't always wear a uniform, and being Ethan Cahill, he never wore a suit to work.

"Batts finished a little ahead of schedule. I'm so happy to get my car back." Her car had been at the repair shop since it was towed the day she was run off the road.

"Yeah. He wanted to get it back to you as soon as possible. I think he's looking for a little reward for all his hard work."

"He loves red-velvet cupcakes. I guess I can make him a dozen." Hope looked out the window as Ethan's truck chugged along the winding road. In her old life, she would have shoved a couple of fifty-dollar bills into an envelope and handed it to the mechanic, but in Jefferson, she was going to extend her gratitude by baking a dozen cupcakes.

"I have some more good news for you."

"Audrey confessed. I'm in the clear." Hope turned her head to Ethan, just in time to see his smile fade. *Shoot.* He'd wanted to tell her about Audrey's confession.

"How do you know?"

"I ran into Reid a few minutes ago, and he shared the information."

"Should I ask how that went?" He glanced over after stopping at an intersection.

Hope shook her head. "No."

"It's all over now." Ethan turned his attention back to the road and proceeded through the intersection.

"No, not really. Sure, Claire and I are cleared of any crimes, but there's still all the fallout to deal with."

"Like what?"

"Harrison's life has been turned upside down. His wife is a murderer. Vera lost her sister." Hope let out a breath and leaned her head against the seat. "I'm having a hard time reconciling everything. For all these years, Audrey lived with the secret of killing someone. I can't imagine that." Three years ago, when she was planning a surprise birthday party for Claire, Hope nearly blew the whole thing because she had a hard time keeping the secret. How did someone keep a murder a secret?

"My guess is that after enough time she managed to convince herself that it didn't happen. Then Peaches turned up and it all came crashing back to her."

Hope nodded in agreement. "Peaches was playing with fire. Once she found out it was Audrey who killed her mother, she should have gone to the police. I'm not saying she got what she deserved. She didn't deserve to die."

"No, she didn't. You're right. She should have come to us and let us handle the situation." Ethan flicked on his signal before turning onto Castle Hill Road. A huge section of the land on the road was in the beginning stages of development by Lionel Whitcomb. The sounds of heavy machines used to move earth rumbled in the distance. According to Claire, that was the sound of progress, but Hope wasn't so sure about that. She wasn't certain she wanted Jefferson to change.

"You know after Audrey stole Wallace's van and drove me off the road, she sent me flowers. You saw them. Then she attacked me in my own home and had the nerve to show up with a fruit basket. Was she remorseful or was she just checking to see what I knew? I thought she was my friend."

"I still can't believe she ran all the way to Wallace's to steal the van and then ran home." Ethan turned the truck onto Commerce Road.

"Well, she ran marathons. Running a few miles around town was nothing for her."

Batts & Sons Auto Repair came into view, and Ethan steered his truck into their parking lot. The one-story building housed a small office and a large garage and all of its bays were filled with mechanics working.

"Audrey betrayed my friendship and she was going to let Claire take the fall for her crimes. I'm hurt and angry and confused. This wasn't exactly how I thought coming home would be like. To be honest, I'm not sure I made the right decision. Maybe I should have stayed in New York."

Ethan parked the truck, then turned off the ignition. He leaned back and looked at Hope. "You really think so?"

Hope shrugged. "I don't know."

"If you had, then who would have cleared your sister's name?"

Now that was a question Hope didn't expect from Ethan. And she didn't have an answer for it.

"Or take in Bigelow?"

Hope glanced over at the dog. He looked happy. He had no idea his first owner was a serial killer. Lucky dog. "So you think I made the right decision to do a little investigating on my own?"

Ethan raised his hand in protest. "Wait, I didn't say that."

Hope nodded. "I think you did."

"No, I think you put yourself into a very dangerous situation by doing a little investigating on your own. But I do think your stubbornness and tenacity helped uncover the real killer."

Hope smiled a triumphant smile. "I did good, huh?"

Ethan sighed and shook his head. "Yes, you did."

A rapping at the passenger window interrupted their conversation. Hope looked over her shoulder. Batts was standing there. She pressed the power button and the window slid down.

"I have all the paperwork ready for you. Come inside." The elderly man turned and ambled back to the garage.

"I should get going. I'll ask Claire to meet me here later when I return the rental. Thanks for the lift." She opened the door, got out and then slid the passenger seat forward to allow Bigelow to jump out.

"See you tomorrow," Ethan called out.

"Don't be late. I've assigned you barbecue duty." Hope wiggled her fingers good-bye and headed for the office with Bigelow beside her.

Chapter Thirty

"These are adorable." Claire picked up one of the paint sample coasters from the table that served as the beverage station. There were four stations set up for the guests out in the yard under a tent, which meant they wouldn't be hovering around Hope in the kitchen. The appetizer station had platters of hot and cold finger foods and bowls of dips and chips, with plates and utensils. Across from the appetizer station, the beverage station was set up with tubs of ice for beer and glass beverage dispensers of iced tea and lemonade and a few bottles of wine and soda. The third station was the dessert and coffee station that was empty at the moment. The final station was for the main meal, and that was what Hope was working on setting up when her sister arrived.

"Thanks. I had a bunch of tiles left from a project and countless numbers of paint sample charts, so I decided to make coasters." With some glue to keep the paint chart and tiles together, sealant to make the coasters waterproof, and felt for the bottoms, she had whipped up a stack of festive coasters. And they'd also made a good DIY project for her blog.

"Why am I not surprised?" Claire studied the coaster. "Are you sure we're really sisters?"

Hope chuckled. "Of course we are. Just because you don't have a crafty bone in your body doesn't mean we're not related."

"These must have taken hours." Claire set the coaster down. She walked over to one of the six tables set up in the tent and pulled out a chair and sat.

"I'm not sure. But they're really all I did for the party, aside from the food." Hope picked up her camera from the table. The housewarming party was going to be featured on her blog the following week, so she needed some photographs of the food, prep work, and lots of the guests enjoying themselves.

"Restraint?" Claire asked in a shocked voice.

"I wanted to keep things simple." Hope positioned the camera above the front of the salad bowl. The vibrant colors of deep green lettuces and bright cherry tomatoes popped, then she tilted the camera up until the bamboo bowl filled the frame. That angle was one of Hope's favorites to shoot. She clicked away until she had far too many photos of the salad bowl, but, in her experience, there were really never enough photos to select from when writing a blog post.

Hope looked over to her sister. Poised and elegant in a blue dress with a green cardigan covering her bare arms from the soft breeze, Claire looked serious. Too serious for a housewarming party.

"What's wrong?" Hope asked.

Claire shook her head. "Nothing. I'm glad we have a moment alone before everybody arrives. I wanted to say, you know, ah—well, I guess, thank you."

"If you really want to express your gratitude, you could give me the pair of Jimmy Choo pumps you just bought." Hope smiled as she set her camera down.

Claire's upper lip curled. "Hmmm . . . not a chance."

"Finally! A front-page story that's not about a boring zoning issue." Drew approached the tent, waving a copy of the *Gazette*.

"That's wonderful, Drew." Hope walked past him on her way into the house. "Good job."

"Thank you." Drew beamed.

"I hope there's a retraction about my being unjustly arrested," Claire said.

"Retractions are only for when we report something incorrectly. You were arrested, we were not incorrect in reporting that."

Hope continued toward the house, leaving those two to hash out their disagreement. Inside the kitchen, she pulled out the dish of chicken and a platter of sliders from the refrigerator. She'd opted to make the sliders because they were fun and kids of all ages loved them. She also made a deep dish of macaroni and cheese because no one disliked mac n' cheese. Ethan would be arriving at any moment and she'd have everything ready for him to start grilling.

"I don't think she invited him." Jane's voice carried from the living room.

"I wouldn't blame her if she didn't," Sally replied.

"Even if she did, how could he show his face here?" Jane entered the kitchen, with Sally behind her. Jane set her purse on the island, then hugged Hope. "Good to see you, dear." She squeezed tightly. She smelled of lavender and hair spray.

"Who are you talking about?" Hope removed herself from Jane's embrace and gave a quick hug to Sally, who was carrying a large basket.

"Detective Reid," Jane answered.

"Oh, no, he wasn't invited." Hope removed the lid from the dish the chicken was marinating in. She'd considered inviting him for a brief moment. Okay, it was more like a nanosecond. Perhaps one day they could be friendly acquaintances. One day in the very far future.

"We brought you a little something." Sally set the basket on the island.

"You shouldn't have. I told everyone no presents." Even though she had told them that, she was excited about the gift. She untied the cellophane wrapping and found the basket full of goodies. At first glance, it seemed like a hodgepodge of gifts, but Hope knew what each symbolized. The bottle of wine was for joy and to never go thirsty, the loaf of bread represented a bounty of food in her home, the container of salt was for flavor and spice in her life, the bottle of olive oil was for health and well-being, and the plant was for her home to always have life. Her breath caught for a moment. With all the love that surrounded her in Jefferson, her home would always have love.

"There's a coin in there for good luck and good fortune," Jane said.

Hope reached out and wrapped her arms around both women for a group hug. She was so thankful for them in her life.

"Knock, knock," a familiar male voice called out from the hall.

Hope released her hold of the Merrifields and moved around the island to welcome Matt to her home. "I'm so glad you could make it today."

"Thank you for the invitation. Your home is charming. I hope I'm going to get a tour." He handed a bouquet of yellow roses to Hope. "These are for you."

"They're beautiful." It had been ages since a man had bought her flowers. She dipped her head and inhaled the sweet fragrance and hoped she wasn't blushing. She told herself he was only being polite by bringing a gift to the hostess. There wasn't anything else to read into the gesture.

She returned to the island, with Matt behind her, and she introduced him to the Merrifields.

"Yesterday Claire drove me around town. Jefferson is a beautiful place." Matt shoved his hands into his pants pockets. His attire was casual, a far cry from his lawyer suits. And she had an unexpected urge to run her fingers through the waves of his dusty blond hair.

"She's an excellent tour guide for this town," Sally said. "But be careful, she'll have you signing a contract to buy a house before you realize what's happened."

Matt laughed. "Thanks for the warning. But I have to admit, I did see a few properties that interest me."

"You're thinking about moving to Jefferson?" Hope asked.

"It would be a weekend house. My practice is in the city. And it would give me the opportunity to keep an eye on you," he said in a low voice that sent a shiver of excitement zipping through Hope.

"Keep an eye on me?" she asked, almost challenging him.

"To make sure you don't find yourself in the middle of another murder investigation," he said in a more playful voice and that settled the shiver resonating within Hope.

"I don't think there'll be a next time," Hope said with confidence. She'd had her fill of sleuthing. Going forward she'd be content with reading mystery novels and working through the authors' clues and red herrings. Yes, fiction was a whole lot safer than real-life investigating.

The French door to the patio opened and Gilbert popped his head in. "There you are, Hope. Buddy and I just got here and I wanted to say 'hi.' He and Bigelow are getting along like old friends. On the way over, I saw Alfred and Maretta pulling up in your driveway. I better go check on the boys and make sure they don't get into any trouble." He ducked back out, closing the door behind him.

Hope appreciated the warning about Maretta and then saw the puzzled look on Matt's face. "That was Gilbert Madison, my neighbor. He's sweet."

"Why don't we take Matt outside and properly introduce him to Gilbert?" Sally looped her arm into the crook of Matt's arm and escorted him out of the house.

Jane followed dutifully and, just before the door closed behind them, Hope heard Jane ask, "Is your wife joining us today?"

Hope shook her head. Jane was going to grill Matt and like the true matchmaker she was she was starting with his marital status. Though, she'd never come out and ask him directly if he was married. She'd consider that rude. Maybe she should go help Matt but he was a big boy capable of handling the likes of Jane Merrifield.

"Since the front door was open, we allowed ourselves in," Maretta stated as she entered the kitchen with a broom in her hand and Alfred behind her. "It's rather informal."

"Well, it is a barbecue, so we're not standing on ceremony." Hope walked to them. Maretta had chosen an ivory-colored A-line dress and changed up her sensible black purse for a peach-colored satchel. She'd tied a floral scarf around her neck, and it added color to her pale face. All in all, Maretta looked very nice, and Hope was happy she'd accepted the invitation to the party.

"It's customary to bring a gift to a housewarming party. This broom is for you." Maretta held it out for Hope to take. "May your home always be clean and free from evil spirits."

"Of course your home is always clean," Alfred interjected quickly and at great risk of Maretta's wrath.

"It's a custom, not a statement on her housekeeping skills," Maretta said.

"Thank you for the gift and for your wishes. Please, go outside where there's food and the other guests. Ethan will be here in a few minutes and then we'll start grilling." Hope set the broom down as the couple headed outside.

Hope returned to her hosting duties and pulled out a reusable container where she stored the cheese for the burgers. Everything was ready for the main course and right on cue Ethan entered the kitchen, holding two bottles of wine in each hand.

"It's about time," she scolded him. "Everybody is arriving. You need to start grilling."

"Happy housewarming to you." He set the bottles on the counter. "Nice broom."

"It's a gift from Maretta."

"Should I ask?"

Hope shook her head. "No." She handed him the dish of chicken. "Start with this and I'll bring out the burgers."

"Yes, ma'am." Ethan saluted and smiled.

"You're the best griller I know, and I appreciate you helping me out today"

"I'm always here for you." Ethan opened the patio door and the sound of cheerful voices and laughter wafted in. Everything she'd ever wanted was right outside. She was one lucky gal.

As she gathered up the burgers and cheese onto a tray to take to the grill, Ethan's words repeated. He'd always been there for her since high school as a friend. Friendships were hard to come by, and they were fragile. Romances were tumultuous and unpredictable. Hope had already been burned by doing something unpredictable when she signed up for the reality show. But it sure was fun while it lasted.

She caught a glimpse of Vera making her way across the yard. Everybody was there finally. Hope pulled open the door and stepped out onto the patio. She paused for a moment to take in the view.

Her friends and family were all gathered. She caught a glimpse of her niece and nephew running from the barn. They loved the chickens and she guessed the hens just got some extra food. Audrey may have done some very bad things, but Hope was thankful for her suggestion to have the party.

"This is where I belong. I made the right decision," Hope said to herself. The picture-perfect moment lasted just that—a moment. All of a sudden, Bigelow came running across the yard at full speed. Buddy followed. He looked like he was cantering with his long hair flowing, and both dogs ended up under the tent with Maretta in their path.

Oh, no.

"Bigelow! No!" Hope shouted.

Maretta screamed as Bigelow, chased by Buddy, raced by her, clipping her just enough to knock her off balance. Her drink sloshed on her dress and just before she landed on the appetizer station and right into the tray of bruschetta, Matt dove to grab her. *Good catch.* A sodden Maretta glared at Hope, but she was too distracted by the mischievous grin from the equally wet attorney.

Yeah, it was good to be home.

Recipes from Hope's blog, Hope at Home

ETHAN'S CRISP CHOCOLATE CHIP COOKIES
Posted by Hope Early

Crispy, thin, slightly chewy, and crunchy. All of that is packed into one little cookie. When you serve up these bad boys, make sure you have filled-to-the-rim glasses of milk and then step back because everyone is going to make a mad dash for the cookie plate.

Makes 3–4 dozen cookies.

    2½ cups all-purpose flour
    ¾ teaspoon salt
    1 teaspoon baking powder
    1 teaspoon baking soda
    1 cup unsalted butter, softened to room
        temperature
    1 cup granulated sugar
    1 cup packed light brown sugar
    2 large eggs at room temperature

3 tablespoons milk
1 tablespoon pure vanilla extract
2 cups semisweet chocolate chips

1. Preheat oven to 350 degrees F. In a mixing bowl, stir together flour, salt, baking powder, and baking soda.
2. Cream together both sugars and butter in the bowl of a stand mixer fitted with a paddle attachment or in a large bowl with a hand mixer. Cream until light and fluffy, about 3–5 minutes. Reduce the speed of the mixer and add in the eggs, one at a time. Add in the milk. Then add in the vanilla. Mix until well combined.
3. Gradually add the flour mixture until just combined, being careful not to overmix. Gently stir in the chocolate chips.
4. Scoop tablespoon-size balls of dough onto prepared baking sheets leaving 2 inches between each cookie to allow for spreading.
5. Bake for 12–15 minutes and cool, before moving to racks to finish cooling. Every oven is different, so I like to bake two cookies first to get the timing down correctly and then fill up the next cookie sheet.

Baker's notes:
1. These are very thin cookies, so you'll want to check each batch baking to make sure they're not getting too browned.
2. I prepare my baking sheets with silicone baking sheets. Parchment paper will work.

EASY-PEASY RICE PILAF
Posted by Hope Early

A funny name for one of the easiest side dishes you'll whip up in your kitchen. No one will ever guess how quickly this dish came together. They're going to be too busy asking for seconds.

Makes 4 servings.

⅓ cup thin spaghetti, broken into 1-inch pieces
¾ cup rice
1½ cups chicken broth
2 tablespoons butter
Salt and pepper to taste
Bunch of parsley, chopped

1. In a medium pan, melt butter over medium heat. Add spaghetti and rice and toast until the spaghetti is golden brown in color.
2. Season with salt and pepper.
3. Add broth and bring to a low boil. Reduce heat and simmer for 18–20 minutes, until the rice is tender. Add extra broth if the pan gets too dry.
4. Fluff with fork before serving. Mix in chopped parsley.

ALL-AMERICAN APPLE PIE
Posted by Hope Early

This pie recipe has been passed down from generations of Early women and I bake it every chance I get because it's simply scrumptious.

Thick slices of apple tucked into buttery crusts, who can resist? Not me! And no one that I know. For added fabulousness, top with a heaping spoonful of vanilla ice cream.

Makes 8 servings.

For the pie filling:
    ¾ cup firmly packed light brown sugar
    1 tablespoon all-purpose flour
    ¼ teaspoon ground nutmeg
    ½ teaspoon cinnamon
    ⅛ teaspoon salt
    1 tablespoon grated lemon peel
    6 cups peeled, cored, and thickly sliced apples
    1 tablespoon lemon juice
    2 tablespoons butter

For the pie crusts (bottom and top):
    2½ cups all-purpose flour
    1 teaspoon salt
    2 sticks unsalted butter, cold, cut into small
        pieces
    ¼ cup ice water, plus more if needed

For the pie:
1. Preheat oven to 425 degrees F. Line 9-inch pie dish with half of the pastry.
2. In a large bowl, combine brown sugar, cinnamon, nutmeg, salt, and lemon peel. Add apples and toss to coat evenly. Spoon apple mixture into pastry-lined pie dish. Sprinkle with lemon juice and dot with butter.
3. Top with remaining pastry. Trim and flute edges. Cut slits in top of crust to allow steam to escape.

4. To prevent over-browning, cover edge of pie with foil. Bake 20 minutes. Remove foil. Bake another 20–25 minutes or until top is golden. Serve warm or at room temperature.

For the pie crust:

1. In the bowl of a food processor, combine flour and salt; pulse to combine. Add the butter, and pulse for about 10 seconds until mixture resembles coarse crumbs. If some larger pieces remain that's okay.

2. With food processor still running, add the ice water through the feed tube in a slow, steady stream, just until the dough holds together without being wet or sticky. Don't process more than 30 seconds. To test, squeeze a small amount of the dough together; if it's still too crumbly, add a bit more water, 1 tablespoon at a time.

3. Turn the dough onto a clean work surface. Divide in half, and place each half on a piece of plastic wrap. Shape into flattened disks. Wrap and refrigerate at least one hour or overnight. Can freeze up to one month. Thaw overnight in the refrigerator before using.

Baker's note: I like to make two batches of pie crust so I have extra in the freezer. Then when I feel like whipping up a pie I have prepared pie crust all ready to be baked.

OATMEAL-CHERRY CHOCOLATE BARS
Posted by Hope Early

These bars are easy to make and are perfect for breakfast, snack, or even dessert. The recipe is flexible, so you can add what you love such as nuts or other dried fruit. You can also decide on how many servings you want based on how big of a bar you cut. Enjoy!

Makes nine 3-inch-square bars.

2 cups old-fashioned oats
½ cup all-purpose flour
½ cup packed brown sugar
½ teaspoon baking powder
¼ teaspoon baking soda
¼ teaspoon salt
½ teaspoon cinnamon
½ cup dried cherries
½ cup dark chocolate chips
½ cup canola oil
2 eggs

1. Preheat oven to 350 degrees F.
2. Spray 8-x-8-inch baking pan with nonstick cooking spray.
3. Mix the dry ingredients in a bowl. Add in canola oil and eggs. Mix well. Add in cherries and chocolate chips. Stir to combine.
4. Spread batter in prepared baking pan and bake for approximately 25–30 minutes until bars are cooked all the way through.
5. Let bars cool completely in pan before cutting.

CINNAMON APPLE BREAD
Posted by Hope Early

Chopped apples, brown sugar, and cinnamon swirl together to make this quick bread an all-time favorite. You'll be able to whip this bread up at any time because it's so simple to make.

Makes 6 to 8 servings (depending how thick you cut the slices).

⅓ cup brown sugar
1 teaspoon ground cinnamon
⅔ cup granulated sugar
½ cup butter, softened
2 eggs
1½ teaspoon vanilla extract
1½ cup all-purpose flour
1¾ teaspoon baking powder
½ cup milk
1 apple, peeled and chopped

1. Preheat oven to 350 degrees F. Butter and flour a 9-x-5-inch loaf pan. Place in refrigerator while you make the batter.
2. Mix brown sugar and cinnamon together in a bowl and set aside. In a stand mixer or large bowl with electric hand mixer, combine granulated sugar and butter until smooth. Beat in eggs, one at a time, until combined. Add in vanilla extract and combine. Add in flour and baking powder in thirds. Then add milk.
3. Remove baking pan from refrigerator. Pour

half the batter into the prepared pan. Next add half of the apple and half of the brown sugar and cinnamon mixture. Lightly pat the apple mixture into the batter with a large spoon.

4. Pour the remaining batter over apple layer and top with remaining apple and the remaining brown sugar and cinnamon mixture. Pat topping into the batter with the back of a large spoon.

5. Bake for 55–65 minutes or until toothpick inserted in the middle of the loaf comes out clean. Cool in pan for 10 minutes before transferring to a cooling rack.

HOPE'S FAVORITE CHOCOLATE CHIP COOKIE
Posted by Hope Early

I know it's wrong to have a favorite cookie. As a food blogger, I shouldn't play favorites with recipes. but I can't help myself with these cookies. Loaded with chocolate chips, these buttery, thick, soft chocolate chip cookies are heavenly. You won't want to miss out on these. Seriously.

Makes about 3 dozen cookies.

¾ cup unsalted butter, melted
1 cup packed light brown sugar
⅔ cup granulated sugar
1 large egg
1 large egg yolk
1 tablespoon vanilla

2 cups all-purpose flour
⅓ cup bread flour
¾ teaspoon baking soda
¾ teaspoon kosher salt
1⅔ cups semisweet chocolate chips

1. Preheat oven to 350 degrees F and line cookie
   sheet pans with silicone baking sheets.
2. Cream butter and sugars together until light
   and fluffy in the bowl of a stand mixer with
   paddle attachment, about 3–4 minutes. Scrape
   side of bowl as needed. Reduce speed of mixer
   and then add in the egg and egg yolk, one at a
   time, beating well to incorporate into mixture.
   Beat in vanilla.
3. Whisk together flours, cornstarch, baking soda,
   and salt in a separate bowl. Slowly add flour
   mixture to the butter mixture and mix until
   just combined. Be careful not to overmix. Stir
   in chocolate chips.
4. Scoop dough by rounded tablespoon and drop
   onto prepared sheet pan, 2 inches apart to
   allow room for spreading. Then drop another
   scoop (approximately 1½ teaspoon) of dough
   onto each cookie. Press together lightly, making sure not to flatten the cookie.
5. Bake for 9–12 minutes, rotating halfway
   through baking, or until cookies have spread
   out and the edges are golden, but the center of
   the cookie still looks soft and just slightly
   undercooked. Every oven is different, so I like
   to bake two cookies first to get the timing down

correctly and then fill up the next cookie sheet.
6. Let cookies cool on cookie sheet for 5 minutes. Then remove to a wire rack to cool completely. Cookies will store in an airtight container for up to 3 days.